Beautifully told, humanity is rev[...]
honest and poignant story o[...]
spiritual wisdom in the face of a[...]
C.F. Dunn, Historical Fiction Au[...]

The Stranger made Psalm 23 come alive for me. It reminded me that God actively pursues us because of His unconditional love for us. He is our Good Shepherd who leads us, refreshes us and gives us all we need. He is our companion along the way and reveals Himself to us through the people we meet along life's journey. Joy creates such relatable characters. Brother Silas has a crisis of faith, and his dream appears dead, but through his experiences he learns what is really important. I can see myself in him and wouldn't be surprised if you too see something of yourself in Brother Silas.
Vicki Cottingham, Author, Blogger and Retreat Leader

A story of faith lost and faith returned; of doubt and the mystery of 'not knowing', and yet understanding that the most important thing is not what we do for God, but our relationship with Him. Thought-provoking, challenging and inspirational; a delightful, page-turning read, and one that will keep the reader engaged till the end.
Sheila Jacobs, Editor and Author

Joy takes us on a journey with Silas, a man who has devoted himself to serving God. But, as in most of our lives, things don't always go as planned. Travel with Silas as he struggles to understand or even know that God is there, as he experiences the feelings of abandonment,

disappointment and failure, to a place of recognising God in different ways and comes to the realisation that a simple faith is better than religion.
Jason Cottingham, Centre Director, Penhurst Retreat Centre

The Stranger

Joy Margetts

Broad Place
publishing

First published in Great Britain in 2024

Broad Place Publishing
Broadplacepublishing.co.uk

Copyright © Joy Margetts 2024

The author has asserted her rights under Section 77 of the Copyright, Designs and Patents Act, 1988, to be identified as the author of the work.

All rights reserved. No portion of this book may be reproduced or transmitted in any form or by any means, electronic or mechanical, including photocopying and recording, or by any information storage or retrieval system, without permission in writing from the publisher.

Unless marked otherwise, all scripture is taken from the New King James Version®. Copyright © 1982 by Thomas Nelson. Used by permission. All rights reserved.

Scripture quotations marked 'NIRV' are taken from the New International Readers Version. Copyright © 1995, 1996, 1998, 2014 by Biblica, Inc.®. Used by permission. All rights reserved worldwide.

This is a work of fiction. Names, characters, businesses, places, events and incidents are either the products of the author's imagination or used in a fictitious manner. Any resemblance to actual persons, living or dead, or actual events is purely coincidental.

The views and opinions expressed in this work are those of the author and do not necessarily reflect the views and opinions of the publisher.

British Library Cataloguing-in-Publication Data.
A catalogue record for this book is available from the British Library.

Print Book: ISBN 978-1-915034-78-6
E-Book: ISBN 978-1-915034-79-3

Books can be purchased from broadplacepublishing.co.uk

*For Lynn, Ruth, Dawn, Karen and Vero,
my travelling companions,
and for Amanda – don't start the
heavenly dance party without us!*

Books in this Series

The Healing
The Pilgrim
The Bride
The Stranger

Each is a standalone story featuring familiar characters.
Available to purchase at
joymargetts.com

CONTENTS

1. Grace Dieu — 11
2. Abbey Dore — 26
3. Hay-on-Wye — 40
4. Hannah and Samuel — 53
5. Hay Castle — 68
6. St Germain — 81
7. The Church at Cregina — 95
8. The Charcoal Burner — 109
9. The Carvings — 123
10. Rhaeadr Gwy — 137
11. Matthew — 153
12. Iorwerth — 169
13. Rachel — 184
14. The Stranger — 199
15. Cennad — 212
16. Stay-a-Little — 226
17. Mountains — 241
18. The Inn — 256
19. Sunrise — 271
20. Home — 286
    Epilogue — 296
    Historical Note — 303
    Author's Note — 305
    Acknowledgements — 307
    About the Publisher — 309

1

GRACE DIEU

1233

The smell of smoke lingered. The dream had been vivid. Silas shook off the disturbing memory and turned over, shifting his shoulders to tease the straw-filled mattress into something resembling comfort. Lying on his side with his back to the ill-fitting door, he drew the thin blanket up over his shoulder trying to shield himself from the persistent cold draft that seeped into the room. Usually, he was so exhausted that sleep came easily despite the limitations of his monk's quarters. With sleep came dreams, recollections of things that in the daylight hours he could forget.

As he lay, eyes closed, hoping that a more peaceful sleep would grace the few short hours of the night that remained, his mind rebelled. In that space between sleeping and waking, where thoughts roam to unbidden places, he remembered. He recalled the panic as the flames took hold. He relived the terror as mounted men swept in and screamed abuse at them in their native tongue. His fellow monks did not understand their slurs, but Silas, weaned at the breast of a Welshwoman, knew full well what they were saying. This was their land, this side of the Welsh border, and their intent was to more than scare. They had come to take, and not just the precious foodstuffs, and any plate or candlesticks left by previous raiders. They had come for hostages.

Abbot John had been their target. The old man had been dragged from his bed, with no quarter given for his pale frailty or hacking cough. Silas had tried to defend him and had been taken himself. They had been unceremoniously thrown onto the back of horses and led away into the night, while their brothers fought bravely to extinguish the flames that threatened to consume the abbey of Grace Dieu.

He remembered the smell of smoke and the taste of fear. The terror of being held by their captors for three days until rescued by ransom. The ordeal had taken its toll on Abbot John. He was freed to return to what was left of Grace Dieu but lingered only a few days with his brothers before slipping away. Silas had grieved deeply, carrying an anger against those Welsh marauders that was ungodly and unforgiving for one called by Christ to bless his enemies. His anger was not only towards the captors, but against God. Yet he would not admit that, even to the priest in the confessional – if the priest ever deigned to step inside the half-destroyed walls of their sad little abbey.

Silas shifted again, aware that he could still smell smoke in his nostrils. It didn't usually linger this long once he awoke from his nightmare. It was acrid and hung in the air around him. As he reluctantly opened an eye, the sting of hot air shocked him into full awareness. This was no memory. He heard a shout; his name being called. As he swung his legs around and grabbed his cloak, he wondered why the dark thatch above him sparkled with bright spots of glowing light. He should run, but a deep weariness of body and soul caused him to pause. Should he just lie down again, cover his head with his cloak, and let the fire take him? He did not have the will or the energy to fight for Grace Dieu again. There had been too many fires, too many raids, too much opposition, too much loss.

A hand grabbed his arm, and the fingers pinched painfully. Silas swung around, raising his other arm to defend himself, and encountered a youthful face, wide-eyed with panic. Cedric! The poor novice had only been at Grace Dieu a few weeks.

'Brother, you must come. The church is alight, and we cannot save it without you. The fire is spreading. Already the stables are ablaze, and the refectory roof is smoking. The thatch above us – look!'

He gestured upwards with his free hand – the one gripping Silas' arm tightened still more. Silas flinched and pulled his arm free. He threw his cloak around his shoulders and slipped his feet into his sandals. His leather scrip was the only other thing he paused to grab, securing the pouch to his belt, before grasping the young man's sleeve and pulling him behind him out into the cold night. The night sky was not as dark as it should have been. The wooden church, the one they had not long finished repairing after the previous raid, was well alight. His brothers had drawn water but no number of perfectly aimed buckets of well water could save the church now. A line of 100 strong men might have; they were but five, four of whom were past their youth and feeble from years of hardship.

A quick glance around, and Silas could see fire had taken hold all over the small compound, fanned by a stiff cold wind that carried sparks easily from structure to structure. He shivered, despite the warmth from the flames. It was a clear and cloudless night. No hope of rain from the heavens to douse the blaze. His fellow brothers stood damp and dishevelled, spaced about like the last few pieces of a well-fought game of chess. They stood, as he did, watching as the abbey and their dreams were mercilessly consumed. At least there was no raiding party this time; a few well-aimed firebrands thrown from outside the fence had done the damage. It might have been the same thugs as before, but it could have been youths or even children, the hatred behind their actions well ingrained. Silas had no doubt that they would be back in the morning to loot what was left. It would not be much.

They would not find him or any of his fellow monks there. Silas made that decision. They were done fighting. They had tried – God knows they had tried – but they had lost the battle. It was time to retreat.

Silas called out and four weary faces turned towards him, each one stained with grime, sweat and tears. He felt the sting of guilt, berating himself that he had slept as they had faced the fire without him. He would not let them down again.

'Come, Brothers!' He raised his voice above the sound of flames crackling and beams splitting.

He turned and began walking, and one by one the others followed. Silas stopped to grab the shafts of an untouched handcart, pulling it into the midst of the little gathering that had formed around him.

'Gather what food and clothing you can, quickly, and do not put yourselves at risk. Only what you or this cart can carry. Forget the animals – Cedric.' The young man was trying to hold on to two terrified hens. 'They must fend for themselves. We cannot take them. We must go now, leave here quickly and quietly. They will expect us to stay and fight the flames, but not this time.'

'Perhaps, God willing, we will return and rebuild Grace Dieu?' Brother Jermaine dumped a bundle of cloth and a small sack of dried beans into the cart. He was wheezing from the effects of the smoke, but his natural optimism shone out from eyes circled by soot. Silas could not hold his questioning gaze. He mumbled something non-committal under his breath and started to move off, pulling the cart behind him.

He could not answer his old friend, as he had no idea any more what God willed. God's will had seemingly brought them here to build their bright new abbey, in this inhospitable and godless corner of the Welsh borderlands. Seven years they had built and fought, prayed and defended, broken their backs in the field, only to have their harvest stolen, time and time again.

Last year's kidnapping of their frail abbot and his subsequent death had almost broken them. Now the abbey was burning to the ground.

To his shame, Silas felt relief. He no longer had the strength or the conviction to fight or rebuild. He was done with Grace Dieu. As he walked away from its burning ruins, a niggling thought suggested that perhaps he was done with God as well.

The brothers fell in behind the handcart, each carrying bundles of belongings, their dark Cistercian cloaks tugged around hunched shoulders, their steps laboured. They looked to Silas for leadership, he knew that. No replacement for Abbot John had appeared at Grace Dieu. The position had never been offered to Silas, for which he was glad; he never had ambition to be an abbot. He had joined the Cistercians as a mature man, with a heart only to serve God and to serve others in community. When called to, he had deputised for Abbot John, happily taking much of the weight of day-to-day leadership from his sickly shoulders out of reverence for the godly man. It still grieved him that such a fine man and leader as John should have ended his days in a failing abbey.

As they made their way north from Grace Dieu, they had only one aim: to get to Abbey Dore, the mother house, before night fell again. However weary they were, they trudged on. The ground was mercifully dry, and the moonlit sky meant well-worn paths were easy enough to follow. By the time the sky began to glow with the first signs of dawn, they had walked some distance.

Silas raised his hand to stop their pathetic procession as they reached a grassy clearing half-hidden from the road by a thick patch of brambles. The grass was damp and cold, but no one complained as they gratefully sank to the ground. One by one, excepting Silas, they wrapped themselves in their cloaks, and slept. Silas sat with his back resting against the handcart, keeping vigil. Hunger was not alien to any of them, not with the Cistercian rule of fasting and simple fare and the scarcity that they had become used to at Grace Dieu. Even so, they would need to eat something if they were going to have the energy to walk the remaining distance to Abbey Dore. A quick look through the meagre provisions that had been rescued from the abbey and Silas realised that the dried beans Jermaine had brought were all they had. A sole flagon of ale would have to be shared to quench their thirst.

The sun was high in the sky when Silas quietly moved around his companions and woke them, encouraging them to take a measured swig from the flagon and a handful of hard beans each to chew on. They ate in silence as they were trained to, but Silas could read their faces. Weariness vied with fear and uncertainty. Most of them had burns on their hands or arms. He needed to get them moving again. Once they could see Abbey Dore they would be comforted.

Would they find a welcome? Or would they be treated as the failures they felt? They had been aware of the rumours, of how their community at Grace Dieu had abandoned the Rule which governed their simple lives as Cistercian monks. There was an element of truth to the tales. It was hard to keep to the strict regimen of Prayer Offices and personal meditation when there were so few of them to work the land and tend the animals, without the help of laymen or locals. It was hard to observe the restrictive dietary rules when foodstuffs of any kind were scarce. If fish caught from the River Trothy was the only thing available, then that is what they ate. There was no immorality; they were conscientious to keep God's law, but their faith had been tested to the limit. Well, Silas knew his had. He did not know for sure where the hearts of his brothers lay.

They stopped again when they found a stream of flowing fresh water. They shared a few more of the beans, but did not linger long. They had been following a path parallel to ancient King Offa's dyke, that marked the boundary between England and Wales, but it was as they crossed the dyke and stepped from Welsh to English soil that they began to pick up their pace. Their journey's end was in sight when the spire at Abbey Dore became visible on the horizon.

Silas recognised the porter, and he recognised them, as they were ushered through the gates and into the abbey compound. Bells were ringing to signal an Office, although Silas could not be sure which one. He was offered a beaker of water, from which he drank thirstily. Beyond that he had no memory. Exhaustion mixed with relief took hold, and strong arms lifted his body and carried him to the infirmary. Kind hands cleansed his filthy body, and a soft voice whispered prayers that lulled him into a deep dreamless sleep.

Silas woke to the sound of bells and by instinct he pulled back the blanket covering him and tried to raise himself up. A firm hand rested on his chest and pushed him gently back down.

'Rest, Brother, you are not required to attend the Offices today. I will bring you some food now that you are awake.' A smiling face framed by a neat tonsure hovered over him.

'What Office is it?' His voice cracked, and a beaker was lifted to his lips. They were parched, and he drank, coughing when the liquid hit his constricted throat.

'It is Sext. Noon. You have slept the whole night and all morning, not even Dore's huge bells have disturbed you.' The monk laughed softly. 'You are the last of your fellow brothers to wake, but they each begged me to leave you to sleep. You are held in high regard, it seems. They knew that you did not rest until they were all within the safe walls of this abbey, and they were grateful.'

Silas looked around the large, light-filled room. The other beds in the infirmary stood empty.

'They all slept well and responded to our ministrations. We tended a few minor burns and cuts and gave you all sleeping draughts. Apart from being underfed and weary, your companions all seem to be recovered and eager enough to join the community in their prayers. You, I think, might need to rest a while longer, and your hands and feet will need some care.'

Until the brother had spoken, Silas had not registered the throbbing in his hands and the pain in his feet. His hands were bound in strips of linen, but he could see that they had bled through.

'Blisters from the handcart. Your feet are not much better. Your sandals have rubbed the skin raw. I am surprised you did not feel the pain as you walked.'

Silas grunted and let his eyes close again as the monk proceeded to expertly change his dressings. The truth was that the pain in his heart hurt far more than the blisters on his hands or feet; a pain that being back at Abbey Dore, and the kind attentions of Dore's infirmarer could do little to ease. He had given his all to Grace Dieu. He had endured hardship, kidnapping and terror. Persevered despite personal suffering and loss. All for the sake of the vision to found a new thriving community. He had been prepared to work hard, serve well, build and help grow an abbey from nothing. Part of a pioneering group sent from this very abbey at Dore. All over Europe, Cistercian houses were being founded and were flourishing, but Grace Dieu had failed.

Now, on top of all else that he had suffered, he was faced with his own personal failure. He was the one who had given up, brought his brothers back to the mother house, left Grace Dieu to burn to the ground. That shame was his. Added to the sense of failure was the feeling of betrayal. Why had God allowed them to fail?

Why had He abandoned the very ones who had given their lives to serve Him?

Even if he had risen to attend the Prayer Office with his brothers, Silas suspected that he would only have been going through the motions. He no longer knew where he stood with God. He was no longer sure he had anything to give. All that he had pledged to God had been thrown back in his face. Grief and pain were his reward. He had honoured his promise to God, but it did not feel like God had honoured His promises in return.

By the following morning, Silas could no longer put off the inevitable, and when the bell rang for Lauds, he was already up and dressed. He knew that he would have to leave the quiet peace of the infirmary as his fellow travellers had, now that he no longer needed care. The next night he would be sleeping in a shared dormitory. He was sad at the thought of leaving kind Brother James, but he was a Cistercian, avowed to live the way of the Rule. That meant sharing in community life and attending the prescribed Prayer Offices.

He made his way to the church through the cloister, joining other silent monks with their heads dipped and hooded. They filed into the quire and he took his place in the second row. He was glad of his short stature, as he mouthed the words of the liturgy. He could hide in what seemed like a crowd compared to the few that had lived and prayed together at Grace Dieu. Around him, he recognised a few familiar faces from the past, when

Abbey Dore had been his home, but shame kept his face averted.

He looked down and saw that his habit now hung loose and reached the floor, covering the dressings on his feet, squeezed painfully back into his worn sandals. There was a time when he had more than filled out his habit, with a propensity to roundness, but the years of lack and hard work at Grace Dieu had stripped the excess flesh from his frame. His once chestnut-brown tonsure was speckled with grey. He felt older than his years.

His hair had grown long, and his pate felt stubbly. He knew he needed to get someone to shave it and redefine his tonsure. He would also need new sandals, and a habit made to fit, now he was back at Dore. All these thoughts strayed through his mind as the worship went on around him. He should have enjoyed being in the church; it was a fine stone building, simply painted with whitewash and red line decoration. Its high glassed windows, pillars, arches and vaulted ceiling were impressive, but to Silas it all felt too much. After the simplicity of their church and worship at Grace Dieu, it felt ostentatious and oppressive to his soul. He was glad when the service ended, and he could leave the church and breathe deeply of the cool, fresh air in the open cloister outside. Yet as the other brothers filed away to their work and tasks, Silas suddenly felt lost.

A figure sidled up to him, touching him gently on the sleeve.

'Come, Brother.'

Brother James spoke in a whisper and led Silas back in the direction of the infirmary. He did not speak until they were safely inside. The infirmarer held his gaze, concern etched on his face.

Silas lowered his head at the scrutiny.

'Silas, I have spoken to the abbot on your behalf. I have been given leave to keep you here with me, to aid me until you are well enough for more arduous work.' He paused, waiting for Silas to respond.

Silas lifted his head, surprised to feel the prick of tears, as he nodded his understanding.

'My brothers from Grace Dieu?' His tongue felt thick.

'Hmm. Your concern for them lingers and although that is to be expected, you no longer have responsibility for their welfare. They have also been allocated less demanding work and will be offered additional meals until their full health returns. They, at least, seem happy to be back with us at Dore. You... I am not so sure of.'

Brother James led Silas to a table and gestured for him to take a seat. He poured something into a beaker from a flagon and handed it to Silas. It was mead – sweet, strong, and flavoured with something floral. Silas took a long drink and felt its warming goodness soothe his unsettled stomach. Its potency made his head swim, so he put the cup to one side. Brother James sat on a stool opposite him.

'I do not expect you to use me as a confessional, Brother, as to what thoughts and feelings plague you. But I would have you know that you can find space and peace here...' He gestured around the infirmary, 'to work out what it is you need to work out. Rest from your worries and leave your friends to our care and to God's.'

Silas took a deep breath, releasing it in a long sigh. He wasn't sure what it would feel like to not worry and fret about his brothers, about abbey buildings and farmland, about where their next meal might come from, or when the next raid would happen. He would try. But if he allowed his mind to let go of all those things that had filled it for so long, he feared what dark emptiness might take their place.

These things I have spoken to you,

that in Me you may have peace.

In the world you will have tribulation; but be of

good cheer, I have overcome the world.

John 16:33

2

ABBEY DORE

Brother James was good to his word. Silas kept his bed in a quiet corner of the infirmary. An aged brother joined them that first night, and the infirmarer made poultices to treat the man's ulcerated legs. Another brother joined them the second night, needing treatment for a persistent cough. Silas helped where he could.

On days when the weather was dry, he enjoyed being in the physic garden. Although the soil was mostly bare and the herbs and shrubs were showing the effects of only just surviving a long cold winter, he could find things to do. It was good to feel of use.

To one end of the garden was a simple wooden hut housing gardening tools and a good selection of knives that Brother James pointed out to him, for cutting and processing the herbs needed for treatments. Dried flowers and leaves hung from the low roof beam and at one end was an old table, covered with bowls, jugs, and a pestle and mortar. There was also a whet stone, so that when rain lashed down, Silas could sit inside and clean and sharpen the blades of knives, scythes and hoes, oiling them when he was done. It was mindless yet satisfying work.

His feet and hands were healing. In the hut Silas had found a pair of old leather gloves which he wore for work. He was also grateful for a pair of soft leather boots Brother James produced from somewhere. Silas did not wear them in company, but when he was alone in the garden or the hut, he loved the warmth and comfort they provided. He kept his old habit. Any time he thought of requesting a new one, he felt uneasy. Just as the Offices meant little to him now, so did the dress of his Order. His clothing covered him and kept him warm; that was enough. An old woollen hooded cloak hung in the hut, not black as he was supposed to wear, but a thick brown, patched-up garment. He wore it in secret, and when he did, pulling up the hood to hide his still untrimmed tonsure, he could imagine he was no longer a Cistercian at all.

A few days after his arrival at Abbey Dore, Brother James found him in the garden hut, with a message that he had been summoned to the abbot's rooms. Silas had not doubted that sooner or later he would be called upon to give an account of his abandonment of Grace Dieu. He did not expect any compassion. He had failed in his mission. If there were punishment to be handed out, he would take it willingly, if it helped assuage his feelings of guilt and self-loathing. He changed his boots for sandals, exchanged his comforting cloak for a clean scapula and made his way through the cloisters to the monks' refectory, then up the stairs that led to the abbot's private apartments. As he mounted the stairs, he could hear raised voices, and he paused before entering through the thick wooden door that stood ajar at the top of the stairway.

'Do as I have asked you and send the reply to Sir Walter as I have written it. He will have my support in this.' The voice rang with authority.

'But my Lord Abbot, is it wise to embroil yourself and the abbey in politics, especially when Sir Walter Clifford stands in conflict with the king and threatens outright rebellion?' His companion spoke in much more measured tones.

'All Sir Walter asks is to secrete some coins and other valuables here with us in the abbey, as surety against the fall of Clifford Castle. He promises to reward us generously. He has lands that will add great value to our holdings if he bequeaths them to us. We cannot sustain our success if we do not strive to expand, Brother Prior, as well you know. He has been a good patron; his own brother lies buried within our sanctuary. He will do well by us, if we but offer our help in this.'

'What if he openly rebels against King Henry? Where does that leave us? That would be treasonous, and I feel it is unwise to take sides in this, my lord.'

There was silence, but not for long. The abbot's voice, when it replied, carried more than a hint of menace.

'You will do as I have asked, and I will be obeyed in this. I hold the power here and I have heard enough. Do you understand? Now leave me...'

Silas tried to melt into the stone wall of the stairwell as the door was flung open and a flustered monk pushed past him. He recognised Prior Anselm; a usually quiet and composed man, good at his job and keen to serve. It was obvious he had been riled from his beet-red face and beaded forehead. He did not stop to acknowledge Silas but hurried past him down the stairs clutching a parchment bearing the abbot's seal. Silas stood for a moment, wondering if he too should leave. He should not have stayed and listened in to a private conversation. If he entered the abbot's rooms now, it would be obvious that he had overheard.

He was leaning against the cool wall, trying to decide what was best, when the abbot appeared in the doorway. He seemed surprised at first to see Silas there, but then his look took a supercilious turn. He did not speak, did not ask if or what Silas had heard, rather beckoned sharply for him to enter, and strode back into the room.

Silas stepped into a foreign world. The room was lavishly decorated with fine wall hangings and silk bed coverings. The bed itself would have been fit for a king, with its finely crafted wooden carvings. Silas had never seen such opulence, certainly never within any of the abbeys he had been to. Abbey Dore was obviously doing well from its land produce and wool sales, and some of that wealth had made it into the abbot's own private domain. Silas felt sick to his stomach with the injustice. They had struggled to live simply, struggled to live at all at Grace Dieu, when all the time the abbot here at Dore was living in comfort and thinking nothing of bartering dangerously with rebellious nobles who stood in opposition to the king. A wave of anger surged through his body; he clenched his fists and willed his lips to stay silent.

The abbot moved behind a table and sat down in a comfortable-looking chair, but did not offer a seat to his visitor. He lifted a lip in a half-sneer as he appraised Silas, and when he spoke it was with a hard edge.

'So, you have come back to Abbey Dore like a cowardly dog, with your tail between your legs.' He leaned forward menacingly. 'You had no instruction to leave Grace Dieu, Brother. No invitation by my hand to return to us. It seems that you took it upon yourself to abandon your post and brought your fellow workers with you. No sign of the eager, pioneering spirit that you left here with.' He narrowed his eyes. 'How does it feel to have failed? It must have humbled you and stripped you of your ambition, Monk.'

Silas shifted but stayed silent. His anger response subsided at the abbot's words and was replaced by the self-loathing he was used to carrying.

It would do him no good to speak, to try to defend himself. He was not sure that he could. He recalled the day vividly when he had left Abbey Dore, proud to be a member of the missionary party that had been chosen to build the new house at Grace Dieu. He had been full of excitement and vision. He had seen it as an opportunity to do something great for God and for the Order. He remembered the energy he had poured out at first, the passion with which he had pursued the dream.

It had all been for nothing, for an abbey that now stood in smouldering ruins. He had heard the sad reports. Little remained of what he and the others had fought to build. No matter that it had always been against the odds; an English mother house, appropriating land from inhospitable Welsh neighbours, and seeking to build within a community that was unwelcoming at best, and openly hostile at worst.

Abbot Adam leant back in his chair, took a long swig from a silver cup and fiddled with the emerald signet ring he wore on his little finger.

'You have been welcomed back to Abbey Dore because it was the right thing to do.' He made an attempt at a smile, but it was half-hearted. 'You are, of course, a brother of this Order, and you must have a home among your own. I thought to demand some penance from you, but I understand from our saintly infirmarer that you and your brothers have suffered, both in your attempts to save Grace Dieu from the flames and from the alleged hardships you have faced. I pray God will reward you for your endurance and will overlook your failures.

'In time, I pray that you will see that your pride led you to this fall, and in true humility you will accept whatever small task God has in mind for you. We will direct you as we see fit. For now, you can return to Brother James and his garden, but make good use of this time to think, pray and consider the character deficiencies that have brought you to this moment of disgrace.'

With that, the abbot rose abruptly from his seat and gestured for Silas to leave.

Disgrace? Was that what this was, Silas pondered as he navigated the stairs, and his path through the refectory and cloisters back to the sanctuary of the infirmary garden. Had he been prideful? Was it his fault that Grace Dieu had failed? Did the abbot really consider his actions a disgrace to the Order? That same abbot who so clearly flaunted his own poverty vows. Silas did not think he could trust Abbot Adam's assessment, nor did he believe the abbot could speak for God.

How did God see it? All Silas knew was that if God was really there, He was not the God Silas had believed Him to be. He had not protected them, had not provided for them, had not prospered the work of their hands, had not saved Abbot John from pain or ignominy. And where was God now? Was He here at Abbey Dore, in that majestic church building, among these well-proportioned cloister arches, in the hymns and prayers of the brothers here? If He was here, then Silas could not sense His presence. One thing was clear and sure in Silas' mind. Abbey Dore was not his home, despite what the abbot had said. Grace Dieu had been more of a home to him, in all its simplicity, than this prosperous abbey ever could be.

He could not stay. He did not want to be here. This life felt alien to him now. How could he come back and behave as if nothing had changed, when everything he loved had been forcibly taken from him? How could he sit in the splendour of the abbey church and lift his voice in praise to a God he neither trusted nor fully believed in anymore? How could he work and serve in a community, knowing that he was likely being judged by others in the same way Abbot Adam had judged him? By the time Silas reached his sanctuary garden, he was already making plans.

A quiet visit to the abbey kitchen in the dark hours of the night, before the bells announced Vigils, allowed him to find a small sack into which he secreted a cup. He added a half-loaf of bread and a handful of dried plums. From a pile of discarded clothing waiting to be laundered, he took a rough woollen tunic, a layman's dress, and from his own garden room, Brother James' leather boots, his gloves and the old woollen cloak. Into his scrip, he dropped the pewter cross and chain that he had always worn under his habit and a short, bladed knife – one that he himself had sharpened and polished to a shine. All this was left stacked ready beneath the table in the hut.

He joined his brothers for the Prayer Office but as they left the church, most to return to their beds for the few hours before Lauds, Silas quietly slipped into the physic garden. In the hut he removed his habit, scapular and sandals, donned his borrowed costume and picked up the few meagre belongings he had gathered. He left through a side gate in the abbey walls, looking back only once to say a silent farewell to the friends he was leaving behind; to those who had returned with him from Grace Dieu and to the kind Brother James who had tried his best to help him. As he turned and walked through the gate into the darkness beyond, it was relief that Silas felt more than any other emotion. He did not know where he would go, how he would live, and if he would ever regret breaking his vows, he just needed to escape.

Silas was not sure how long he walked. His feet had gone from being sore, to painful, to numb with cold, despite the boots. His cloak did little to keep out the biting wind, nor the icy rain that began to fall. The sun had started to breach the horizon, but dark clouds scudded above his head. He walked on, uncaring, and did not see the tree root that crossed his path until he found himself awkwardly sprawled in the dirt. He lay there, winded, and thought for a moment that perhaps he could continue to lie, his cheek resting against ice-cold mud, his legs twisted behind him. The shape of something hard and unyielding pressed into his chest, so he heaved himself up until he was sitting half-upright. His last rebellious act on leaving Abbey Dore had been to steal one of Brother James' flagons of mead, and it was the only thing he felt any guilt about.

Silas pulled the flagon out, relieved to find it undamaged by his fall, unstopped it and took a deep swig. He glanced behind him, down the path he had come, but it was silent. A sudden anxiety that he might have been followed gripped him, but he shook the feeling away. He was sure no one had seen him leave, and even when they did find him missing, he was unsure any would care enough to pursue him. He tore a chunk of bread off the loaf he had taken from the refectory kitchen and ate it. He would have to ration what he carried, as he had no coin and no idea where he would find food when what he had ran out. He also needed to rest, out of sight of the road for his own peace of mind.

The trees were fairly dense, but it was too early in the year for leaf growth, so there was no foliage to offer much in the way of protection. However, the great oak whose wayward root had stopped him in his tracks, had grown and twisted in such a way that a natural hollow had formed where its trunk met the ground. Silas crawled over and was grateful for his short legs and malnourished form as he bent to fit in the confined space. With his hood up and the hem of his cloak covering his feet, it was as sheltered as he was going to get. Whether it was the infirmarer's mead, or his night flight catching up with him, in that cramped space, just feet from the weather-blown path, he slept soundly.

Silas woke to a strange chattering sound. The wind had died down and the clouds dispersed. The late winter sun cast its watery warmth in his direction, and he was grateful for it. From the sun's position, he reckoned it was almost noon, and his stomach rumbled in agreement. He wasn't sure where the chattering had come from, but it was somewhere close by, and as he stretched out his painfully bent legs, something russet red flashed by. Now the chattering noise was closer. Whatever the creature was, it wasn't happy. Silas inched his way out of the hollow and turned to find himself face to face with a squirrel, perched on a nearby tree root, clutching an acorn in its paws.

Silas was surprised to find his face crease into a half smile; he had wondered if his mouth had forgotten how to do that lately. The squirrel was animated and seemingly unafraid. Something had stolen its home, and it was not happy about it. Silas knew only too well how it felt. He stood up awkwardly, feeling the effects of his deep, damp, cramped sleep, and tried not to make any sudden movements. The squirrel stopped its agitated chattering but was watching him, beady-eyed. Silas slowly retrieved his sack and scrip and backed away until the squirrel, obviously happy that the intruder was far enough away, dove into the hollow, to enjoy his acorn in the very spot where Silas had slept.

Silas walked away, allowing himself the slightest of chuckles. He was thankful for the light moment the squirrel's antics had afforded him. He was also glad of the improved weather. He could hear birds singing to each other, no doubt as grateful as he for the respite from the rain and the sun's welcome light. It was still cold, though, and the sun wasn't warm enough to make much difference to the damp weight of his clothes. He needed to freshen up and he was thirsty, and not for more of Brother James' potent mead. He needed to find a fresh water source.

He walked on, following a route that was not much more than a track. He was glad for that; wider roads would have attracted horses, wagons and travelling strangers that he was keen not to encounter. He didn't expect a search party to have been sent out after him, but he needed to get further away from Dore, needed not to be recognised. The thought of being dragged back spurred him on and he picked up his pace as his stiff muscles eased.

The track rose up an incline that grew increasingly steep until it levelled out and he recognised the raised earthwork of a man-made dyke. He had inadvertently rediscovered Offa's boundary. He had not considered where he was headed, but now he faced a decision; to stay in England, or to cross over into Wales. Despite his terrifying experience of the Welsh at Grace Dieu, he still felt an unmistakeable draw towards the country of his birth. The *hiraeth* siren was strong, he mused, as he climbed up onto the dyke, finding the rocky path along its ridge still passable. He chose to walk it for a while. Being stuck between one country and the other, in the middle of the troublesome Marches, felt symbolic of where his heart and mind lay. He was neither monk nor layman. He did not know which way to go. Should he continue to run from his contained monastic life, or find his way back? Try to find his God, or just to let God find him? If He truly existed. It was easier to not think, to not make a decision, to just keep walking.

The sound of running water made him stop. He listened and followed. Stepping down from the dyke path and around a large rock, he found a stream on the other side, trickling over mossy stones to where it formed a small pool in a stony basin. Silas sank heavily to his knees and removed a glove, cupping his hand to gather some water and bring it to his mouth. It was sweet, cold and much needed. Silas removed his other glove and retrieved the cup from his sack. He held it in the stream until it was half-full, and then lifted it to his lips and drank deeply. The second cupful he tipped over his head. The icy water shocked the breath from him, but it felt good. He shook his head and ran his hand over his scalp. A thought seized him. He focused on the pool and could see a rippled reflection of his face, lit by the high sun above him. Taking the knife from his scrip, he held it to his scalp and scraped as gently as he could. He watched his tonsured hair fall away from his head. It was not the best knife for the job, and he could not see all his scalp, but he worked methodically around his hairline, feeling as he went, wincing when the blade scraped skin as well as hair. When he was done, his head felt lighter, and his heart also felt strangely relieved. He could be whoever he wanted to be now. Brother Silas lay in clumps of hair around his feet.

Lo, I am with you always, even to the end of the age.

Matthew 28:20

3

Hay-on-Wye

The dyke followed the ridge of the bluff, and Silas continued to walk along it. From his vantage point he could see for some distance. The day wore on, and as his sore feet began to stumble on the path, he saw the outline of a meandering river at the base of the rise. The river flowed into a settlement with a large castle enclosure at its centre. The castle had a tall, imposing, completed stone gatehouse to one end of it, but otherwise looked to be in a state of disrepair.

Silas realised that the dyke had led him to the castle and settlement at Hay. He had never visited, but Hay's reputation proceeded it. Sitting as it did on the border, and in the heart of the tumultuous Marches, it was an important castle for whoever had control of it. For years, the king of England had held it, or rather the powerful de Braose family had held it for him. That is until William de Braose, the last Lord of Hay, had crossed the Welsh Prince, Llewellyn. William had been caught in a compromising situation with Llewellyn's wife, and finding himself at the mercy of Welsh law, had been summarily judged and hanged at Abergwyngregyn, the Prince's Welsh stronghold. Llewellyn had then ridden south and attacked Hay Castle, causing major damage. Silas had heard the rumours and now could see the evidence for himself.

Silas had no desire to enter the town, but Offa's path ended there. He would need to find a river crossing somewhere and it made sense that there would be one in Hay. He stepped off the dyke as the sun began to sink in the sky. Clear skies meant it was likely to be a frigid night and he needed to find shelter; somewhere he could wait and watch until he deemed it safe to enter Hay and walk its streets unnoticed. He finally found a large rock to rest his back against. Even with his cloak wrapped tightly around him and a deep swallow of Brother James' mead in his stomach, the cold soon began to permeate his clothing. He dared not light a fire and risk being spotted from the town below, even if he had the energy to do so. He waited and watched and shivered, periodically forcing his tired legs to raise himself from the ground and move his body, stamping his feet and rubbing his arms vigorously to try to warm himself. Eventually, fatigue took over and he dosed fitfully, until some deep remembrance within him woke him at the early morning hour of Vigils.

He moved gingerly. The shivering had stopped but now his legs, arms, hands and feet felt numb. He had to stand up; he knew he needed to get his blood flowing. Silas reached again for the mead, took a swig and chewed on a dried plum. He thought of his brothers and how they would be forcing themselves from their warm beds to attend Vigils in the cold abbey church. He longed for the warm bed, but not for the Prayer Office.

It did feel strange to not pray as he woke and as he ate. The habit of prayer had been well entrenched even before he entered the Order. He had prayed morning and evening, and before every meal, as his mother had taught him. He had spoken to God and had even thought he had heard Him speak back. He had been sure of his faith and dedicated to deepening it. He had served and worshipped God for as long as he could remember. Silas could make himself repeat the familiar words, he supposed, but something within him rejected the thought. He just could not do it.

He shook himself out of his musings and forced his body upright. He was not sure that his frozen feet could bear his weight, and he swayed slightly as they burned. He gasped and tried to stamp the pain away, shaking his hands vigorously at the same time. If anyone had come across him at that moment, he was sure they would have either laughed or shied away in terror. An owl's solitary hoot startled him, and he spun around panicked, but he was alone.

Eventually, he bent to pick up his meagre belongings and hobbled to a vantage point from where he could see the outline of the settlement below. All seemed quiet. Now was as good a time as any for him to creep down and see if he could find a bridge or ford. He still had no idea where he was headed, but he did not want to be where people were. He hoped to pass through Hay's streets unnoticed.

A lone cockerel crowed as he reached the edge of the town, and he could see the sky was beginning to lighten. He urged his legs to move a bit quicker. There were no other signs of life, and he avoided passing too close to the castle, where he imagined sentries stood guard. As soon as he could, he ducked behind the dwellings that lined the river edge. He followed the riverbank but there were no obvious crossing places. In fact, the river was wider than he had imagined, and flowed, dark and ominous, beside him.

He had walked almost the length of Hay, skirting yards, squeezing between buildings and wading through reed beds, before he realised that there was no bridge, no shallow ford. Finally, when he had almost given up hope he came to a natural beach. On the shale lay three upturned coracles tied loosely to a stake dug into the shore. Silas sat down on the grass where it met the shale. This was not what he had imagined. The thought of trusting himself to one of those unsteady vessels terrified him. How badly did he need to cross the river here? Could he chance walking further to find an easier way? He knew enough about coracles to know that they were not easy to manoeuvre, and the river was flowing fast. He could imagine how cold and deep its waters were.

He heard another cockerel crow, and the sound of someone hitching a horse to a wagon not too far away. He had to decide. Either he slunk back into the shadows of Hay and hid somewhere until he could make his escape back the way he came, or he could take his chances with one of those little boats and try to get across the river. It did not seem much of a choice. He heaved himself up and wrestled a coracle free from its mooring and into the river shallows. He should have removed his boots, and it might have been sensible to remove his heavy cloak also, but he did not have time to think about it. He threw his belongings in and then half-fell into the vessel, clasping the oar in his free hand. Surprisingly the coracle floated, and he eased into a kneeling position and anxiously dipped the oar into the water. Its tip met with the riverbed and Silas pushed the boat further away from the shore, until he felt the current take it. He heard a yell and running feet and turned to see a figure of a man on the riverbank. He was shouting and gesturing, but Silas could not catch what he was saying. It made no difference, because he could not turn back now. He had little control over the coracle. The river was winning, and he was nowhere near either bank.

It took all his effort to keep the bobbing vessel afloat. Fear clenched his stomach as water sloshed over the edges and soaked his legs. He felt the freezing cold creep above his knees and knew he was in trouble. If the coracle capsized in the fast-flowing river, weighed down with his tunic and heavy cloak, Silas knew he would sink like a stone. The oar struck something beneath the surface and was torn from his hand. Silas leaned over the side to try to grab it, but the current swirled it away, and the coracle tipped precariously. He sat back onto his knees, gripping tightly to the sides of the boat. He was wet, and cold, and terrified. The buildings of Hay were now barely visible behind him, and he could see no signs of habitation on the riverbank. He felt the hopelessness of his situation. Like Jonah in the belly of the whale, he was helpless, held captive by his own foolish decision, carried away to who knew where with no knowledge of how this would end.

'God', he cried. 'Help me!'

The coracle spun and his stomach heaved. He was being tossed about and it was taking all his remaining strength to keep himself upright. At least the whale had spewed Jonah out eventually, onto a beach, alive to rethink his choices. He bowed his head and screwed his eyes shut. If this was to be his end, he would not fight it. He was done. Perhaps it would be quicker to just toss himself out of the coracle and let the freezing river waters take him. His arms, his legs, his back ached. He let go of the sides of the coracle, and sank down, curling into a ball at the bottom of the boat. Tears of despair mixed with cold river water as the coracle continued to swirl and bob.

He heard splashing. Then he felt the coracle lurch and come to a sudden stop.

'Oh-hh! A m-man! 'Tis a man, M-Mother!'

He heard more splashes and felt the coracle being pulled along by strong hands. He raised his head slightly and opened his eyes. In the early morning light, he could see that his rescuer was tall. Young and strong too, by the ease at which he pulled Silas ashore. As the coracle hit the beach, a face appeared unnervingly close to his own. The eyes were bright, inquisitive, and paired with a crooked smile.

'C-c-come now, like M- M -Moses in the bulrushes you... are... rescued! Though I be no p-p-princess of Egypt!' His rescuer laughed and gripped his arm. Silas struggled to stand. The coracle may have come to rest on solid ground, but he still felt like he was being tossed to and fro. He was soaked to the skin and shivering violently.

'Now then, Samuel, take some care. The poor man is drenched and frozen.' A woman wearing a simple white wimple and veil, and a worn blue cloak, reached out to steady him as he stepped out of the coracle. Her face was pleasant but marked with deep lines.

'Come.' She smiled briefly. 'Let us get you to our hearth and see you warm and dry. Samuel will bring your things. He thought only that one of John Boatman's coracles had got loose and floated downstream. He did not think he was stepping into the Wye to retrieve a boat complete with passenger.'

All the time she was speaking she was gently guiding Silas along, her hand light on his sleeve. He wanted to say something, but he could not find the energy to speak. He concentrated on putting one stumbling foot in front of the other until he was leaning against the wall of a good-sized but simply built thatched house. It stood on its own, surrounded by trees and river reed beds. The woman stepped around him and pushed open a wooden door. A stream of white smoke escaped and with it, the promise of warmth.

'Come inside.' She led him through the doorway. The sun had not risen enough to pour much natural light through the small window openings, but as the woman threw peat onto the fire, the flames blazed and Silas could see enough to make out a large living room, furnished and well kept. He felt her come behind him, and a firm hand pushed him down onto a chair. He was so close to the fire he thought it might singe him, except that the steam rising from his clothes was evidence enough that he was likely too drenched to burn.

He sat staring into the flames, his body still quaking. He could hear bustling, and cupboards being opened and closed, and then the woman was back with a pot that she secured onto the pothook that hung over the fire.

'It won't take long to heat that stew, and then you can be warmed by it from the inside out. In the meantime, you might want to rid yourself of those wet things. Here, my late husband was bigger than you, but these will serve you well enough while we dry yours.' She thrust a bundle into his hands.

He coloured as the thought crossed his mind that he had not undressed in front of a woman for many, many years. When he looked up, however, she had gone, and the young lad stood in her place, a lopsided grin on his face.

'M – Ma will be seeing to the m-milk c-c-cow. I will h-h-help you. H-here.' The young man began to untie Silas' cloak at the neck.

'Thank you,' Silas croaked, and then cleared his throat as he stood to have his tunic pulled over his head. 'You are very kind, Samuel.'

The lad held out the dry tunic, helping Silas to manoeuvre it over his head and outstretched arms. It was thick and surprisingly soft, made of green dyed wool, trimmed with red thread in stitched designs around the collar and cuffs. A fine garment by all accounts, and warm. Silas was grateful as he sat back down heavily on his seat. The lad was then at his feet, tugging at his soggy boots. Silas did what he could to help until between them they had removed the offending articles.

The door swung open behind him.

'Don't put those cold feet too close to the fire or you will find they will heat too quickly and burn fiercely.' The woman had returned and was pouring fresh milk into a beaker. 'Here, this is warm from the cow and will sustain you until we can get food into you.' She handed it to him and then glanced down at his feet. She could see, as he could, that his barely healed blisters had reopened. His palms too were raw and bleeding.

Silas held the beaker carefully in his hands, which were now throbbing as the numbing cold was leaving them. A heavy blanket was placed around his shoulders, and he sipped the milk gratefully.

'Can I ask who shows me such kindness?' Silas was surprised to find his eyes pricking as he watched the lad hang his wet things from pegs well positioned in thick oak beam rafters. There was something slightly odd about the way the boy moved, as there had been in the way he spoke. A slowness, a deliberateness, an awkwardness. Yet he had proved himself strong and capable enough.

The woman leaned over the pot and used a wooden spoon to stir whatever it contained. The aroma that drifted up made Silas' mouth water. She spoke as she stirred.

'You have found yourself in the home of Hannah and Samuel Carpenter. My husband passed not two months since, so we manage alone.' She paused then and glanced up as he watched her. Her eyes were moss green and shone with kindness. 'It is just as well that I still had Daniel's best tunic. I meant to sell it; God knows we could use the money it would bring, but I have not been able to bring myself to do so.' Her voice cracked. She stood upright and wiped her hands down her apron front.

'Well, I thank you both, for my rescue, for your care, and for the borrow of the tunic. It is indeed a fine garment, and this - a welcoming home.' He tried to smile reassuringly.

Samuel had come to sit by his knees, long legs twisted beneath him, a broad grin on his open face. His eyes were the same shade as his mother's and bore the same look of kindness.

'

'Tis good to have c-c-company. C-c-can I have stew again, M-Ma?'

She laughed softly. 'You have not long had breakfast, and this was meant for our supper tonight. But I suppose you can eat with our guest.' She busied herself with a ladle and passed Samuel a steaming bowl. She dished a bowl for Silas but glancing at his hands, pulled up a stool beside him, and lifted a spoonful to his mouth with her own hand. It felt strangely intimate to Silas, who had no choice but to open his mouth, like a weaning child, and accept the proffered food. As he received the spoon's contents into his mouth, it tasted so good he had to fight the urge to sigh with satisfaction.

When his bowl was empty and taken away, Hannah proceeded to busy herself, binding his hands and feet with clean linen strips.

'I am no healer. These wounds look beyond my wisdom to treat, but at least the linen will keep them clean.' She stood back to assess him. 'Now you look a mite better, but also like you might fall off that chair with exhaustion at any moment. Can you move, do you think? Through that doorway is where the cow lives when we bring her indoors, and above it is a loft where Samuel has his bed. There is a ladder, but I think if we can get you up there, you will find it comfortable enough. You can sleep, and then when you are rested, you can tell us why you stole one of John Boatman's coracles, and where you thought you were heading in it. I don't know why God brought you to our door,' she paused. 'I am not in the habit of taking strangers in... especially men...'

She turned questioning eyes on him.

'I am a stranger, but I am safe. You need not fear.' He held her gaze, until she nodded almost imperceivably. He continued, 'I will take you up on your offer of a bed, but when I have rested and my things are dry, I will leave and not inconvenience you further.' He stood unsteadily and Hannah and Samuel were there, one either side of him, holding his arms and helping him towards the doorway.

'You have somewhere to be, when you leave here, I presume?'

Silas could not answer her, and she did not push him. Only as he reached the ladder and placed his bandaged hands on the uprights did she speak again.

'Can we at least know your name, Stranger?'

'I am Br...' He hesitated and shook his head. 'Forgive me. My name is Morgan. Morgan ap Bedwyr.' Names from his past, from before he gave up his wealthy home and prosperous family to live a life of devoted simplicity.

She stared again, her eyes too knowing, then turned away as Samuel helped him up the ladder and onto the shelf. Once there Silas found a clean, soft, straw-filled mattress. He allowed himself to lie down and close heavy eyes. He felt, rather than saw, Samuel move to cover him with the weight of a thick blanket. The slightly sweet smell of cow was the last thing he registered as he let his aching body sink into oblivion.

Peace I leave with you, My peace I give to you;

not as the world gives do I give to you.

Let not your heart be troubled, neither let it be

afraid.

John 14:27

4

Hannah and Samuel

Shouted greetings and the sound of cartwheels bouncing over rutted ground woke him. He was warm and felt more rested than he had in days, but as he stretched his arms and legs, they reminded him of the miles he had walked and of his fight with the river. His limbs were stiff and aching, and his hands and feet, although no longer throbbing, were sore. He slowly raised himself up. He needed a drink, and to find out if his clothes were dry. As if reading his thoughts, a hand appeared at the top of the ladder clutching a beaker of water, which he leaned over to take thankfully. His host had stepped onto the first rung of the ladder to reach him but had averted her face to preserve his dignity.

'I heard you stirring.' She spoke in a hurried whisper. 'Forgive me for intruding, but I wanted to warn you to stay where you are. That is John Boatman outside, come to reclaim his lost coracle. Samuel went into town to tell him that we had found it but made no mention of finding you in it. John is not a bad man, but he might not take it too kindly if he knew we were sheltering a boat thief!'

Silas took a deep swig of the cool water when she had gone. He moved quietly, pulling his body as far away from the edge of the loft as he could, until he was curled up against the rear wall under the sloping thatch. Fully awake now, he could feel his heart pounding and trained his ears for sounds of anyone approaching. What would happen if he were discovered? He had been observed, after all. The boatman would know that the coracle Samuel had retrieved hadn't been empty when it left the beach in Hay.

He knew the penalty for thieving. He could lose his hands or worse, find himself strung up from a hangman's noose, but no one approached the spot where he hid. He could hear only the sounds of a weighty object being hauled up and onto the cart. The boatman's voice was loud and sounded jolly more than angry, although Silas could not distinguish his words clearly. The man did not seem in any hurry to leave, as Silas waited and shifted uncomfortably.

Finally, he heard the clunking of wheels turning and a shouted farewell. A sigh of relief escaped as he carefully slid across to the top of the ladder and lowered himself down. This time it was a grinning Samuel that greeted him as his feet painfully touched the ground. Samuel had Silas' still damp boots in his hands and cheerfully helped him to pull them on. Silas gingerly followed the boy out of the house and into the bright daylight. The horse-drawn cart was already some distance away down the track from the house and he felt his body relax.

The relief of not being found was tinged with guilt. Not only had he stolen and almost destroyed another man's property, but here he was now imposing on the kindness of strangers and causing them to sin by omitting the truth of his presence. No true man of God would countenance such things. He needed to be gone from this place soon, and no longer subject others to the consequences of his bad choices. He was not safe to be in company, despite the reassurances he had given Mistress Carpenter.

His resolve to leave was threatened almost immediately as Samuel re-emerged from the doorway of the house with a pair of fine-looking trout dangling from his hand.

'J-J-John Boatman s-s-said I d-d-deserved a reward!' He held up the fish to display them in all their glory, almost stumbling over with excitement.

'Humph.' Hannah came out of the house behind him. 'More likely trying to impress me with his largesse.' She smiled, not quite as wide a grin as her son's, but it did reach her eyes. 'It means we have something for supper now, in place of the stew that you two finished this morning. Cooked over the fire with some fresh bread to accompany it, this will make a fine feast.'

Silas opened his mouth to explain that he could no longer stay but the words would not come. His stomach rumbled audibly which made Samuel laugh and brought a smile to Silas' own face.

'Wash and gut those fish for me, Samuel.'

Hannah pointed her son in the direction of the river and then gestured for Silas to sit on a bench placed against the exterior wall of the house. He noted that although made from pieces of simply split tree trunks, the bench was sturdy and well made, the seat sanded to a smooth finish and oiled, the joints secure. Hannah sat down with him, a respectable distance between them. The sky was clear, and a weak sun gave a little pleasant warmth, although it no longer sat high in the sky. Silas realised that even if he were to leave now, he would not get far before nightfall, and there was still the river to navigate. He had already failed to get across it once. He was also still wearing his borrowed clothes. He shifted self-consciously.

'Your things are almost dry.'

It was uncanny how she seemed to read his mind.

'Thank you. I must not impose on your hospitality. Perhaps I might eat with you and then find some shelter nearby for the night, before continuing my journey. Samuel must have his bed tonight.'

She turned to look at him. It took her a moment to respond, her face hard to read.

'Your hands and your feet need to heal before you try to journey further. Your presence here is no imposition.' She paused. 'Can you walk a few paces with me?'

She stood and held her hands together in front of her, waiting for him.

Silas pushed himself upright with some effort. She was right. He was in no state to travel; he could barely move. That became evident as she rounded the other side of the house, and he hobbled after her. Before them was a building he had not noticed before, not as large as the house but similarly constructed with a high-pitched thatched roof. It had one large doorway with two doors that opened back on their hinges. As they reached it, Hannah hung back to allow him to see inside. The floor was covered with wood shavings and the air redolent with the smell of freshly cut wood. A large workbench filled much of the interior, and stacked all around it were items of furniture, most of them unfinished. There were also sawn lengths of wood in different stages of being worked and stacks of cut logs. On the workbench itself was a large wooden box, most likely a trunk in the making. Silas moved closer and reached his finger out to touch the smooth surface and then he gasped. Carved into the side of the box was the most intricate design of twisted flowers, leaves and birds. It was beautifully done, the work of a truly gifted craftsman.

'He died suddenly.' She stepped up beside him and reached out her own hand to caress the wood.

He felt the sudden need to step away, as if imposing on a moment of intimacy. She stood there for a minute before sniffing and quickly withdrawing her hand, burying it in the wide sleeve of her gown.

'It is a beautiful piece of work. I am sorry for your loss.'

'Daniel was proud of it, to be sure. He did not get to make such fine pieces often, but Lady Eve had commissioned this, and one or two other pieces. That was before the castle was attacked, and before Daniel...'

She moved past him and reached her hand out to touch what appeared to be a chair back, decorated with the same elaborate carved design as the trunk. It was leaning against the wall, the seat and legs of the unfinished chair lying discarded beside it.

'Can I ask what happened? Was your husband killed when the castle was attacked?'

She spun around at his words. A look of pain on her face.

'No. Daniel had no heart to fight. He was a gentle man, and kind. He would not have raised a weapon to anyone.' She dipped her head and let her veil half-cover her face.

Silas chided himself. What business was it of his how her husband died? There was proof enough here that she had loved and lost.

'Forgive me.'

She raised her face to him.

'Do not concern yourself, *Brother.* It is your nature, and I dare say your custom, to ask questions that probe to the heart of a matter... He died suddenly, in his sleep, leaving his work unfinished, my heart wounded, and Samuel fatherless. Our only consolation is that he has gone to God. Of that, we are sure.'

He drew a sharp intake of breath when he heard how she addressed him. He felt suddenly trapped and, needing to distance himself from her, he stepped backwards. Her hand reached out to grab his sleeve. She dropped her voice to a gentle whisper as she leaned close.

'We all carry secrets, Brother, and I have no wish to know yours, unless you need to tell me. But I knew from the moment I saw the state of your poorly shaved head, and the sandal marks dug deep into your feet, that you were a monk. Your clothes are not your own, and the pewter cross in your pouch hinted at a life of devotion... Come, sit. You look ready to drop.'

She was right. Her words had drained the blood from his face.

She half-tugged him further into the workshop to where a bed base stood against the back wall. It had the unmistakeable fine carvings of the other pieces of her husband's work. It too was unfinished – it had a base and four corner poles, but the finely carved headboard stood leaning against the wall beside it.

'This is what I was going to show you.'

Straw had been heaped onto the bed base and covered with blankets.

'I was going to offer you this... very fine...' her face twisted in wry grin, '... bed to use, for as long as you need for your feet to heal. It is not as warm in here as in the house, and you cannot have a fire, but there are more blankets and more straw.'

Silas sank down onto the side of the bed. His head was spinning. She knew that he was a monk, but she didn't need to know more? She was still willing to shelter and help him? He felt something catch in his throat and suddenly it became hard to take a deep breath. He dropped his head into his hands, cringing as the pressure of his face on the bandaged sores made them sting. Did he have any choice but to stay, knowing that she held his secret? He felt so weary, down to the very bone, and here was kindness, warmth and shelter.

She stood quietly watching him, saying nothing. Her presence alone was soothing. Eventually Silas raised his head to meet her gaze.

'I thank you for your generosity, your kindness and your discretion.' He looked away, and as he caught sight of the workbench, and the unfinished trunk, he suddenly knew he had the answer.

'I will stay until my hands and feet are healed enough for me to leave. Please let me repay your hospitality. This,' he pointed to the trunk, 'and the chair, and the bed; let me finish them for you. I do not have the skill to carve, not like your late husband had, but I can make solid joints and am well used to handling wood and tools.'

He thought back to all the work he had done at Grace Dieu; all they had taught themselves of wooden construction to build and repair the God-forsaken abbey and its contents. They had needed to be self-sufficient. At least the skills he had acquired there could be reused for some good here.

She walked back over to the unfinished trunk sat on the workbench and raised her fingers to trace the carving again.

'While it sits here, it is as if he is still here. Just gone out for a few hours but coming back to finish his work later.' She spoke quietly. 'It deserves to be finished. All the pieces he was working on do. They will sell for a good price, and that is what he would have wanted. He would never have wanted to leave us in need. Our food stores have run low, and I have had no work. I used to take in laundry from the castle when the ladies were in residence. They trusted me with their fine pieces. But that ended when they left.'

She dropped her hand and stepped away from the workbench, turning to face him again.

'Can you do it? Samuel will help, but he is not... he can't handle the tools skilfully, his hands will not always behave as he wants.' She sighed deeply, and compassion welled up within him.

She was bearing a heavy weight, dealing with her own grief and with a son whose limitations affected his prospects. And with the threat of poverty looming. He would help her as much as he could. He had nowhere else to go.

'I believe I can finish the furniture, and I will gladly engage Samuel as my helper. He is strong to lift and carry, and my hands and feet are weak yet.' He studied his bandaged hands again, and saw that the wounds were still weeping, staining the linen that bound them. 'I also think Samuel could help me make these better. Do you have any mint growing nearby, and would you have any honey left in your store?'

She bobbed her head. 'Yes of course. We'll find Samuel and he can aid you. I am glad you know what your wounds need.'

That was one more skill that life at Grace Dieu had taught him.

She led the way back out into the now fading sunlight.

The herbs and the honey helped heal his blisters, although it was some days before Silas could use the tools he needed to. He had tried wearing his gloves, but found he could neither grip nor handle chisel, hammer or fine saw with them on. While Samuel was keen to help, his awkwardness meant that lifting and carrying was about all he could do. As the days passed, and Silas ate well-prepared simple food, sat in warmth in the evenings at the hearthside, and then slept restfully in the fine unfinished bed, he found his strength returning and his body healing. He kept his mind focused on the things before him in the present, and not on what had gone before or what might be in the future.

He was glad when he could take up the tools and concentrate on working with his hands. Labour was a great distraction, and Samuel good company. The lad had such a sweet nature and was bright and intelligent, despite his physical limitations.

One evening when the boy had gone out to bring the cow in, Silas took the opportunity to ask his mother about him.

'Has Samuel been afflicted since birth? I have seen a child with similar awkward speech and movement before, but she did not live beyond her early years. Her parents rejected her as being cursed. She was mistreated and uncared for. Some in her village even believed her demon-possessed and the local priest tried exorcism. When, at last she was taken to the monks at the abbey, there was little that could be done for her by the infirmarer. She lies buried in an unmarked grave there.'

He cursed himself when he realised that Hannah was staring into the fire with bright tears rolling down her cheeks. Why had he shared that particular story?

She sniffed and ran a hand around her face, catching the stray tears. She spoke softly in answer to his question.

'I thought I would die giving my son life. The labour was long, and he refused to come for too many hours. When he was finally born, the midwife had to cut him from me and cut the life cord from around his neck. He was not breathing. We thought it had all been for naught, my pain and suffering. He was handed to my husband who held him and breathed his own breath into him, and prayed and prayed, until finally my boy took his first breath. Then we laughed and praised God, the giver of life.

'As he grew, it was obvious that he was different. His speech and his movement did not come as easily as they should have. We knew there would be no more children from my broken body, so he was all we had to lavish our love and prayers on. He grew healthy and strong, but always with the same strangeness of speech and movement. We saw he was bright, and special, but those around us were quick to laugh, judge, and even fear him. So, Daniel sold his woodyard in the town and moved us out here, close to the river, far enough away from the people of Hay who did not understand our son. We were happy here, and Samuel continued to flourish. But then Daniel died... and now I fear for our boy again. What will become of him, if anything happens to me? It is a worry that keeps me awake at night.'

She glanced at him, her eyes pleading for an answer. He wished he could console her, give her some well-versed scriptural word of hope, but he had none. He could have offered to pray for her and her son, but that was not something he could promise to do either. He did not think himself on speaking terms with God, and any prayer would only amount to empty words.

He watched Samuel more attentively over the next few days as they worked together. The trunk now had a fixed hinged lid, which had been worked to a smooth shine. It only needed an oil and polish, and it would be done. Silas had encouraged Samuel with the oil rag, but the lad found the circular movement too difficult, so now he was just watching Silas as he worked. He was sitting on a sawn-off piece of tree trunk, his back to the open door, using a stick to make a series of lines in the sawdust that lay on the mud-packed floor.

Silas was curious. 'What are those lines, Samuel? Do they mean something?'

The boy looked up, with his usual lopsided grin.

'I-I'm c-counting,' he said.

'Counting?' Silas tried not to sound or look surprised. 'What are you counting?'

'The n-number of c-circles you make with your hand. I l-love c-counting. Sometimes I c-count the clouds, or the c-cries of the g-geese on the river. I once t-tried c-counting the bits of d-dust that float in the air.' He laughed. 'I l-lost c-count.'

Silas chuckled. 'So, you like numbers?'

'Yes. My p-pa taught me. I c-can't write them b-but I c-can see them in my head, and I c-can make marks, look.'

Silas put down his rag and came over to the boy. He had an idea, and he wasn't sure where it had come from.

'If a farmer has 100 sheep and he takes forty-three to the market, how many will he have left?'

Samuel grinned. 'Fifty-seven.'

'If a farmer has 100 sheep, takes sixty-seven to the market, sells twelve to his neighbour and loses one, how many will he have left?'

Samuel giggled but needed no thinking time. 'Twenty,' he answered.

'If a farmer has 200 sheep and buys fourteen more, then sells twenty-five and loses three, how many will he have left?'

Silas was still trying to work it out himself, but Samuel was there before him.

'The f-farmer will have 186 s-sheep.'

Samuel laughed so hard, he tipped himself off his seat and onto the floor. Silas couldn't help grinning as he reached out his hand to help the youngster up.

'What is so funny?'

'I t-thought you would be a-asking me about the f-farmer who had 100 s-sheep and lost one. The s-story in the Bible[1]. That would have been too easy a s-sum for me. All those s-sums were easy.'

Silas helped him take his seat again and sat down on the floor next to him. The joy the lad carried was infectious.

'I think you are very clever with numbers,' he said eventually, and watched as Samuel registered the compliment. His face flushed with pride.

'My p-pa always s-said so.'

They sat in silence for a few minutes. Silas thinking about how they could possibly harness Samuel's gift for numbers. Was there a way he could use his skill and find paid work? As he sat pondering Samuel's need, Silas' mind couldn't help going to the parable he had inadvertently paraphrased. Jesus' story of the lost sheep, and the shepherd who had searched high and low until he found that lamb and brought it home. The sheep that had left the comfort and safety of the fold and gone out on his own. The shepherd who had persisted in caring and loving that lost sheep, finding it and carrying it back on his shoulders. The story spoke to his soul in ways he was afraid to admit.

---

[1] Luke 15:4-7

What man of you, having a hundred sheep, if he loses one of them, does not leave the ninety-nine in the wilderness, and go after the one which is lost until he finds it? And when he has found it, he lays it on his shoulders, rejoicing. And when he comes home, he calls together his friends and neighbors, saying to them, 'Rejoice with me, for I have found my sheep which was lost!' I say to you that likewise there will be more joy in heaven over one sinner who repents than over ninety-nine just persons who need no repentance.

Luke 15:4-7

5

Hay Castle

From inside the workshop, Silas heard John Boatman arrive; the clatter of the wheels, the whinny of the horse, and the thud as the man dismounted from the driving seat of the cart. He heard him shout a greeting and heard Hannah's softer response, but he stayed hidden. The trunk stood finished in front of him on the workbench. Silas ran his hand over the lid, pleased with how well it had turned out. Despite his lack of expertise, the finished piece was fine enough to grace any well-appointed room. And it was worth much to his host family. It needed to be sold, and it seemed they had found a prospective buyer. The chair was also finished. That was not quite as finely done, as Silas had not had much experience with a lathe. The legs were turned with a simple design. But the carved back was so beautiful that the plain chair legs did not detract from it. It would sell too, Silas was sure. He was glad to have been able to do this much to repay Hannah's generosity.

There was still the fine carved bed to finish and construct. That would take a while longer. Once that was done, Silas would take his leave. Not just because he would no longer have a bed to sleep on, but because he was finding himself becoming too attached to both place and people. He had promised that he would be gone when he was well, and his hands and feet had long healed. His soul had some way to go, but the kindness he had received from Hannah and Samuel had helped to comfort him. He knew he could easily stay, but he would be another mouth to feed, and they had barely enough. With the sale of the furniture there would be enough to see them through a few months, and Silas had in mind another way in which the family might support themselves that wasn't dependent on him.

He could hear footsteps approaching. He pulled his hat down low on his head so that it covered his still stubbly pate. They had hoped that by wearing the borrowed hat and Daniel's green tunic, Silas would not remind John Boatman in any way of the man who had stolen one of his coracles less than a month past, but still his heart thumped, and his palms felt sticky. Hannah had made it known that a Welsh cousin of Daniel's had arrived on her threshold and, finding her alone, had stayed to offer his skills as a woodcrafter. She would be introducing Silas by his own given name, Morgan. Morgan ap Bedwyr.

They appeared around the door; a slightly nervous-looking Hannah, followed by a large man, with a look on his face that could be described as wary in the least, if not openly suspicious.

He approached, leaving Hannah in the doorway. Close enough to look as though he was leaning in to examine the trunk, also close enough for Silas to catch the narrowing of his eyes as he looked him up and down. Silas swallowed hard, anticipating the worst.

'Excellent!' John's voice was loud and booming. 'The trunk will sit well in the castle's newly refurbished rooms; I am sure of it. You were right, Mistress Carpenter, Master St Germain will pay well to buy these for Lady de Braose.' He addressed the lady, but his eyes did not leave Silas' face. Silas shifted his feet.

John turned and spoke directly to Hannah, a smile transforming his face.

'Best give that boy of yours a shout. I dare say your *cousin*,' the word brought a strange edge to the boatman's voice, 'and I are strong enough to carry the trunk to the cart. We might need Samuel to steady the horse as we load it on. Dory can be skittish.'

Hannah paused and looked from John, with his smile, to Silas, who stood mute, his whole body trembling slightly. She seemed to take a moment to make up her mind, and nobody moved, until finally she turned away from them and swept up her skirts to leave. As soon as she was out of sight, John spun around, and his large form loomed menacingly. Silas stepped back, despite his resolve. He willed his legs and back to straighten. He was never going to match the man in height, but he knew he could defend himself if called on. He had learned to fight on the docksides of Bristol, where his father's warehouses had often been targets for thieves. He clenched his fists tightly.

'I do not know who you are, *cousin* of a man who claimed no Welsh family while he lived. Nor do I know what you do here, wearing a dead man's clothes, working on a dead man's creations, and living with a dead man's wife. I warn you, you are not the only man hereabouts who has designs on getting their feet under Hannah's table, and their body in her bed.'

So that was it. Silas almost choked with relief. He hadn't been recognised as the coracle thief, instead he was being sized up as a competitor for Hannah's hand. He breathed easily for a moment, before realising that it wasn't actually that ridiculous an idea. He already felt admiration for the woman who had taken him in. For her gentleness, wisdom and kindness. For taking him in as a stranger and asking no questions of him. For keeping his secrets and not exposing him. For giving him a bed, a purpose, food to feed his body and a warm fire to sit by in the long evenings. Many a man would look for nothing more. But, he reminded himself, he was not just a man. He had taken vows. Breaking free of abbey life had been one thing. Breaking his vow of celibacy was a whole other issue. He didn't know why the thought troubled him so much.

He realised that John had not moved. All the time that Silas had been musing he had stood with his hands on his hips, probably expecting an answer. Silas allowed himself a small smile, releasing his fists from their grip. He wasn't going to give the man the satisfaction of knowing the truth. Meeting John's gaze, he spoke clearly and firmly.

'It will be Mistress Carpenter's choice as to which, if any, man shares her table or her bed. As far as I can see, she is well able to judge for herself. Be it you, or I, or any other. So, step aside, John Boatman, and let us get to the task in hand.'

He made a point of brushing up against the man's elbow as he pushed past him, only then realising that Hannah had stepped back into the workshop. He could not be sure what she had overheard, but the look on her face was not a happy one.

'Samuel has hold of Dory, and they and the cart are stood waiting for you. Is there a problem?'

She had one hand on a hip and was giving them a look similar to one that Silas had last seen on his mother's face when he was a young boy.

'No, no. No problem.' John was nodding and dipping, dancing in his efforts to placate her. He was soon stood on the other side of the workbench and between them the two men covered the trunk in sacking and lifted it from the table. It was solid and weighty and took some manoeuvring to get onto the cart and secured with ropes. The chair followed, which was less heavy but still somehow needed both of them to carry it. Neither would allow the other to take the full weight, like two playmates fighting over a child's toy. It must have been comedic to watch from Hannah's perspective. Silas was definitely enjoying himself playing his part. If John wanted to see him as a rival for Hannah's affections, that was better than him finding out his true reason for being there. Or who he really was.

Finally, the furniture was loaded, and Silas made the decision to climb up into the back, with the excuse of watching over the load. Samuel was coming with them, and it was far better for him to sit close to the boatman when there was so much antagonism in the air. The lad clambered up onto the driver's seat and John smiled genuinely at him. Silas wondered then if he had read the man wrongly. Perhaps he might be a good husband for Hannah, and father for Samuel. He was surprised at how much the thought disturbed him.

The ride into Hay did not take long. They entered a very different town to the one Silas had encountered last time he had crept along its silent streets. Houses and shops lined the wide road that led to the slight mound where the castle stood. Some of the doors and shutters opening onto the street revealed shops selling meat and crafted goods. Men and women called to one another, children ran and squealed, and dogs barked. There was other traffic too. Loaded donkeys, a small herd of sheep being driven down the centre of the road, and a huge cart bearing large chunks of cut stone being pulled by two great horses. The driver of this particular vehicle was standing on his perch, whip in hand, yelling at the shepherd to move his flock to one side to let his cart pass.

'Stone for the castle. We'll get in behind him as he parts the sea for us,' John chuckled as he pulled Dory over, and sure enough the stone-filled cart with its fierce driver, caused livestock and people to scatter.

They pulled to a stop before a busy gatehouse. There were sentries on guard, but they were allowing workmen through and women carrying baskets of food and linens. The stone-filled cart was waved through but as John clicked the reins to galvanise Dory to follow, a blunt-faced guard stepped in front of the horse, his halberd raised, and Dory shied. John pulled hard on the reins and spoke calmly to the horse. He tipped his forehead in deference to the guard and made to get down from his seat.

'Halt. Stop there.' The voice was heavily accented, but not with Welsh. He sounded Norman French. 'What business have you here?'

John sat down heavily on the driver's seat, so heavily that Samuel was almost catapulted off the other side. The lad giggled and Silas could have sworn that the guard's face softened a touch.

Silas slipped quietly from the back of the cart and walked over to take Dory by her headcollar. The sentry watched his every move but did not challenge him. Perhaps he presented less of a threat with his diminutive form.

'I am Morgan, and this here is my *friend*,' he emphasised the word slightly, 'John Boatman, who lives here in Hay, and plies his trade providing river crossings for any who may need them. He is a fine coracle handler.'

As he was speaking, he was glancing between the guard and John, and was satisfied to see John turn his head slightly to one side and half-smile at his words. The guard was unflinching.

'Also with us is Samuel Carpenter, son of the late Daniel Carpenter, a fine craftsman, well known locally. His pieces of furniture have been commissioned for the castle before. See here.' He stepped over to the cart to fling the covering back from a corner of the trunk. The guard tensed for a moment and pulled his halberd down so that the end was perilously close to Silas' nose. He must have seen under the sacking to the piece of furniture beneath, as he relaxed his stance. 'We were hoping to show this trunk and a magnificent chair to the man overseeing the rebuilding and refurbishing of the castle. I believe Roget St Germain will want to see these pieces and acquire them for the private rooms of Lady Eve de Braose?'

The guard had forgotten him for a moment. He pulled the covers further back and was admiring the trunk with both eyes and hands.

'A fine piece of carving. I have only once seen the like,' the voice was almost a whisper. 'A cabinet, carved with the same design, sat in the great hall in the days of Lord William, God rest his soul. I noted it because the leaves looked so real, as if they had been plucked straight from an oak tree and encased with wood. Your master's work, you say?'

'My late cousin's work, yes. I am here on behalf of his widow, and his fatherless son.' He indicated Samuel. 'All we ask is the chance to show these fine pieces to the steward and let him decide whether they are worth the price we would need to feed and clothe his family in their time of need.'

The guard turned his attention back to Silas then, and looked over at John, still sat mute, and at Samuel fidgeting beside him. He nodded.

'Wait here.' He spun and strode away.

John let out a long breath. 'Well, you certainly charmed the man, *friend*. I think you may well have gained us entry. Look.'

The guard was already coming back to them.

'You can come. Master St Germain will see you and the furniture. But you,' he pointed his halberd full at John. 'You, Boatman, will stay with the cart and leave the castle precinct, once the furniture has been unloaded. There is too much activity in there,' he tilted his head in the direction of the castle, 'for you to stand idly by with an empty horse and cart, getting in the way.'

Roget St Germain was a man of average height, but he carried himself as if he were much taller. Broad in shoulder, with dark hair trimmed close in the Norman style and a clean-shaven face, he had the bearing of a man who meant business. He seemed to carry an innate authority, and there was a look in his eyes that defied challenge. He had made them wait, standing together in a large room scattered with workmen all at different tasks. Some were whitewashing freshly pointed stone walls, some were hammering at planks to build a raised dais, others were scuttling back and forth carrying wood, baskets of nails or pails of water.

As the steward was engrossed in conversation with a flustered-looking man holding a drawing of some sort, Silas used the time to take in the room. It was once a great hall, most certainly, but the high roof above him was in the process of being replaced, and dark soot stains marred the upper regions of the walls. He remembered the stories of Prince Llewellyn taking his vengeance on his wife's supposed lover, venturing over the border to fire his castle fortress. William de Braose had caused this destruction, and his actions had reverberated along the Marches. Now it seemed that King Henry had ordered the castle rebuilt. Its position was strategic, and the English needed to make a statement concerning the security of the borderlands. It seemed that Lady Eve de Braose, William's blighted widow, was to have a hand in the rebuilding works. Roget St Germain served her. The king might have financed the rebuild, but a de Braose steward was managing it.

Finally, the man himself strode over to where Silas stood. Samuel had long since got bored and was watching the painters. He was not speaking but he seemed to be using his fingers to count. Probably counting the strokes of the painter's brush, Silas mused to himself.

'So, this is the trunk and chair I have heard so highly praised.' The steward bent to examine both and seemed to approve. As he straightened, he narrowed his eyes slightly at Silas, his mouth a hard line.

'I know this work, and I knew Daniel Carpenter. There is no question, the lady will want both pieces, and anything else you... who exactly are you?'

'I am Br...' He was flustered by the man's gaze. He mentally shook himself. 'I am Morgan ap Bedwyr, cousin to the late Daniel of whom you spoke.' Silas instinctively stepped back and lowered his head slightly. St Germain's very presence seemed to demand it.

'A Welshman? Ha. You might have been better to keep that fact secret, especially in the confines of this place.' He laughed, but it was a short and shallow laugh.

'I have lived most of my life on the English side of the border.' That was the truth. 'I am subject to the king and bear no ill will to any born of English or Norman blood. My only cause to be here today is to see Daniel Carpenter's widow and son well done by.'

Silas pulled a reluctant Samuel over to stand by his side. The boy fidgeted but stayed silent. He too seemed overawed by St Germain.

The steward glanced at Samuel and nodded slowly.

'I will offer a good price for both pieces you have brought today, enough to provide generously for a good man's family.' There was a distinct softening of his features as he spoke. 'I can see they have been finished by another hand. Yours?'

'Yes'.

'You are not as skilled as he was, but the work is good enough. Are there any more pieces?'

'A fine carved bed, yet in pieces. Mistress Carpenter believes all three pieces were commissioned by the Lady de Braose, before...' Silas hesitated.

'The fire? Yes, and before your cousin's untimely death. Yes, I remember. Can you finish the bed also?'

'I believe I can, but it may need to be assembled here in place, and I might need the help of one of your own carpenters to do that.'

'That can be arranged. I will pay you for that once the bed is completed. The lady's solar above,' he pointed to a stone stairwell, 'is almost ready for habitation. She will be beyond pleased to find it furnished with such fine pieces. It is a shame that Daniel Carpenter is not alive to work with us here. I could do with a man of his skill, and his commitment to task.' A wry smile softened his features yet more, and he let out a sigh, seeming to relax his body. 'Your father was a good man,' he was addressing Samuel, 'and we mourn his loss. But not as much as you do, I don't doubt.' He placed a large hand on the lad's shoulder, and Samuel stumbled slightly.

'May I speak with you on one further matter?' Silas wanted to draw St Germain's attention back to himself, as Samuel's limbs began to twitch, and his head was moving slowly from side to side in agitation. 'In private, if possible.' He was aware of too many eyes watching the lad, anxious of what reaction his strange movements might engender.

St Germain seemed to pause for just a moment but then moved with purpose. 'Follow me, and bring the lad.' He strode towards an open doorway, and Silas grabbed Samuel's arm. As he crossed the room, the steward glared, and the men returned to work. If there were whispers, they were not heard. The steward had full command here.

When He, the Spirit of truth, has come, He will guide you into all truth...

John 16:13

6

St Germain

The doorway they followed the steward through led to a small square room with two glassless windows placed high in the outside wall. It was dominated by a large rectangular table, strewn with parchments, scrolls, quills and other detritus. In contrast, the narrow pallet bed positioned along the far wall was neatly made; so neat that Silas wondered if it had ever been slept in.

Roget St Germain leaned against the table and stretched his legs out in front of him. There was a solitary chair, but he did not offer it to either Silas or Samuel. Samuel unselfconsciously wandered over to where a large, banded trunk sat and lowered himself to sit on it. Now they were away from the noise and bustle of the great hall, the lad seemed more relaxed. He was more in control of his movements and his face bore its more normal half-grin.

'What is this private matter you needed so desperately to talk of? As you can see,' he gestured at the tabletop behind him, 'I am a busy man.' It was said with tired resignation, rather than with irritation.

So, these were the man's meagre private quarters. Silas could only imagine how little time and space the steward actually got to himself. At least he had this private space, although probably not to rest much, by the state of the room.

'I am sorry to take up your time, but I wanted to speak to you about Samuel here. The pieces of furniture we have brought to you will earn some much-needed coin for him and Daniel's widow, but not long-term provision. Samuel,' he glanced over at the boy, 'is not physically able to do what his father did.' St Germain followed his gaze. 'I think you understand.'

Samuel's attention had been taken by a spider weaving its web in a shaft of sunlight. He was transfixed by the creature's movements, oblivious to the conversation going on concerning him.

'I do.' It was said in just above a whisper. 'I had a sister. She too had trouble controlling her movements and speech. She was no less intelligent than any of us, but not physically strong. She was hidden away from prying eyes and malicious tongues, and then sent to the convent when she was twelve. I never saw her again.' He paused and took a steadying breath. 'We heard she had died from a fever within weeks of coming under the care of the nuns. I believe it was being separated from her family and shut away from the world that likely killed her. She was such a kind and loving soul, always smiling in that strange way, always happy. I loved her.'

As he had been speaking, Silas had watched a mixture of emotions cross the man's face. He found himself thanking God for the extraordinary coincidence of this man understanding Samuel's affliction first-hand. And then he checked himself. He wasn't sure he was ready to offer his thanks to God, if God was listening to him at all.

He realised then that St Germain was watching him, waiting for him to speak. 'Samuel is intelligent. Very clever with numbers. He can add and subtract in his head faster than you, me, or most men.'

The steward slowly levered his frame from the table and wandered over to where Samuel sat.

'You are good with numbers, lad?'

Samuel grinned.

'You will need to stand so that I can open the trunk you are sitting on.'

Samuel stood awkwardly and they watched as St Germain removed a ring of keys from his belt and inserted a large key into a lock at the front of the trunk. The lock sprung open, and he lifted the heavy wooden lid. Inside were more documents and letters and what looked like a bound book. To one end of the trunk sat a smaller wooden box, with iron banding and its own lock. This box, and the bound book, the steward carried to the table.

'Here.' He beckoned for Samuel to come and used a smaller key to open the coffer. It was full of coinage, some loose, some in bags. Clearing a space on the table he dropped a handful of mixed coins on the table, silver whole pennies, and half and clipped coins. There were one or two gold nobles there also.

'You know your coins, boy?'

Samuel grinned again and bobbed his head.

'Tell me. If I were to offer to pay for all three of the finished pieces of furniture that you and Master Morgan here have brought me from your father's workshop, the sum of two pounds in total and gave you twelve shillings of that today, and then promised to pay the remainder over the next six months, in equal payments, how much would I be paying your mother each month? Here, use these to help you count,' he indicated the coins on the table.

Samuel did not move towards the coins, he just tipped his head to one side and looked at the steward quizzically for a moment.

'F-f-fifty-six pence, or f-f-four shillings and eight pence.'

'Remarkable.' St Germain had leaned over to pick up a quill and was making quick ink marks on a scrap of parchment, doing his own calculations, but Samuel was far ahead of him.

'Can he write? Make marks?' St Germain moved to the back of the table. Sitting in the chair, he pulled the bound book towards him. He opened it to reveal what looked like a meticulously kept list of accounts written in neat columns.

'I am so far behind with this.' He rubbed ink-stained fingers through his hair. 'I have been trying to pay the workers and merchants, but it takes so much of my time to keep up with payments and recording them. I had a clerk, but he was stealing from me and had to be removed.' He spat then, and Silas shuddered slightly. He could only imagine what that 'removal' might have looked like. These were cruel times.

The steward fixed a hard stare on Samuel then. 'Are you honest, boy?'

The lad nodded his head so vigorously his whole body shook. 'And will you, Morgan ap Bedwyr, stand surety for his honesty?'

Silas could not admit that he might not be around much longer.

'I can attest to his honesty and good nature. His mother and father have brought him up to be God-fearing.'

He picked up the quill that the steward had dropped and moved to offer it to Samuel. The lad seemed to focus all his concentration on the object, lifting his hand and taking it from Silas. His hand shook and tiny drops of ink splattered on the tabletop.

'Can he sit? He finds it easier to control his hands if he does not have to think about the rest of his body.'

St Germain stood quickly and offered his seat to Samuel. The lad sat heavily, and a loud sigh escaped him. He giggled, but then he was all concentration, as he pushed the ledger away and pulled the same scrap of parchment that the steward had written on towards him. He had the quill in his right hand, and resting his left elbow on the table he used his left hand to support his right. Cautiously, he made ink marks on the parchment. It wasn't neat and it wasn't tidy, but it was clearly recognisable: 4s 8d.

'I have been teaching him, but only with sticks and dust. This is the first time he has held a quill!'

Silas felt his chest almost burst with pride. He realised how much Samuel had come to mean to him. 'I believe with time and with practice he could write faster and with more clarity.'

St Germain stood with his arms crossed across his chest. 'I can use him. I will not have much time to teach him, but if he can do the accounting in his head as quickly as he did just now, and if all I have to do is write the figures down until he is good enough to do it himself, that will be of great help to me. And the wages will be a help to his mother, no doubt.'

'You have already promised a generous amount for the furniture. Would you pay Samuel also?'

The steward made a dismissive gesture. 'The price I offered for the pieces is no more than I would expect to pay a master carpenter in my employ for six months of work.'

He took a bag of money from the coffer and added a few coins to it, handing the bag to Silas.

'How long do you think it will take you to finish the bed?'

'Maybe a fortnight, with help, as you promised.'

'Good. Then for the time it takes you to complete your commission, I will expect Samuel here at the hour of Prime every day. He can return to his mother, and complete whatever tasks she might have for him, after noon. It will only be for a few hours a day, and on a trial period. If we work well together then I will keep him on and pay him a wage. Are we agreed?' He looked from Silas to Samuel.

Silas was watching Samuel too. This was not his decision to make. The lad looked thoughtful for a moment, before holding out his hand to St Germain, who took it, with a barely suppressed smile.

'A-a-agreed!' Samuel shook the man's hand once, with some force.

'Now I must get back to more pressing things.' The steward released his hand from Samuel but did not step away, placing a hand on the lad's shoulder as he ushered him towards the door.

'I will see you tomorrow, Samuel,' he said smiling, but as the three of them stepped back into the busy great hall, all signs of geniality left the steward's face, and his hand dropped from Samuel's shoulder. He shot Silas a fleeting look and then strode away into the melee, leaving them to find their own way out.

Hannah's incredulity at both the amount the steward of Hay Castle had been willing to pay for Daniel's furniture and for his kindness towards her son, brought tears to her eyes. Silas had observed how she carried her grief with such quiet dignity, but on their return, she stood with tears rolling down her cheeks, a brightness in her eyes that took years off her. Silas handed her the coin bag and was shocked at how much he wanted to take her into his arms and share her emotion. He knew deep down that he could not stay. He could not afford to allow his blossoming feelings of affection for this woman to complicate things. He would finish the work on the bed as he had promised and take his leave.

A large wagon appeared the day after his visit with the steward and two burly men helped him load the pieces of the bed onto it. He threw in some tools and climbed into the wagon with them. As promised, less than a fortnight later, the bed was finished and stood proudly in Lady de Braose's newly appointed solar. A gifted seamstress had been commissioned to make fine drapes to enclose its sides, and linens had been procured to dress it comfortably. Silas had wanted to stay to see it all completed. He was proud of the part he had played in its construction. He wanted Hannah to see it completed also.

He purposed to mention this to St Germain. He had come to find the steward in his room to tell him that his work on the bed was done, and to see what the outcome of Samuel's work trial was to be.

He found the two bent over the accounts ledger and it was Samuel who was making the entry. His writing had improved, although not as neat as the scribe who had worked on it before. It didn't seem to matter to St Germain, whose face wore an indulgent smile.

They both looked up as Silas entered.

'Ah, Morgan ap Bedwyr. Have you come to check on your cousin here?' St Germain slapped the lad on the back and the quill flew from Samuel's hand, sending ink spray across the newly scribed page. Samuel jumped to his feet, and a look of alarm crossed his face.

'I-I-I'm sorry!'

But St Germain was laughing. 'Don't trouble yourself. I spray ink all the time.' He placed a more gentle hand on Samuel's shoulder, encouraging him to resume his seat. 'As you can see, Samuel here is doing very well and I have never had a clerk with a quicker mind, or a more pleasant manner. He works hard and he makes me laugh. Both things that I am sorely in need of! He and I have agreed that he will continue to come to work with me, six days a week, from daybreak till noon. I will pay him a shilling a week, on top of what I have promised Mistress Carpenter in monthly payment for the work you and her late husband have done.' He moved around the table. 'Is the bed completed?'

'It is, and I think both you and the lady will be pleased with it. Especially when it has been dressed and draped.'

'What will you do now? Will you try your hand at other pieces of furniture? I could find a place for you here among my carpenters.'

Silas peered over the steward's shoulder to see Samuel with his head still lowered over the ledger, quill in hand, all his concentration taken by the job he was doing. He dropped his voice to just above a whisper.

'I thank you, but I must move on, as I feel I have stayed long enough here. I have yet to tell the lad – or his mother – of my plans.'

A quizzical look crossed the steward's face momentarily. Then he gave the slightest of nods.

'Before I leave, I think Mistress Carpenter would take great comfort in seeing her husband's pieces completed and in their rightful places. To see where her son works would also encourage her heart. Could that be arranged?'

'Of course. I will see to it.' The steward was still unsmiling, but Silas imagined he could see understanding in the man's eyes.

Silas took his leave and while waiting to accompany Samuel home, made a quick visit to John Boatman's yard. The large man did not seem overly happy to see him, but when Silas explained what he wanted from him, his demeanour towards him changed instantly. Arrangements were made, and Silas knew what he must do. It would be hard, but it was necessary.

That evening, he smiled and conversed with Hannah, enjoying her well-prepared food and the warmth of her fire, as he had for too many evenings. She was talking about Daniel, how he had developed the designs he used in his carvings, what the symbols meant. Silas was interested and tried to focus more on what she was saying, rather than on the fact that he might never hear her voice again. She showed no signs of knowing what was in his mind. Nor did Samuel, for which he was grateful. He could not bear to think of how Samuel would react. He was comforted by the appearance of St Germain's affection for the lad, and double-comforted that he knew that both mother and son were no longer penniless or friendless. He had helped in that.

'The oak leaves. You must have noticed those, of course.'

He forced a smile, grateful for the distance between them and the half-light. The fire flickered but did not flare to reveal the sadness she might have seen in his eyes.

'Oak trees were important to him. He used to tell us how his mother had sat him on her knee as a boy and recited verses from the Psalms to him. She had been brought up by nuns and had been well-drilled in the scriptures. His favourite had been one about a tree planted by waters, that stood strong and bore fruit.[2] He said it made him think of oak trees, that stood strong, with huge roots, so that even when the wind blew fiercely, they stood firm. He loved it when acorns appeared. He would laugh and say, "Look, the trees have weathered another year and are still bearing fruit."'

'He was strong like that, you see. His faith was so unshakeable that even when we were weathered by storms, some painful, some terrifying, he never wavered. "God will provide," he would say to me. "He has promised, and He will do it. He even looks after the birds and makes sure they are fed, so He will look after us."[3] He started to add tiny sparrows to his carvings to remind me.' She laughed to herself. 'He even carved one here on the beam above where I store our food.'

She pointed above her head. Silas could not make it out in the dim light, but he had noticed it previously and

---

[2] See Psalm 1
[3] See Matthew 6:26

had traced his fingers around the edges of Daniel's fine carvings. They were so beautifully lifelike. He had deeply admired the man for his skill, and now something deep inside him also admired him for his simple faith. Silas desperately wanted to understand how a man could live, and die, in such faith, despite all his family had endured.

If he allowed himself to ponder further, he knew self-condemnation at his own faithlessness would likely follow. He chose not to linger on the thought of a God who was faithful, and how Hannah's husband had found the secret of trusting in Him.

'That's why I know he is with God now. He lived so close to Him in life, he must be with Him in death. Do you not think so, Brother?'

Silas lowered his head in thought, but at her use of the title his head shot up. He could not find words to answer her but forced himself to nod.

It seemed enough for her. But as she continued to speak of her late husband, one thing had become paramount in Silas' mind. Whatever he had imagined he might feel for the woman who sat opposite him on the other side of the hearth, to her he was still a monk. Still a brother, still a man wedded to the church. If he needed confirmation that he had to leave, he had it now.

There was scant light in the sky when Silas rose from his bed. He shook the blankets that had covered the straw-filled sacking, his hastily constructed bed to take the place of Daniel's fine one. He folded them and to the pile added Daniel's tunic and hat. He dressed in the same tunic and hooded cloak he had arrived in and pulled the worn leather boots onto his feet and gloves onto his hands. The only other thing he took with him was his scrip with his knife, cup and pewter cross stowed inside. If Hannah had known he was leaving, she would have insisted on sending him on his way with a sack of provisions, a bundle of Daniel's clothes, and probably some coin as well. But he could not leave with anything more than he had arrived with. It did not seem right.

The house was quiet, and the animals too, as he stole away, down to the wide, mist-shrouded river. He shivered as he stood on the bank, but then the coracle appeared out of the gloom with the unmistakeable bulk of John Boatman deftly handling its oar. He pulled into the muddy beach where Silas stood, then climbed out.

They did not speak as John Boatman held the vessel for Silas to clamber into and then climbed back in himself. It was barely big enough for the two of them. Silas smiled wryly. He was leaving Hannah with something more; his bones had begun to fill out with her generous hospitality.

Before he knew it, they were on the other bank of the river and John was stepping into the reeded shallows. He held the coracle with one hand and held out the other to Silas. Only then did he speak.

'I think I know this river, and how to get across it, better than you, Stranger.'

Silas sent him a sidewards glance. 'And I am grateful for that,' he said, clambering up the bank and walking away, not once looking back.

Are not two sparrows sold for a copper coin?

And not one of them falls to the ground apart

from your Father's will.

But the very hairs of your head are all

numbered.

Do not fear therefore; you are of more value

than many sparrows.

Matthew 10:29-31

7

The Church at Cregina

Jumping into the river shallows and wading through the reed bank had filled his boots with water and soaked the hems of both tunic and cloak. Still he walked on, trying to put distance between himself and a place that had begun to work its way into his heart. As the sun rose, the clouds thickened, and the rain came. It seemed apt. Silas didn't know where he was going, or what lay ahead of him. He was back to being homeless and purposeless, and the rain matched his mood. He trudged on, finally finding what looked like a drovers' trail and deciding to follow it. He knew he was going deeper into Welsh territory as the terrain got hillier.

The track wound between dense woodland and rounded hillsides, with the occasional open field inhabited by huddling sheep. He felt for them; he could find no shelter from the weather either. He lost track of the hours, as there was no reason to stop. He had brought no food, and he only needed to hold his cup out for a few minutes to have enough rainwater to slate his thirst. He knew how to fast. Abbey life had taught him that.

He met no one, and kept his head hooded and lowered so that for much of the time his sodden boots were all he saw. One foot in front of the other, the monotony a good distraction from the thoughts and emotions that threatened. He could have wondered how Samuel and Hannah would have reacted to finding him gone. He could have pondered what, if anything, John Boatman would have told them. He could have longed for company on the journey, for the community he used to know. The loneliness might have been an impetus for trying to connect with God again. But he didn't want his heart or mind to go to any of those places. Better that he just kept plodding on, letting the rainwater soak him and the clouded skies and looming hills shield him.

Eventually, he knew he had to stop. His legs were no longer complying, and sheer exhaustion threatened. He had no idea how far he had walked, but it seemed that the sky had got yet darker. The invisible sun was setting, and still the rain fell. Silas stopped and stretched his aching back. His last steps had been particularly hard work. The path had climbed and now he stood on a small peak. Breathing heavily, he dragged his soaked hood from his head. It was then he saw it, down in a valley below him. Whitewashed against the dark trees surrounding it, a stone building of some sort. He could see no light from its windows or smoke from a roof hole, but even if it were abandoned, it might offer him more shelter than the open trail. He could also hear running water, the unmistakeable sound of the down rush of a fast-flowing stream.

Maybe this building was the start of a settlement, built beside a natural water source, in the lea of the hills. It was worth investigation.

Only as he got closer did he realise that the stone building stood alone. And there was a reason for that, one that made his heart sink. He had walked all those miles, thinking he was distancing himself further and further from his past life, not seeing another human soul all day, and here, in the middle of the wilds of Wales, he found himself faced with the unmistakeable form of a small church. He desperately looked about, but there were no other buildings, no farms, no homesteads. He shook his head and resigned himself to the fact that unless he took shelter here, he might have to walk miles to find it elsewhere. He was shivering violently and knew he had to be sensible. If the church had a dry interior, at least he might prevent himself from dying of exposure by stepping inside its doors.

The church was rectangular with a double glassed window at one end and an arched wooden door halfway down its side. There was no porch; Silas would have preferred to rest in that, if it meant not actually stepping inside the sanctuary. He tried the handle, and the door sighed and creaked as it swung inwards. The church was dim, but sweet-smelling rushes covered the floor. There was a simple altar placed under the end window, and the start of what looked like a wooden rood screen in the process of being fitted across the nave. Silas stepped inside and closed the door behind him. He immediately felt the relief of being out of the wind and rain, but the stone walls gave no warmth or comfort. There was no way he could chance lighting a fire inside, even though there were tall tallow candles on the altar. There was also a thick, embroidered altar cloth. Silas stood before that altar for some time, trying not to look at the wooden crucifix that stood on it. What he was contemplating doing would probably be considered sacrilege by those he had once called brothers. Would God judge him for it? He laughed bitterly. What did he care what God thought anyway? Why worry about offending the Almighty when he felt abandoned by Him already?

He stepped up to the altar, carefully picked up the candles and placed them on the floor. The wooden crucifix made him hesitate and strangely he felt he had to close his eyes as he took the weight of it in his hands. This Christ crucified. This Jesus. This had once been the centre of all he believed. When had it ever become about all the other things? When had it become about rules and vows and lives of service? When had it become about pouring yourself out until you felt broken inside and out? Those things had soured his once simple faith.

Take up your cross.[4]

He remembered the words of Jesus, and as he bent to lower the crucifix to the floor beside the candles, he

---

[4] Matthew 26:24

crossed himself, unsure why, except that it had come naturally.

Take up your cross.

Hadn't he done that? Hadn't he taken up the cross of suffering for the sake of Christ? Been obedient to the call to forsake all and follow Him? It hurt him deeply that God seemed to have abandoned him, in the light of all that. Had all that self-sacrifice been for nothing?

He pulled the altar cloth from the table. It was heavy and thick. He dragged it to a far corner, where he would not have to look at the desecrated altar table. Shedding himself of his wet cloak and tunic, he threw the altar cloth around his shoulders and lowered himself to the floor, tucking the ends of the thick embroidered material around his feet. He leaned his head back against the cool stone and closed his eyes. He was spent, and he was hungry. He was lost and alone. But at least, here in this simple church, his cold body was wrapped in warmth.

He must have slept. He had dreamt, he knew that. The dreams had been disturbing and hard to make sense of. Snatches of his past life, interwoven with scenes of Hannah and Samuel. And in every scene, he had seen the faint shadow of a wooden crucifix hovering over him. He gingerly stretched out his cramped legs and found a shaft of sunlight warming the rushes beside him. That meant two things. Firstly, that the rain had stopped, for which he was grateful, but also that it was well past dawn. He did not want to be discovered by anyone as he was, almost naked except for the fine altar cloth that he had wrapped around himself.

Silas found his still-wet clothes and dressed, cursing himself for not thinking of hanging them up the night before. He could see the whole church clearly now, and the half-constructed rood screen had finely carved features. He could have hung his clothes from any one of a number of decorated finials. Even more sacrilege to add to his account, he mused as he dragged his damp boots on and secured his scrip to his belt. He felt his stomach cramp painfully. He needed to find food and fresh water. He needed to keep travelling. But first he must put the altar back as he had found it. He moved quickly to replace the sacred pieces, trying not to think about how the priest, or his congregation, would react if they knew what he had done. Hoping that they wouldn't wonder at the marked creases in the cloth that he could not rub smooth, he was grateful no one had found him.

He made his way to the door, turned the heavy latch and glanced back to check that he had left no sign of his visit. He did not see the reed basket on the doorstep until he stumbled over it. It tipped over and out of it rolled a loaf of bread wrapped in clean linen and a small, stoppered flask.

Silas stepped back into the dark doorway and looked around anxiously. There was no sign of anyone in the immediate environs of the church and yet someone had been there. Someone had left the basket with its contents. He glanced down at the half-unwrapped loaf of bread and his stomach rumbled. The flask looked like a wine flask – he had seen many of them in different styles and sizes in his father's warehouses.

He waited for a few minutes more, and then decided to act. He snatched up the basket, placing the bread and bottle back in it, and tucked it under his cloak. Pulling the heavy door shut behind him, he half-walked, half-ran away from the church, into a nearby copse of trees.

He stopped at the bank of the river, still swollen from the previous days' rain. Today the sun was high, and he could already feel its warmth drying out his clothing. Song thrushes sang from the trees, and yellow celandine opened in greeting to the spring sunshine.

Silas no longer cared whether he was observed, or that he had probably stolen someone's provisions. He sat down with his back to a tree and unstopped the bottle, sniffing it before putting it to his lips and taking a swallow. It was wine, and the finest quality. He knew from its aroma and the feel in his mouth, as much as from the taste. There was a time, long ago, when he could have pinpointed the grape and the region it came from. Strange to find such rich wine so simply presented. It was strong and made his head swim slightly.

The bread, when he tore into it, was good too. Freshly baked, soft and faintly warm to the touch. He ate more than half of it, before he made himself pause; he might need further sustenance later. So, the bread was rewrapped in its linen and pushed into his now bulging scrip. He drank deeply of the wine again, enjoying the way it warmed him from the inside, its effects less potent now that bread lined his stomach. Bread and wine. He grimaced. Had he partaken of the elements of Holy Communion without meaning to? Well, his soul might not have been fed, but his body felt a great deal better. He dismissed any lingering feelings of guilt or unease and blessed the soul who had unknowingly met his needs.

Re-emerging from the trees into the churchyard, he looked again for any signs of human life. There was no trace. The path to the church was muddy from the rain that had fallen the day before, and yet the only footsteps visible in soft soil, now hardening under the warm sun, were his own, going to and from the church. A feeling of unease crept up his back and he spun around. But there was no one there. Silas placed the basket and empty wine bottle back on the step where he had found them and walked away. He resolved that at the next settlement, he would enquire as to the name of the church and of the priest and offer to pay for what he had stolen. Yet he had nothing to pay with, except his pewter cross and chain, and something made him baulk at parting so easily with that. It may not be worn around his neck any longer, but he still carried it on his person, as a remembrance of a past life, if nothing else.

He did not meet any other travellers or see any other habitation. The church had obviously been built to serve people, and was well maintained, so it was strange that for miles Silas saw no one. He was no longer following a clear path. Maybe he had just veered away from where people lived, or was this one of those places where the Welsh lived high in the hills, hidden, unseen, and yet seeing all? He trembled at the thought that he might be being watched. Yet no one challenged him or crossed his path. The bread and wine sat comfortably in his stomach and the sun warmed his back. His legs were still feeling the effects of his wet trudge the day before, but they loosened as he walked.

Before long, he threw his cloak from his shoulders and was enjoying the feel of the sun on his head. His hair was growing back slowly, greyer and patchier than his tonsure had been. He had let his beard grow too in the weeks since leaving Dore, and that too was more grey than brown. He was glad not to have to keep company with strangers, looking as he did like a vagabond, and yet, he did not relish being alone either. His thoughts strayed to Hannah and her warm hearthside and kind smile, but he checked himself with a resigned sigh. He had been right to leave. Even if she had felt more than friendship for him, which he doubted, his heart was too broken to give away. She deserved more.

Being in community was what he was used to, and he couldn't bear the thought of walking on alone. He had to find somewhere to rest. He began looking more intently for signs of human life. Maybe there was a farm that needed a labourer? He could turn his hand to most things; Grace Dieu had taught him how to raise both crops and farm animals. He was no stranger to hard work. He walked on, the sun behind him, walking westward and then north as the sun reached its peak. As he walked, he remembered snatched memories of his father's lilted accent, and his mother's sweet singing voice. *Hiraeth* – the feeling of being called back and drawn into the heart of the land of your ancestors.

The land embraced him, but he had still to meet any of its people. He wondered if they too would embrace him. He tried to remember some words of the language he had spoken around his parents' hearth. Tried to practise the sound of them rolling off his tongue. His steps had slowed, so he stopped by a stream to take a drink and break off another hunk of bread, sitting to watch a pair of wide-winged birds dipping and soaring against the bluest of skies. He envied their freedom. And yet, surely he was free now? Nothing or no one held him. He was free to do whatever he wanted, go wherever he desired. That was freedom, wasn't it? So, why didn't he feel free? Why did he still feel burdened? Perhaps if he could soar in the sky as those birds did, he could shake off the weight of what had gone before. Perhaps he would be able to get a wider perspective, a clearer understanding of the events of his life. But those birds were buzzards, birds of prey, and any minute now one of them would swoop and strike and death would come. There was purpose to their high flying, and he had none. How would it help him to look back or to look forward? To dwell on what had been and what might be? He had only the heart capacity to live one day at a time.

He got to his feet and moved on. The sun was now going down, turning the sky into a rich display of fiery reds, vibrant pinks and purples. He needed to find shelter for the coming night. At least the sky was clear, but that meant the air would cool. It was still early enough in the year for an overnight frost. Silas shuddered at the thought. A forest of trees loomed to his right, and he decided to head for it. Even tree cover was better than nothing.

Approaching the trees, he crossed a wide man-made track that seemed to skirt the edges of the wood. The unmistakeable odour of smoke hung in the air. He could not see if the smoke was coming from inside the forest, but finding a narrower track, he decided to follow it. The track took him deeper among trees that loomed high against a darkening sky. Very soon, he would be unable to see very much at all.

Had it been a mistake entering the wood? He could feel his heart pounding and it wasn't just from the exertion of picking his way along a fairly well-marked track that was now decidedly boggy underfoot. This deep into the forest, the sun hadn't reached where the recent rain had. Stumbling more than once, Silas wondered if he should turn and retrace his steps. Dark shadows loomed, and he shivered, glancing around and finding himself assaulted by menacing branches on all sides.

He heard a high-pitched bark, and a sudden rustling, and then something big and hairy was at his feet, growling threateningly. Silas froze and tried to stand stock still, but his whole body was quivering with terror. He held his hands up out of the way in case the creature snapped, but it did not jump. Instead, it circled him sniffing and growling until suddenly it stopped and sat in front of him, its mouth open, panting, but showing no teeth. Silas took his chance to try to step away. As he did so, the dog jumped to his feet and growled again.

'Wolf, what have ye found there? More rabbits?'

Behind the voice appeared a man. He was stocky and walked with a distinct limp. Silas could not clearly see his form or face in the dim light. The man approached, sniffing the air. He pushed the dog aside, and came uncomfortably close to Silas, peering into his face.

'A stranger, eh, Wolf?'

He addressed the dog and not the man. The dog stopped growling and instead pushed his nose up against the scrip hanging from Silas' belt. It still contained a crust of bread. Silas didn't know whether to reach down and release his scrip or keep his hands up above his head where he had lifted them. Both man and dog reeked of smoke and sweat, and Silas tried to pull back from their close scrutiny.

The man grabbed the dog by the scruff of the neck and pulled him down into a sit beside him. The dog sat, his eyes fixed on his master, his tongue lolling, as if waiting for the order to attack.

Silas held his breath.

'Lost, be ye?'

The question startled him. It was not asked roughly. He released his breath and lowered his trembling arms, clasping them across his chest. Just in case the dog snapped.

'Ye best speak, Stranger, as I can see very little. When the sky begins to darken, so do my eyes. Just as well my sniffer still works.' He sniffed loudly. 'Come, now, and I'll take ye back with me. I mustn't leave my fires for too long, or else the whole forest might go up.' He cackled then, and coughed, and spat. 'Wolf, lead the way.'

He whistled and the dog began trotting down the path. The man followed behind, without waiting for Silas to move. Silas watched them and before they were out of sight, he made a hasty decision. This was the first human contact he had had for two days, and he wasn't at all sure that this human was safe, but he would rather take his chances with this strange man and his dog than be left alone in the dark forest at night.

Then Jesus said to His disciples,

'If anyone desires to come after Me, let him

deny himself,

and take up his cross, and follow Me.'

Matthew 16:24

8

The Charcoal Burner

Silas followed the dog and the strange man hobbling and wheezing behind him, until suddenly the narrow track opened into a wide clearing. Here was the source of the smoke. Two sources, in fact. The gap in the trees allowed in enough of the dying sunlight for Silas to distinguish the outline of a large domed charcoal pile, with a plume of smoke rising from its centre. A few feet away was a small open fire, burning well, adding to the smoky haze.

'Come, Stranger. Come now into the firelight so as I can get a better look at ye.'

The man grabbed Silas firmly by the arm and unceremoniously pulled him over to the fire and down until the flames illuminated his face.

'Ah, ye look like a man in need of a good feed.' He released him then and sat himself down on what curiously looked like a one-legged stool. He reached over and picked up a lidded iron pot, placing it at Silas' feet.

'Sit. Sit, man.'

Silas obeyed, unsure what he was letting himself in for. On his feet he could have still run, but he was weary, and the fire was warm. He was going to risk it.

'That, in the pot, is the remains of the rabbit Wolf caught for me this morning. Well-cooked and falling off the bone, it is. That there dog,' his host gestured to Wolf, who in the light of the fire actually looked less like a wolf and more like a lanky-legged dog, but big enough to still be a threat. 'He thought he would be getting what was left over. I dare say ye might save him the bones.'

The ground felt cold and damp, and Silas inched a bit closer to the warmth of the fire. He leant forward to lift the lid from the pot and the unmistakeable sweet aroma of charred cooked meat assailed his nostrils.

'Eat, man. Eat!' The man had thrown a thick stick on the fire and was poking it with another. It flared comfortably. Silas did as he was told, reaching his hand into the pot.

The rabbit was good. It did indeed fall off the bone, and Silas ate hungrily. All the time, a pair of round glowing eyes watched his every move. Panting, drooling and shifting, the dog was finding it hard to be patient. Silas put him out of his misery by throwing him a leg bone. The bone was crunched and demolished by strong teeth in no time.

The dog came back to him and the pot, and disconcertingly chose not to leave his side. He was a tall, rangy dog, and somewhere in his ancestry, Silas supposed, there could have been a fine wolfhound. But

Wolf was less hound, more mangy mongrel; friendly enough, now that Silas had been welcomed and fed by his master. Perhaps too friendly for comfort, as his long lolling tongue and potent breath were poised uncomfortably close to Silas' face. He was glad when he could throw the last of the rabbit bones some distance away from where he sat, and the dog trotted after them.

All the time Silas had been eating, the charcoal burner had sat hunched over on his odd stool, singing to himself, his hands busy with something.

'Thank you for the food,' Silas said, finally, wiping greasy fingers down the edge of his tunic. He didn't feel the need for good table manners here.

The sun had now set completely. The moon had risen, and a multitude of stars lit the sky above the clearing. Silas' eyes began to adjust to the dark. The man held a small knife in one hand and was whittling away at a piece of wood. Suddenly, the man stood and put his work down. He hobbled to where a long pole stuck up out of the ground. As he pulled it from the earth, the end of the stick shone in the firelight, and Silas could see a spear-like iron tip, sharpened to a point. He felt a sudden rush of fear, stumbling as he hastened to stand. Had he been lulled into eating at this man's fireside, only to be speared?

The man turned and his eyes in his soot-stained face were bright. His mouth spread in a wide grin showing a set of surprisingly white teeth. Silas began to back away as the man lifted the spear, looking like some ancient warrior in his fur lined boots and thick black cloak. Silas looked around, panicked, for a way of escape, but he couldn't see clearly the way he had come. The dog too had jumped to his feet and a low growl was emitted as Silas pushed the dog away.

'Ha!' The man lowered the spear and then almost doubled over with laughter, cackling and roaring until the resultant coughing fit made him stop and draw deep breaths. 'I'll not be for spearing ye, Stranger. This here is for me to poke the pile. I can't see the colour of her smoke, but I can smell that she be burning too hot. She needs poking in a few places, that's all. I am sorry to have afeared you, but it did make me laugh.'

Silas held a hand over his heart, while Wolf stepped over and licked his other hand. He bent double to catch his breath, waiting for his heartrate to slow. As he did so he felt an unfamiliar bubbling rise from deep within his chest, and suddenly, he was laughing too. He laughed long and deep, until tears rolled down his cheeks and he had to stagger back to his spot by the fire. It was too long since he had belly-laughed, and it was releasing and exhausting all at once.

'Here, Stranger.' The man returned from his task and held out a cup of water and a cloth bundle to Silas. He took the cup and drained it, and then found the bundle to be a large rolled up blanket. It was not clean, nor sweet-smelling, but it was thick and as he wrapped it around himself and laid down, he felt its comforting warmth.

'Thank you,' he muttered, willing his eyes to stay open. The flickering flames of the fire were mesmerising.

'Now ye can rest, Stranger, and Wolf here and I will watch over you. This here pile needs watching and may well need poking some more. But I promise ye I will not poke ye!' The charcoal burner cackled again.

Silas was beyond caring what happened to him as weariness took him into a deep, dreamless sleep.

A wet tongue licking his face woke him. He opened his eyes to find Wolf standing over him, his breath warm and pungent. He really was the ugliest dog Silas had ever come across, and the dark soot stains on his coat did nothing to improve his overall appearance. But still, there was something strangely endearing about the beast.

He sat up, pushing the dog to one side. The fire he had slept beside had long since died, but the charcoal pile was still smoking in the early morning light. There were also the remains of two further charcoal piles, obviously spent, and several piles of freshly cut lumber ready to start another. A rough lean-to had been constructed to one side of the clearing. It had three sides and a roof, but the front was open to the elements. Was that where the charcoal burner lived? Or did he have a home elsewhere?

As if imagining him into being, the charcoal burner appeared, and Silas could finally get a good look at his host. His age was hard to determine, his face, hands and hair being liberally covered in soot and grime. But the slowness of his movements and the slight hunching of his frame indicated he wasn't a young man.

'Ah, ye be awake? I have porridge cooking on the pile.'

He used steps cut into the earth covering of the pile to climb up to where the smoke-hole was still blowing out large plumes of dark-grey, acrid smoke. He clambered down with the same iron pot that had held the rabbit the night before.

'Placing it by the fire hole cooks it well enough, but it does come with added smoke.' The charcoal burner grinned, put the pot down between them, and then from somewhere under his cloak produced a wooden spoon.

'Ye eat first, being our guest, then Wolf and I will finish it.'

Silas shrugged the blanket from his shoulders and dipped the spoon into a slightly grey-looking porridge. He scooped up a spoonful and hesitantly put it to his lips. It was hot, and it was smoky, but Silas had tasted worse. He ate a few mouthfuls before handing the spoon back to the charcoal burner, uncomfortable under the scrutiny of two pairs of bright, soot-rimmed eyes.

'Can I ask you your name?' Silas asked as the man stood and shovelled porridge into his mouth, oblivious to the heat coming off it. He tipped the remainder out onto the ground for the dog to finish, burped loudly and ran a filthy hand across his mouth.

'Iorwerth, at your service.' He swept his arm forward in a parody of obeisance.

'Well, I am grateful for your hospitality, Iorwerth,' Silas smiled, wondering if he too now had a soot-covered face.

'Will ye be telling us your name, Stranger?'

Silas thought for a moment. Who was he? Who did he need to be here? He opted for his Welsh identity.

'Morgan.'

'Morgan, eh? But not native to this land by your accent?'

'Born here, but only lately returned.'

'Ah, I see. And perhaps we could ask why ye were trying to get yourself lost in our woods.' He paused, but then continued. 'But it is not my way to pry. I have lived long enough to know that a man's secrets may be all he can hold on to.'

He settled himself again on his strange one-legged stool. Silas sat on the hard ground, but even that looked more comfortable than Iorwerth's perch. His curiosity got the better of him.

'Why does your stool only have one leg?'

'Ha. 'Tis simple. I have to sit for many, many hours, watching over my precious pile. Now, ye try to stay awake all night and all day for many days on the stretch. When I need to rest my legs, I sit on this stool. If I drop off, I drop off! If ye get my meaning. I fall asleep and I fall to the ground. Soon wakes me.'

It made perfect sense.

'But you don't tend your pile alone, surely?' Silas knew enough about charcoal burning to know that the burners usually worked in groups.

'That is my lot now,' Iorwerth sighed. 'I had two sons once, and we worked the piles together. But now they are gone, and I am left. What is it the good book says? "The LORD gave, and the LORD has taken away; Blessed be the name of the LORD."'[5] He was quoting Job.

The words from his mouth stung a little too close to home. Silas, surprised that a simple man would know the scriptures that well, tried to bury the challenge to his soul.

'I am sorry for your loss,' was all he could manage.

'Oh, they left of their own accord. One to fight for the Prince... He lost his life in a forest skirmish some miles north of here. The other left to pursue a different life. He told me he would make his fortune on the high seas and come back for me. But that was nigh on five years hence and he has not yet returned. Not saying he never will, but I leave that to God.' He shifted and sniffed. 'It's not a glamorous life, being a charcoal burner, but it is a skilled one. My biggest regret is that both my sons had been taught well how to tend the piles. Still, they could not bear the isolation of living apart from folk. And we are not highly thought of in polite company.'

There was truth in that. Charcoal burners, by the very nature of their work, were forced to live on the outskirts of society – yet were essential in producing a commodity that supposedly better folk relied on.

---

[5] Job 1:21.

'Have ye ever been wed, Morgan?'

The question startled him. He was never usually asked that. But, of course, Iorwerth did not know his background.

'No. Never married.'

'Ah. I never thought to marry. What woman would choose to live this life?' He gestured around the camp. 'But then Mair came along, as much as an outcast as I. I feel safe telling ye of our secret. The babe she carried in her womb was the consequence of a bad man who took her by force. Her fine family did not believe her tale and cast her out. Like you, she wandered into my forest and into my camp. And she ended up staying. I was a much younger, stronger man then,' he grinned briefly, and Silas caught a glimpse of that same good-natured young man. 'I worked the piles with my uncles, and they were glad of a woman's presence in the camp. She stayed and became my wife. We raised her son as our own, and then had another together. She died before my sons left.'

A sadness crossed his face, but his eyes were bright as Silas watched him. He took up his knife and the piece of wood to whittle at again.

'I don't know why I be telling ye all this. Except that I don't have company much these days.'

'I am sorry for the loss of your wife.'

'Yes. It pained me deep in my soul. But I still had much to live for. The L{\sc ord} gave... and so on.'

Silas shook his head, and it must have been observed.

'Ye don't believe in the words of the good book, then? My Mair, she did. She taught me that scripture, well-read she was, and educated. She always said that she believed that whatever calamities befell us were not the fault of God, but the result of the cruelty of humans. She believed wherever there was bad, there was always good. Something to be thankful for. And that, coming from a woman who endured much.'

He stopped working the piece of wood and handed it to Silas. Silas looked down and to his surprise found himself holding a beautifully carved animal. It was unmistakably a deer, like the ones that most likely roamed the forest.

'This is fine work, Iorwerth. How did you do it? I watched you last night and this morning and you hardly glanced at the wood in your hand.'

'My eyes are failing. Too many years working in heat and smoke, I don't doubt. I don't see much now. Less at night. In the daytime I can see the outlines of objects and people. I can see to poke the pile, and light my fire. I am so familiar with my surroundings that we get by, me and Wolf.' He sighed. 'I long learned to carve by touch, Morgan. This shape I have recreated many times. I have more. Come, see.'

He stood awkwardly from his stool and Silas wondered again at how Iorwerth coped with the physicality of his profession. To have grown sons he must be older than Silas, who for a moment could not recall how old that was exactly. He felt that he had lived a thousand lifetimes in the last few years. He raised himself up from the ground, his own bones creaking as he did so.

Iorwerth walked over to the lean-to. As Silas approached, he could see that it was lined with shelves full of Iorwerth's carvings. They were tiny, small enough to hold in the palm of a man's hand, with a couple of larger pieces leaning against the cobweb-laced back wall, sheltered from the elements. Animals, that were all instantly recognisable – hares, rabbits, deer, horses, even the odd dog or two. Each had been carved to a smooth surface and Silas could not help but reach out to stroke a hare that had been carved to look like it was ready to jump, its rear legs extended, and its ears raised in alarm. So lifelike, Silas almost expected it to jump away from his hand.

'These are magnificent.' It was said in an awed whisper, and he felt drawn to pick up one after another of Iorwerth's carvings, replacing them each with care.

The charcoal burner stood watching him.

'Forgive me,' Silas began to feel uncomfortable under the man's silent gaze. He backed away from the animals, raising his hands in apology.

Iorwerth raised his own hand to touch his work. 'It is nice to be able to show them to someone who appreciates them.' His lips lifted in a half-smile. 'A secret of mine that not many get to share. Most of my visitors come for my charcoal, not to see what else the wood can produce. I started to make them as a way of filling the long hours. The more I made, the better I got at likenesses. Mair loved them, and my boys played with them. I couldn't bring myself to stop working on them when my family were gone. Now I think they perhaps have become my family. They live here with me.'

He bent to retrieve a medium-sized box from a low shelf.

'Here, let me show ye something else. This was Mair's favourite. I don't carve images of men and women much, but she asked for these in particular.'

He lifted the lid of the box and Silas gasped. Nestled on a bed of wood chippings were the most honest and beautiful depictions of familiar figures that he had ever seen. The Madonna holding her child, the upright figure of Joseph. His hands felt drawn to the third form and he reached to take a simple crucifix from the box. It was not large, it almost fit in his two hands, but the carving of the figure of the dying Christ on the cross was exquisite. Silas gazed at it as it lay in his hands, and a sudden wave of emotion brought a tightness to his throat and tears to his eyes. The piece was beautiful. Its simplicity speaking far more than the most elaborately fashioned altarpiece. He reverently traced the side of the cross, not daring to even touch the figure depicted on it.

However hard he had tried to deny his faith, despite all the things he still had against God, seeing His Son so movingly portrayed in His moment of death touched his soul, and perhaps deeper than that. For something deep, deep within him was responding with an emotion that he could not deny. He might have chosen to close his mind and his will to God, but His spirit still responded. He recognised that and wanted to weep.

Instead, he swallowed hard and placed the crucifix gently back into the box.

He turned to find that he was alone. He could see Iorwerth tending the pile. The smoke was still burning thick and grey, and it hung low in the air. Silas lifted his sleeve to wipe his smarting eyes, but it wasn't smoke that had caused them to sting. He stumbled away from the charcoal burner's treasure trove and made his way towards the shelter of the trees. He would not go far; he dared not, as he knew he could easily get lost. But he needed to find a place where he would be unobserved.

Just as the laughter had welled up unbidden from within him the night before, so he could now feel the wave of something very different threatening to overwhelm him. It felt hard to breathe. He staggered into the embrace of the forest. Sinking down at the base of a large craggy oak, and leaning his head back against the rough trunk, finally he let the tears come. Waves of grief, loss and pain poured out of him, tinged by something else. A realisation that he could no longer deny. The God who loved him and gave Himself for him had not deserted him. He still lived inside of him, by His Spirit. His faith might feel dead, his mind might still struggle to understand it all, but the truth was that Iorwerth's simple representation of Christ's sacrificial death had connected with Silas' broken spirit. It released a wave of something sweet and healing, a flicker of hope that perhaps he was not lost after all.

If you love Me, keep My commandments. And I will pray the Father, and He will give you another Helper, that He may abide with you forever – the Spirit of truth, whom the world cannot receive, because it neither sees Him nor knows Him; but you know Him, for He dwells with you and will be in you.

John 14:15-17

9

THE CARVINGS

The weeping drained him and after it subsided, Silas just sat quietly listening to the sounds of the forest. Stretching his legs in front of him, he allowed himself to relax and drift off into a doze. When he finally opened his eyes, the sky had lost its cloud covering, and long, probing sunbeams poured through the leaf canopy. Birds sang as they built their nests in the treetops, small creatures scurried through the tall ferns that covered the forest floor and insects buzzed by.

He was finally disturbed by the sound of a rather large creature. With a single woof, Wolf sprung into his private space. This time he came with his whole body waggling with barely contained excitement, and his long tongue lolling. His swishing tail disturbed more than Silas, as the ladybird that he had been observing make its way slowly up a long fern frond, flew high into the air without the need of its wings.

'Oh, Wolf!' Silas couldn't help smiling as he tried to ward off the wet and less than fragrant ministrations of the dog's tongue. He levered himself up using the tree trunk behind him, and then bent to give the dog a head rub. As he stood, stretching his back and arms, the dog spun around and woofed again. Sure enough, through the trees came the sound of someone approaching, whistling as he came.

'Ah, so Wolf found ye again!' Iorwerth laughed, but his eyes spoke of something else.

Silas smiled reassuringly. 'He did, but I would have found my way back soon enough. I was not trying to get myself lost. I am sorry if I troubled you.'

'No, no. I was not troubled. We know these woods well enough to find ye if ye had wandered further.'

He turned, and without saying more, walked back the way he had come. He obviously expected both Silas and the dog to follow, which they did. However, it didn't take Silas long to realise they were walking in the opposite direction from the camp. He was debating whether to mention the fact when he realised that they had stepped out of thick undergrowth and were now walking along a narrow but well-beaten track.

Iorwerth was some feet ahead when he suddenly halted and raised his stick in the air. Silas and Wolf both stopped at the signal. After a tense, silent moment or two, the charcoal burner lowered his stick and waved them on. The track wove around another large oak and to the left, until before them stood a small rectangular wooden cottage. Its thatch had seen better days, but the walls and door looked sturdy enough.

'I thought I heard something, but 'twas probably only a stag helping himself to some of my roof. He skittered off when he heard you two coming!' Iorwerth grinned, and then led the way to the door of the house, lifted the latch and creaked it open. Silas followed while the dog busied himself trying to pick up the scent of the deer.

Iorwerth had gone inside, and Silas bent his head to follow him through the low doorway. Inside, the cottage was dark and musty. Cobwebs hung from beams, and pieces of thatch hung from the roof. Iorwerth coughed.

'Open the window, would ye, Morgan.' He indicated a wooden-shuttered square in the wall beside the door. 'We need some air in here, and more light. I am struggling to find what I came for.'

As Silas pulled the shutter open, more light did indeed fill the space, but it was still dim. A table with a bench seat was pushed against a side wall, and opposite it were two raised bed platforms, one covered by a thin mattress that had seen better days. A circular hearth was visible in the centre of the room and a large cupboard stood against the back wall. This simple space had once been a home. Iorwerth and his family had lived here, not in that poor shelter at the camp. By the look of it, it had been lovingly built and well-furnished at one time. It had also been long neglected.

Iorwerth was scrabbling around in the cupboard. 'Here,' he said finally, handing Silas a small sack.

'That is flour, I hope. I keep a stock of dry goods here, 'tis safer than in the camp. As we have a guest, I thought we could make some bread over the fire. I have some fish that I smoked, if it is still good.' He reached up into the top of the cupboard and pulled a leathery-looking whole fish off a hook. He sniffed it and grunted. 'Smells of smoke and nothing bad. I think we can trust it.'

He dangled it from his fingers in Silas' direction. He was right, it did not smell offensive.

Iorwerth closed and barred the cupboard. He looked around the cottage once more, lingering over the area where the beds stood, before turning and heading outside. Silas closed the window shutter and followed him.

'Pull the door and make sure the latch has settled. We don't get human intruders, but animal thieves... well they can be troublesome.' He began walking back the way they had come, and Silas fell in beside him. He was curious.

'You don't use the house now – to live in, I mean?'

'Sometimes, when the weather is very bad, and when I can leave the piles, I take shelter there. It was a happy, joy-filled place once, and holds many happy memories, but being there brings to mind what I have lost. I find more comfort in my fires and my smoke, and in sleeping under the stars.'

Silas understood. He had returned to Abbey Dore but found no comfort. It had been a familiar space, and it had offered him shelter, but it had not eased his soul. Now here he was, living like a vagabond, a wandering stranger, in the company of a simple outdoors man and his mangy dog. And it felt strangely good. Simple, uncomplicated.

On their return to the camp, Iorwerth engaged him to help with poking the piles. He taught him how to make holes at certain intervals around the circumference of the dome, and what the changes in colour and smell of the smoke emanating from the fire hole meant. He showed him the skill of stacking logs to start a new pile, how to arrange them so that they would not collapse inwards but burn slowly and evenly when fire was set. Silas was fascinated and content to be useful, but all the time his attention kept returning to Iorwerth's collection of carvings and the inadequate shelter that protected them.

Later, as they sat together by the fiercely burning campfire, their bellies full of simple flatbread and surprisingly tasty smoked river trout, Silas decided to broach the subject he had been thinking on.

'Why do you not keep your carved pieces in the cottage, away from the risks of fire, and out of the elements?'

Iorwerth looked up from where he had been stoking the fire and gave Silas a strange look.

'Why do ye ask?' he said. 'If they are lost or damaged, I can easily enough replace them. They are worth little.'

Silas did not agree and had been considering the potential value of the carvings. He was formulating a plan, but he wasn't ready to share it with the charcoal burner yet. He sensed the subject was closed, as Iorwerth rose from his stool and moved away from the fire to relieve himself.

When the man returned, Silas changed tack. He waited for Iorwerth to settle on his stool again.

'When will the charcoal be ready? And where does it go when it is done?'

Iorwerth glanced across the fire at him, his face unreadable. He reached into his pocket for his knife and proceeded to work away at a small section of tree branch.

'If the weather holds and it continues to burn steadily it will be ready to be shifted the day after tomorrow, which is Friday. A carter comes from Rhaeadr Gwy once a week and I try to have a load ready for him.'

Silas had noticed that there was no wheeled vehicle in the camp, apart from a handcart not dissimilar to the one he had pulled away from Grace Dieu.

'Do you ever go into town with your load?'

'No. No need.'

'You don't need to purchase supplies?'

Iorwerth was concentrating on the wood in his hands and not meeting Silas' gaze.

'The carter brings me what I need. Which is not much. Normally I have only myself and Wolf to feed.'

The silence hung between them for a while. All Silas could hear was the soft scraping of blade on wood, the snores of a sleeping dog, and the occasional crackle or spit from the fire as it reached a damp piece of kindling.

'Rhaeadr Gwy...' He had heard of the place but knew little about it. 'Is it a market town? Are there tradesmen and workshops?'

'It is, and there are a few. I don't know how it compares to your English market towns, but it is busy enough. Helped by the wool trade hereabouts, and the abbey that has brought work in.'

Abbey? Of course, they were close to Cwmhir – a well-established Cistercian abbey, similar in size to Dore. How had he forgotten that this country was now riddled with abbeys? After all his wanderings, he had found himself within miles of one.

Iorwerth stopped whittling and looked at him intently.

'Why the questions, Stranger?'

Silas cleared his throat and thought quickly. He wasn't about to share his past with this man, however kind and welcoming he had been.

'I must move on soon, and I need to know where I am heading.'

Iorwerth nodded slowly, but his eyes never left him.

'I may be dim-sighted, Morgan, but what I do see is a man shifting in his seat. Not used to lying, perhaps?'

Silas sighed. 'You are perceptive. I am actually in no hurry to move on, because I have no idea where to go next. And I have enjoyed your simple hospitality.' He looked down at Wolf, who was now lying warm against him with his head resting on Silas' lap. 'You have both been friendly to me, without knowing who I was. You have shown kindness to a stranger, and it is humbling to me. I was only thinking of how I might repay your kindness in some way. I have nothing to give you that is worth anything to you. Except perhaps...' He was unsure how to explain his thoughts. 'When the carter comes for the charcoal, I will ask him to take me into town with him, and I will also ask you if I can take one of your carvings with me.'

Iorwerth sniffed. 'You can take as many as you want. Except the ones in the box. They will stay here with me, for Mair's sake.'

He turned away, wielding his spear to tend to the charcoal pile again.

Friday morning dawned cold and misty, for which Silas was grateful. Iorwerth had deemed the charcoal ready the evening before, stating that by the smell of the smoke, it was now burning blue. Silas had seen the change in colour of the smoke and wondered again how the charcoal burner managed so well with his sight impaired.

Iorwerth had damped down the remains of any fire in the fire hole, and almost straight away began to gently pull the pile apart, removing the layers of soil from the dome with a rake-like tool, to expose the precious carbonised wood beneath. Silas had tried to help, but once the daylight had died, they both conceded that they would have to complete the job in the morning.

They rose early and set to the task in hand. It was warm work. Silas blessed the cool, wet mist that hung in the air as sweat poured from his brow, and the still steaming charcoal made his legs and arms glow. By the time the sun had risen high and hot enough to burn off the mist, the charcoal was all laid out and the pile no more. Silas was filthy and worn out, but also strangely proud of the part he played. If only the abbot at Dore, or even his fellow brothers, could see him now. The thought made him snigger. He who once had taken pride in his appearance, in his work for God, in his adherence to the Rule and to his vow. Now the simplest of humble tasks had left him with a feeling of deep satisfaction. Although he had done little except be a manual labourer. All the skill in creating this perfect batch of well-made charcoal was Iorwerth's.

Not long after noon, the carter appeared, his long, low cart pulled by one of the biggest horses Silas had ever seen. The man driving the horse was not small either. Broad and tall, with a thick, dark beard and wide-brimmed hat, he hollered a greeting as he jumped from his perch.

'Iorwerth! Are you ready for me, old man?' The voice was loud but not harsh.

'Twm Carter, ye be as old as I am.' Iorwerth held out his hand to the man who loomed over him. The carter shook it firmly before heading over to examine the charcoal.

'Good, good. Won't take us long to load – especially as you have taken on help. About time too.' He glanced in Silas' direction.

Silas stayed silent and Iorwerth laughed.

'Ah, him? He is just a harmless stranger that wandered into our camp a night or two back. Wolf has taken a liking to him, haven't ye, boy?' The dog woofed in agreement and came over to stand beside Silas, wagging his tail.

'Well, if that daft dog of yours likes him, he must be safe enough. Come,' he gestured to Silas, 'grab a shovel, and we'll make light work of this.'

He grabbed the headcollar of his carthorse, gently pulled her into place so that the cart was alongside the charcoal and unloaded a pile of large empty sacks. All three of them began to shovel the charcoal into the bags, and the pile began to reduce considerably.

'I came here to you first this week, and I am glad I did, Iorwerth. You have a good quantity and quality of charcoal here, and I will get a good price for it.' Twm was shovelling away without seeming to lose breath. Silas was finding the work much harder.

Iorwerth stopped at the carter's comment and rested his arm on his shovel handle. He wiped a grubby sleeve across his brow.

'I am grateful to ye, Twm,' he said quietly. 'How does Gruffudd Ddu do now?'

'Well, he has his boys, and that means he can tend two piles to every one of yours. Still, your burning skills are superior to his. He lost a whole pile last week to the flames because of lack of care.'

'It happens.'

'Hmm. Doesn't happen to you so much.'

Iorwerth bent back to his work. Silas was curious and itching to ask for more information. It was obvious that Iorwerth had a competitor, and he wondered what that would mean for the man, especially if his eyesight, or general health deteriorated more. Whoever this Gruffudd Ddu was, he had help, and Iorwerth didn't.

When the task was finished Silas was grateful to be handed a rag and pail of water. The water was not clean, but it was cleaner than his eyes and face. He had to make himself look more presentable, as he was still planning to ride back to Rhaeadr Gwy with the carter. He cleaned himself up as best he could, put his cloak around his shoulders and tied his scrip to his belt. Twm and the charcoal burner were standing by the cart. Silas saw Twm hand Iorwerth a sack of provisions, before clapping each other on their backs and making their farewells.

Iorwerth turned as Silas approached the cart. He handed Silas two small wooden figures – the hare he had so admired, and another of a deer.

'I have asked Twm Carter to take you into town. He is willing enough. Take these with ye, as my thanks for your help with the charcoal. I have enjoyed your company almost as much as Wolf here has.' He reached down to fondle the dog's ears. Wolf had come to sit beside the charcoal burner and was leaning against his legs.

'Thank you,' Silas said. 'For these and for everything.'

He wasn't sure what else to add. Iorwerth thought he was leaving, and that was for the best. He wasn't sure himself if he would see the man or his dog again. He had a plan, and this time he had even prayed that God might help him in it. He was still unsure of where he and God stood, but he hadn't been praying for anything for himself. Just that he might make a difference to this kind man's life.

Twm was already in the driving seat and reached down a strong arm to help pull Silas up beside him. He clicked the reins, and the horse pulled away, seemingly undeterred by the weight of the load she drew. Silas did not look back as they trundled down a wide track that must have been the one that had drawn Silas into the forest before he lost his way. He wondered now if Providence had led him there. He would never have sought to keep company with a charcoal burner, or to sleep outside with a dog curled against his back, or to break a sweat loading charcoal onto a cart. Yet he felt a quiet peace in it all. And had made a new friend. Well, two, if he included Wolf.

'Iorwerth told me not to ask who you were or where you are from, as a man is allowed to keep his secrets.' Twm gave him a hard stare, but then raised an eyebrow. 'That is your right. But you look like a man intent on doing business, and I think it may have something to do with those figures you are holding so reverently.'

Silas looked down at the hare and the deer in his hands. He was amazed by the workmanship, the beauty of them. Yes, they sat well in his hands, but he did not plan to keep them.

'Do you know of anyone in Rhaeadr Gwy who might be interested in selling these for me?'

'Hmm? So that's it. Does Iorwerth know your plan, to sell the gifts he has given you?' The carter did not seem happy, and Silas shifted uncomfortably. The horse plodded on regardless.

Silas forced a smile. 'Oh, I don't want to sell them for me. I want to sell them for Iorwerth. He sees them as having little value. I disagree.'

'In that case, I think I do know someone.' The big man turned his attention back to urging the carthorse forward. 'Yes, I think I know just the man.'

Then the King will say to those on His right hand,

'Come, you blessed of My Father, inherit the kingdom prepared for you from the foundation of the world: for I was hungry and you gave Me food; I was thirsty and you gave Me drink; I was a stranger and you took Me in.

Matthew 25:34-35

10

Rhaeadr Gwy

Rhaeadr Gwy was not a big town. Nothing like Bristol, or Hereford, or even Hay. It was built around a crossroads, and where the four roads met, the land had been levelled and cleared to form a rough market square. Buildings were dotted along the streets, most of them wooden built, and low level, with simple thatched roofs. The charcoal-ladened cart passed a couple of shops with shutters thrown open. One displayed a meagre selection of leather goods. From another, the tempting smell of freshly baked bread wafted on the breeze. A painted sign indicated another house where ale could be bought, and as they trundled on, a distinct smell assaulted Silas' nostrils indicating a tannery was not far away. There were people going about their business, children playing on rough areas of grass, and a shepherd herding a straggly flock of sheep. Although there were one or two other wooden vehicles, it was far from bustling.

Twm Carter pulled up alongside a fence that stood at least a tall man's height. It was solidly built with no gaps between its wooden slats. It seemed to be forming one side of a sizeable enclosure or compound, as at one end it turned in at right angles. At the other end of the fence stood a two-storey building that had one large window facing the street and a smaller window on the upper floor. Both windows were shuttered closed. In the fence was a solid double wooden gate, also closed. If this was a business, it seemed strange to Silas that it was shut up in the middle of a working day.

Twm jumped down from the driver's seat and pulled on a cord hanging beside the gate, which released a tuneful bell chime. He glanced back at Silas, grinning, and sure enough, before many minutes had passed, one of the gates opened to reveal a tall, slim lady of middle age. She was dressed in simple grey with a snow-white veil, and to all intents and purposes could have been mistaken for a nun. Her clothing gave her an austere look, but at the sight of the carter she smiled, and it softened her face. Her voice, when she spoke, was also surprisingly soft.

'Good day to you, Twm Carter. Have you some charcoal for us? We are so grateful. We are keeping the gates closed while the forge is out of action. Please, come, bring the cart in.' She moved gracefully to swing back the other gate.

It opened into a wide, enclosed yard. The building Silas had seen from the road stretched back to form one side of the rectangular enclosure. The windows of the finely built house on the side within the enclosure were unshuttered, and a solid wooden door stood ajar within a wide doorway. The back of the yard was lined with outbuildings, and as Twm pulled the cart in, a pony peered out of a stable doorway, whinnying a greeting. In the far-left corner of the compound, a large forge sat cold and unattended, with a smith's anvil and tools laid out around it.

Silas kept his seat as Twm led the horse and cart and then helped their host to close the gate behind them.

'As you can see, our fires are calling out for fresh charcoal.' She indicated the forge with a nod of her head. 'But then, we are also lacking a smith. Einion has been called home to see his mother, who is sickening. God heal her soul.' She crossed herself daintily. 'Come. Let me serve you refreshments. You and your friend.' She turned her attention more fully on Silas who suddenly felt acutely aware of his dishevelled state. He hastily jumped down from the cart and straightened his tunic.

'Thank you, Mistress Goldsmith.' Twm turned his attention to the charcoal. 'We would be grateful for some cool water to slake our thirst, but let us first unload what you need. Will you take the whole load? It is Iorwerth's finest.'

'Call me Rachel, Twm. We have known each other long enough.'

She seemed to take a moment to examine his wares, and then a further moment to decide. 'We will take half the load today, Twm, and will pay you a fair price as always.'

She turned with a swish of her woollen skirts and disappeared into the house.

'Come on, help me with this, Stranger. Then I will introduce you properly and you can see if you can get a fair price for those other goods that Iorwerth has produced.' Twm led the way to the rear of the cart.

Silas bent his back to the task of helping to unload the very charcoal he had loaded earlier. Soon he was hot and filthy again, and longing for the promised cold water. Some warm water to wash his hands and face would be doubly welcome.

As if reading his mind, Rachel reappeared, carrying a large tray bearing a fine pewter jug and cups, and a dish of fine white wafers. She lowered the tray onto an upturned barrel. Silas looked at his hands with dismay. He wanted to avail himself of the refreshments on offer but even wiping his hands on the sides of his rough tunic would not rid them of the sweaty grime. He felt uncouth in the presence of such fine provisions, and of the lady who had provided them. Twm came over, wiping his own dirty hands on an equally grubby rag.

'Matthew?' Rachel's voice rang out clear and strong.

Out of the same doorway, a man appeared. He was as slim as she was, and half a head taller. He had the same pale face and dark eyes, and the dark tunic he wore added to his pallor. As he approached, he was smiling. He carried a large jug and basin, and had a clean towel thrown over his arm.

'I'm sorry. My apologies, friends, Rachel. I was just waiting for the water to heat up, using a very inadequate fire for the task. I should have come and grabbed some of this fine charcoal. Here...'

He knelt and poured steaming water from the jug into the basin, which he had placed on the ground, close to Silas' feet. He stood again and lifted the basin to hold it before Silas at waist height.

For one heart-stopping moment Silas had thought the man meant to wash his grimy feet! He wondered why he had even thought that. Of course, the water and towel were for his hands and face. He dipped his hands into the almost-too-hot water and bent his face over the basin to splash it clean. It felt so good. As did the soft, clean towel, which was markedly less white when he had finished his hasty ablutions. Then the man, Matthew, moved over to Twm to offer him the washing water.

Silas still felt less than clean, but when Rachel approached him, at least he could reach out washed hands to take the cup. He helped himself to a wafer, savouring its delicate honey sweetness.

'Who is your friend, Twm? Will you not introduce him?' Matthew had put his basin down and helped himself to two of Rachel's wafers. She shot him an indulgent look.

Twm had shoved several of the delicacies into his mouth at once and looked suddenly abashed. He gulped some water from the cup in his hand.

'He goes by the name of... what was it?'

He looked at Silas, who shifted uncomfortably. All three of them were watching, waiting for his response.

'M... Morgan. Morgan ap Bedwyr,' He managed to stammer out.

Twm raised an eyebrow. 'Yes. Well, I found him at Iorwerth's camp; seemingly he had wandered into it a night or two back. He had made himself useful, though, while enjoying the charcoal burner's simple hospitality. And Wolf seemed to have taken a liking to him, so he can't be all that bad, whoever he is.'

'If Wolf approves, that is good enough for me.' Matthew laughed and held out his hand to Silas. 'You are welcome to our yard, Friend. I am Matthew and this is my sister, Rachel. As you can see, the smithy is quiet. Our brother-in-law will be gone a few days. He too would have welcomed you if he had been here.' He turned back to Twm. 'You have more deliveries to make?' He nodded towards the remaining charcoal in the cart.

'Yes, I think I might take this to the abbey.'

Silas felt his hair bristle at the word.

'Ah, yes, good, I need to go and pay Abbot Julian a visit, but I have some things to finish for him first. Will you go with Twm, Morgan?'

Silas was lost in his thoughts. He had visited Abbey Cwmhir once and knew of its kind abbot. Julian had heard of their struggles at Grace Dieu and had written to Abbot Adam at Dore, asking for more resources for their beleaguered abbey, and for greater leniency towards their keeping of the Rule. Silas had been grateful for his intervention, but it had not achieved much.

'Morgan?'

Silas was startled back into the present. He cleared his throat to answer, but Twm answered for him.

'No, he only asked me to bring him to town, and to point him in the direction of someone who might be interested in what he has to sell. So, I brought him to you.'

'Oh?' Matthew's eyebrows rose and his high forehead crinkled. His hairline had receded with age, and where once it perhaps had been as dark as his eyebrows, it was now smattered with grey. His intense stare made Silas feel uncomfortable, but there was no hostility in the man's gaze.

Silas found his scrip hanging from his waist and fished out the two small figures he had hastily stored there. He extended both hands, one of the pieces nestling in each. Matthew stepped forward and took the deer from him. He brought it close to his face, twisting and examining it intently, as if it were the finest of jewels.

'Yes,' he whispered, half to himself. 'This is beautiful. So wonderfully fashioned and so lifelike.' He turned to Rachel. 'What think you, sister?'

He handed the figure to her, and she studied it. 'Lovely, and I can see it would take some embellishment, as I think you can too.'

'Yes, indeed. Here, along the back.' He traced the markings that resembled the white spots of a fallow deer. 'And perhaps the eyes. Yes. And the other?' He turned back to Silas, his eyes shining. 'A hare!' He took it from him. 'Again, so finely done. The work of a true craftsman. Is this your work?'

'No, no. Not mine. Iorwerth's.'

'The charcoal burner did these? A hidden talent indeed! How is it that we did not know he could make more from wood than fine charcoal?'

He did not wait for an answer, but taking the deer back from Rachel, he turned and set out to return to the house.

'Matthew?' The voice rang clear and true again. He stopped and turned, seeming to be surprised at her call. She laughed. 'You cannot start work on them until you have paid Morgan for them. Or paid Iorwerth?' She sent Silas a quizzical look.

'Oh dear. Of course. My apologies,' Matthew hurried back, looking flustered. 'Yes, of course. Only I think these could be worth a great deal more if I could work on them. Do you think Iorwerth would entrust them to me and my craft without payment? When I have finished, I can sell them, and he can have a far greater share of the profit?'

He was asking Silas, who was unable to reply. Iorwerth had no idea that he was trying to sell the pieces. They had been given to him as a gift. He didn't know this man or what he intended to do with the carvings, but he had nothing to lose.

'There are more.' He wasn't sure why he said it. 'Iorwerth... he has made many more. Hundreds, possibly. Many as fine as these.'

'Has he?' Matthew was definitely interested. 'I would love to see for myself. But for now...' He glanced up at the sky, which had begun to cloud over. A few drops of rain fell. 'Twm here needs to get on his way, and I need to work. Will you stay, Morgan?'

Twm was already on the driver's seat of his cart, and Rachel was hurrying to open the gate for him. Silas felt stuck. He had nowhere to go – not with Twm to the Abbey, that was for sure. The rain was beginning to fall more heavily.

'Here, Morgan, follow me.' Matthew was already scurrying back towards the house. Silas stood for a moment watching Rachel close the gates behind Twm's departing cart. She turned and walked briskly towards the house.

'Come inside, Morgan. Out of the rain.' Matthew stood in the open doorway, waiting for him, having let Rachel pass. Silas looked at his grubby tunic, the cloak he had grabbed from Twm's cart, now slung untidily over his arm, and his filthy boots. Reluctantly he followed them inside the house, stopping just over the threshold.

The interior was dim, but he could see it was an elegantly furnished home. He felt even more uncomfortable in his unwashed state as he looked around a large room fitted out with a table, benches, and a number of fine, high-backed chairs. A charcoal brazier stood to one side, but it was barely alight. A high open window let in daylight, but also brought a damp chill to the room.

'I would like to work on these, while you wait, and show you what is possible.' Matthew moved towards a narrow open doorway that led off one side of the room.

'Will you sit, Morgan?'

Rachel indicated one of the high-backed chairs, its seat covered by a plush cushion. Silas felt his face flush. His stay at the charcoal burner's camp and his physical labours had left its mark on both skin and clothing. He doubted that he smelt too good either. He hesitated.

'Wait,' Matthew shoved the carvings back into his hands, gestured to Rachel, and then they both withdrew through another wider doorway, leaving Silas standing in the middle of the room, uncertain of what to do next.

Matthew reappeared within moments, with a steaming basin of water, and a rough blanket slung over his arm. He placed the basin on the floor by the chair that Rachel had offered Silas, and then placed the blanket over its seat so that it draped over the arms and fully covered the cushion. He touched Silas' sleeve.

'Sit please, it does not bother us that you are mired by living outside, but it seems to be bothering you. Here, let me take your cloak,' he spoke in low tones as he plucked it from Silas' arm. 'And if you want to remove your boots you can soak your feet here.' He indicated the basin.

Silas sat down heavily and immediately relished the softness of the cushion beneath him.

'Can I take Iorwerth's carvings from you? Will you trust me with them?'

Silas suddenly felt drained of all energy. He gratefully handed the pieces to Matthew and leant back in the chair. He should have kicked his boots off and made use of the warm water to soak his feet, but it felt like too much effort to do so. He felt chilled and pulled the edges of the rough blanket over his arms and knees and closed his eyes for a moment.

He did not hear his hostess re-enter the room to shutter the window or restock the charcoal in the brazier.

Silas awoke with a start, feeling awkward for having dozed off, a stranger in a strange house. Yet again he had been shown kindness. It did not escape him that he had so far met only good people on his travels. Was that God's doing? He did not know why Matthew and Rachel had welcomed him into their fine home.

He stretched his stiff neck and back, easing himself to the edge of the chair and standing slowly. The heavy work of charcoal shifting had taken its toll on his muscles, as had sleeping upright in a chair.

'Ah, you are awake.' The figure of Matthew bobbed into the doorway. 'Come and see what I have done.'

He ducked back through the door and Silas followed him into what was obviously a workshop. It was bathed in light but not from its single large window – the one that faced the street – which was securely shuttered and barred. Instead, several tallow candles burned brightly. On a shelf above a wide bench were a number of half-finished pieces: cups, jugs, plates and dishes. Silver or pewter, Silas could not be sure. A large cupboard to one side was banded by iron with a huge chain and lock to close it.

Matthew was standing by his workbench with his hands on his narrow hips, a broad grin on his face. There, between two candles, stood Iorwerth's deer. In the candlelight, two tiny round green eyes glowed, and a pattern of delicately placed pearl-white spots shone along its back. It was stunning.

'Mother of Pearl,' Matthew said, and then picked up the deer and held it worryingly close to a candle flame. 'Can you see? The eyes I have decorated with green agate.' He excitedly put the deer down and reached for the hare. 'This one, I will set him on a plinth of silver-embossed wood and place a piece of lapis lazuli in his paws. Can you see how it will look? In your mind, at least?'

Silas drew a deep breath, and let it out, closing his eyes against a sudden rush of emotion.

'Are you quite well?' A firm hand grasped his arm, and he opened his eyes to see a worried face peering into his own.

'Yes, yes, please excuse me, Matthew. I ...' he didn't know how to explain it. But he knew his soul had been touched by beauty.

'Sit, please.' Matthew pulled his stool up behind Silas' knees and he allowed himself to sit. A cup was thrust into his hand. Water again, but that was good, and Silas drank it gratefully.

'Forgive me,' he managed. 'I think perhaps I rose from my rest too quickly.'

'Hmm,' Matthew looked at him knowingly. 'Or perhaps you are carrying a weight on your shoulders, an unseen burden, that is wearying your soul and body.'

Silas drew his eyebrows together, and shook his head, ready to deny the truth of Matthew's words. Yet he knew he could not.

'I see it,' Matthew whispered. 'Because I too have carried unseen burdens, have been so weighed down of soul that the slightest thing of joy or beauty could tip into overwhelm.' He smiled and moderated his voice. 'You are welcome in our home, Morgan, and if we can do anything to lighten your burden, we will.'

Silas felt tears pricking and swallowed. He could not unburden himself on these poor, unsuspecting people. What could they possibly know of the pain he had endured, of the life he had left behind, here in their comfortable home, safe behind high fences? What would they know of fights lost, dreams crushed and faith abandoned?

Matthew had returned to his bench and was once again admiring his handiwork.

'I think this would make a fine love token. The hare, too, when it is done. You say he has more?' He didn't wait for Silas to answer. 'Has he perhaps made any human likenesses?'

Silas took another deep drink of water. 'Yes, he has fashioned likenesses of the holy family, and...' he almost didn't want to mention it, '... a beautiful depiction of Christ on the cross. More pleasing than any other crucifix I have ever seen.'

'Ah. And you have seen many perhaps? As have I.'

Again, he did not wait for Silas to answer, and he was glad of that. How could he tell this man how many crosses of wood, silver and gold he had seen. All the years he had held onto a faith that seemed to have slipped away. His hand went instinctively to his scrip, and he felt the pewter cross within. He made a sudden decision.

'Here.' He put his hand into the scrip and took out the cross. 'Would this be enough to pay for the stones you have used to beautify Iorwerth's deer? If you would take this, then I can leave you with a clear conscience.'

Matthew took the cross from him but did not look at it; rather, he studied Silas' face.

'Iorwerth gave me the figures as a gift. He did not ask me to sell them for him. It was my idea, an attempt to pay him back for his kindness to me. I only intended to get a coin or two for them, that I could give to Twm to take back to him. I did not know what value you would see in them, and now you have added gems to them...'

'Morgan! Be at peace. I will take your cross in payment if it soothes your conscience. But on the morrow, I will go myself to the charcoal burner's camp and show him what I have done with his work. I will give him a good price for them and offer to take more to work on. I would especially love to see his holy figures. I know Abbot Julian at Cwmhir would love something like them for his own private apartments, if not for the abbey church. He appreciates the simpler things but is not averse to a little embellishment.'

'He will not sell them.' Silas felt the rush of guilt for even mentioning Iorwerth's figures.

'Then I will not offer for them. But he might be persuaded to make more.' Matthew grinned and winked. 'Will you stay under our roof tonight, at least? And perhaps you will accompany me to Iorwerth's camp tomorrow? The rain is lashing down outside now, and we could not sleep peacefully knowing you did not have shelter.'

Rachel had appeared in the doorway. 'I agree with my brother. Will you stay with us?'

Silas looked from one kind face to the other, and found himself nodding, as the sound of the rainstorm outside hammered out any last vestige of resistance in him.

Then the righteous will answer Him, saying, 'Lord, when did we see You hungry and feed You, or thirsty and give You drink? When did we see You a stranger and take You in, or naked and clothe You? Or when did we see You sick, or in prison, and come to You?' And the King will answer and say to them, 'Assuredly, I say to you, inasmuch as you did it to one of the least of these My brethren, you did it to Me.'

Matthew 25:37-40

11

MATTHEW

'Will you be comfortable enough here?' Matthew glanced back at Silas. They were standing in a simple, clean room, with fresh rushes strewn on the floor and a raised pallet bed along one wall. A small window was shuttered against the weather. They had come through Rachel's well-equipped kitchen and into the blacksmith's living quarters, a separate single storey building that had been added on to the side of the house.

'You are most welcome to use this room in Einion's absence. The other door leads directly outside to the courtyard. Einion's water trough will be full with all this water falling from the heavens. If you would like to remove your tunic and cleanse yourself, you can borrow this.' He plucked a garment from a peg on the wall.

'It is a spare tunic of Einion's.' He held it up and chuckled. 'It may be large on your frame, but it is better than you trying to squeeze into one of mine.'

Silas gave a small smile.

'Thank you,' he said and took the proffered item.

'Rachel will be busy in the kitchen for a good while, so you will not be observed.' Matthew turned and left through the narrow door that led to the rest of the house, closing it firmly behind him.

The charcoal brazier in the main room burned with a pleasing warmth. Silas was thankful for the heat source as his skin still tingled. He had quickly scrubbed his head, chest and arms outside in the freezing rainwater, and donned the borrowed tunic, which dwarfed him. His belt did enough to keep him from tripping over its hem. At least he felt a little more presentable, and smelt a great deal better as Matthew ushered him in.

A large, single tallow candle in a simple holder had been placed in the centre of the table casting a cosy welcoming glow. A fine silver candlestick also stood on the table, holding not one, but seven narrow candles, as yet unlit. Silas was surprised to see it. He knew what it was; he had seen one before, in the house of a Jewish money lender in Bristol.

Rachel appeared, wearing a clean white apron over her dress, and carrying a lidded pot. 'Please, show our guest to the table, brother.'

She hurried out and Silas took a seat on the bench behind the table. Tendrils of steam and a delicious savoury smell emanated from around the edges of the lid of the pot. Rachel reappeared with a stack of trenchers in one hand and a large platter in the other. Both were placed on the table. The aroma of freshly cooked fish assailed Silas' nose, and his mouth watered. Rachel had gone and come back yet again, this time with a tray bearing the same pewter jug and cups she had produced earlier, and a collection of spoons of different sizes.

She laid them down and moved to the end of the table where the candlestick stood. She picked up a spill from the table and lit it from the tallow candle. Silently she lit the seven candles one by one, blew on the spill and then covered her eyes with her hands. Quietly she prayed. It was in Hebrew, but Silas could make out words that he could recognise; '*Baruch*', blessed, '*Adonai*', Lord, '*Shabbat*', Sabbath.

He shifted uncomfortably in his seat, but there was something peaceful, holy even, about this simple Jewish ceremony. Was it lawful for him as a Gentile to eat with Jews on the Sabbath? He smiled to himself at the irony of it all. What would the Cistercian brothers say if they could see him now?

As Rachel finished praying, she took the seat beside her brother, and then bowed her head, as did Matthew.

'Thank You, Almighty God, for Your provision for us, for the guest at our table, and for the gift of Your Son, Jesus Christ. In His name. Amen.'

Matthew raised his head, and his eyes met Silas'. One corner of his mouth lifted in a half-smile. Silas was confused. He remembered how he had witnessed Rachel cross herself earlier and recalled Matthew's interest in Iorwerth's carvings of the holy family and the crucified Christ. Was this a Jewish home or a Christian one? Or both?

He had no time to voice his questions, as Matthew handed him a trencher that Rachel had piled with savoury lentil stew and a piece of fish. Silas smiled his thanks.

'Eat, please.' Matthew gestured enthusiastically and then tucked into his own meal.

Silas ate in silence, trying to make sense of what he had just observed and heard. Only when the dishes were finally cleared and his stomach satisfyingly full, did he attempt to voice his confusion.

'Your prayers? Rachel prayed a Jewish blessing, but then you blessed the food in the name of Christ.'

Matthew let out a short laugh, and Rachel smiled.

'I'm sorry if our strange habits confused you, or made you feel uncomfortable. We were born Jewish. Some of the ceremonies and rituals we were brought up with, still hold meaning for us. We like to honour our heritage in small ways, behind closed doors, even though we both follow Christ now. We are not confused, I assure you.' He grinned, pushed his empty trencher away from him, and wiped his fingers and mouth on a piece of cloth. 'Would you like to know our story? Come, let us sit closer to the brazier in more comfortable chairs. It is a wild night out there. Our story may entertain you for a while, before we retire to our beds.'

Silas followed him and sat in the chair that he had vacated earlier. Matthew sat opposite him, placing the large candle on a stool between them. The *menorah* still shone brightly from its place on the table. Before long Rachel joined them, her apron gone, but with a thick woollen cloak tucked around her shoulders.

Matthew leaned slightly forward in his chair and rested his hands in his lap. His eyes were bright in the candlelight as he began his tale.

'Matthew is my Christian name; my given name was Levi. We came to Rhaeadr Gwy as fugitives, in my father's time, when Jews were being openly persecuted for their faith. We left a thriving business in Oxford and ended up here. Needless to say, the business suffered from the move. There was not much call for a goldsmith's craft here, nor the numbers of wealthy clients we were used to. My father tried to bring in trade by pretending that we were Christian, and offering for sale Christian artefacts, plate, icons and reliquaries to churches and abbeys.

I thought at the time it was greed that motivated him, but looking back I can see now that he was terrified. Fearful for his family, for our future; scared of us being found out and of what would happen if we were. I believe he had the best intention, in trying to protect us and provide for our security, but he did not always do things honestly. For years, he insisted that we denied our Jewish heritage and traditions, in order to stay safe. He made money out of our Christian neighbours and created this home for my mother, sisters and myself. He even went as far as sending me to a priest for Christian instruction. That turned out to be a mistake on his part.'

He and Rachel exchanged a knowing look.

'You found Christ?'

'Well, I am not sure I quite "found" Him, but I was interested enough to go looking. It was not what that priest taught me, but how he showed Christ through his own life. His humility, gentleness of spirit, honesty – so seemingly different from my father – and his own confidence in his faith, those things impressed me. I found my heart warmed to both the man and the message he taught. I even went on a pilgrimage to immerse myself in the Christian faith.'

Silas was impressed. Matthew had done something he had longed to do but had never had the opportunity. Perhaps he should go on pilgrimage. Would it help him find his faith again?

'Did the pilgrimage lead you to faith?'

'I thought it had. I tried to live what I imagined the Christian faith to look like. On that journey, I met men and women who followed Christ, and their faith challenged me. But I was twisted in my understanding. I thought following Christ required self-abasement, rule-keeping and a version of self-righteousness that left me judgemental of others, unloving towards my family and generally unpleasant to live with.' A look of pain crossed his face.

'That was a long time ago.' Rachel placed her hand over her brother's.

'Yes. It was, and I am not that man now,' Matthew added quietly.

'Can I ask what changed in your thinking?'

Matthew's description of the Christian life sounded a little too familiar to Silas. He had observed this in the lives of others but had also given great value to rule-keeping and self-sacrifice himself. Those things had engendered an unhealthy pride and self-confidence. Was that why his failure at Grace Dieu had cut so deep? He let the thought go as Matthew continued speaking.

'I was forced to abandon my pilgrimage before its completion. At the time I came home angry; angry at my father for falling ill and angry at my mother for summoning me home before I had experienced all the pilgrimage had promised. I was annoyed that I was the only son, expected to take on my father's business so that my mother and sisters did not starve. I was lacking in grace and not at peace in my soul. I had failed to prove myself a good Christian, in my own mind.'

He paused and reached out to add some charcoal to the brazier from a wooden pail situated by his chair.

'I am not proud of the young man of my past,' he whispered, as he sat back again.

Silas understood what it felt like to be angry and disappointed – in himself, and in the circumstances forced upon him.

Matthew took a deep breath and let out a long sigh. 'It is a good thing that God does not leave us in the messes we create for ourselves, is it not?'

He glanced over at Silas as if expecting him to answer.

'God is good,' Rachel added, when the silence had lingered. 'Shall I continue your story, Matthew, and make it ours?'

Matthew smiled at her. 'Of course.'

'Matthew came home to see our father, who was dying, but he was too late to hear him speak again. Father had fallen into a deep stupor from which he never woke, dying within hours of Matthew's return. That was a hard time for all of us. Grief was mixed with anxiety as we realised that we had been kept in the dark about the sorry state of the business. Matthew soon discovered that debts had not been paid while my father had spent lavishly on this building and on fine things. We believe that he fully intended to make good on what he owed, but his sickness came before he had the chance. He was a hard man who had suffered much, but fitting our home out in comfort spoke of his care for us. We only wish he had been more prudent, as when those debts were called in, we were left almost destitute. More unsafe than ever.

'Our "salvation" came through the abbey. In more ways than one. A commission came our way for a fine set of silver plate for the abbey church, a bequest from a wealthy patron. Matthew went to discuss the making of it with the abbot over several visits and met a young monk there. Brother Julian, as he was then, was clever and knowledgeable, but also kind and sensitive, and the two developed an unlikely friendship which has lasted until today.' She smiled at her brother.

'While visiting the abbey, Matthew also heard of a young man, a gifted blacksmith who had been apprenticed to an older man and thought to inherit the business. But he had been cheated of it by the blacksmith's family and had returned to Rhaeadr Gwy with just his anvil and tools. Julian introduced Matthew to Einion and between them they came up with a plan to combine their businesses. Having a blacksmith and a goldsmith on the same premises meant shared costs and shared customers. It is an arrangement that has worked well for years and kept a roof over all our heads.'

'I spent hours with Julian,' Matthew took up the story again. 'I asked him every difficult question I could think of. I challenged him and watched how he responded to me. He brought everything back to the cross. He would not be diverted. For him, it was all about Christ's death, what it accomplished, and our personal response. Slowly I came to realise that I had it all wrong. To be like Christ was not to force myself to behave in a certain way, to try in my own effort to be a good Christian. All that God required was for me to accept the death of His Son and to submit to Christ's Lordship in my life. Once I had repented of my wrong thinking, and for the myriad sins of my past, I needed only to receive the forgiveness He offered and commit my life to Him. When I did that, I knew He had changed me, on the inside, by His Spirit. He is still changing me. It is His job to make me more like Him.

'It didn't take long for Sarah, my sister, and I to see the change in Matthew,' Rachel continued gently. 'Our mother saw it too. One by one, we came to understand who Jesus was and what His death meant for each one of us. Sarah believed first. By then, she and Einion had formed an attachment and wanted to marry, so she submitted to Christ before they said their vows. I was slower in seeing the truth. Our mother never spoke openly of her heart position, but she asked us to call for the priest as she was dying. That was a comfort to us all.'

'So that is our story, and now it is late.' Matthew stretched out his long legs and yawned.

'Your sister, Sarah?' Silas knew the likely answer before he had even asked the question.

'She is with Jesus, as is her unborn child.' Rachel stood and pulled her cloak more tightly around her, shivering slightly. 'The rain has definitely chilled the air.'

She took up the *menorah* from the table and began to move towards the door.

Silas looked to Matthew, but he was staring into the flame of the solitary candle still burning on the stool between them. He said nothing to disturb the man's contemplation, and he stood, feeling his bones complain as he did so. He followed Rachel from the room and into the kitchen that ran almost across the full width of the house. It was unusual for any homes other than the grandest to have separate kitchens to the main living area. This was a luxury indeed and was obviously Rachel's domain. A large stone hearth with an oven was built into the back wall, and the smoke hole above it was unusually encased in stone, rising up the wall above the fire. Silas had heard of such constructions – *chimneys*, they were called – a device that took the smoke from the room and directed it straight out through the roof.

Rachel placed the menorah on the kitchen table and took one of the lit candles from it, fixing it into a simple pewter candle holder. She held it out to him, and Silas took it.

'May God grant you peaceful sleep, Morgan,' she said softly, before turning and heading towards a wooden stairway at the far end of the kitchen.

Sleep did not come easily. Maybe because he had dozed earlier or maybe because of the stories Matthew and Rachel had shared. They had known suffering and loss, yet their faith burnt bright, unlike Silas' candle, which had long since spluttered and died. Silas lay on the bed in the dark, listening to the sound of the rain falling relentlessly outside.

Finally, he sat up and went to where he had thrown his soiled tunic in a heap in the corner of the room. He had meant to rinse it when he bathed himself but had not lingered at Einion's water trough for longer than it took to splash himself with water and throw the blacksmith's huge tunic over his head. It had still felt public, even in Matthew's enclosed yard, and he was anxious not to cause his hostess embarrassment.

Silas forced his feet into his cold boots. Throwing his cloak over his head, he lifted the bar on the door. It opened to reveal a deluge to rival Noah's flood. Water was falling in sheets from the sky and pouring from the roofs of the stables and outbuildings. The packed earth of the compound had become a lake that came almost to his ankles. Silas stepped back into the relative warmth of the room and closed the door. He could wait to rinse out his tunic – maybe he should have just left it out there in the rain. He threw it and his now wet cloak, back into the corner it had come from.

He drew off his sodden boots and raised his legs up onto the bed. The blast of cold wet air had chilled him, so he pulled the blanket up over his shoulder and turned to face the wall, curling his body for warmth.

Sounds of cooking and food preparation coming from the kitchen woke him. Light was streaming through the crack in the shutters. Still the rain fell, and the air felt damp, even inside. He wandered into Rachel's kitchen and the warmth of the well-stocked fire hit him.

'Good morning, Morgan.' Rachel was stirring a huge pot of creamy white porridge over the fire – a very different kind of porridge to the one Iorwerth had served him. His thoughts went to the charcoal burner, and how he might be faring in this weather. He would hopefully be using his cottage to see out the rainstorm. There was no use trying to burn charcoal in this.

Matthew appeared. He too must have been thinking about Iorwerth.

'I am not sure we will be able to get to the charcoal burner's camp for a few hours yet. The roads will be impassable.'

'Eat, break your fast, both of you. Iorwerth is not expecting you, so there is no hurry. We see a lot of rain here, and it will pass. The ground will dry out quicker than you think, but it is a nuisance while it lasts.'

Rachel placed two bowls of steaming porridge on the wide, rough table, and Matthew pulled up stools for himself and Silas. Matthew paused and bowed his head, moving his lips in a silent prayer, and Silas bent his own head. He managed a silent 'Thank You'.

He was grateful. For the dry roof over his head and for the food. The porridge was rich and thick and sweetened with honey and dried fruit. It was so delicious. How Matthew and Rachel kept their slim figures with the quality of food at their table baffled him. Matthew made short work of his meal, and then stood to let his sister sit and eat hers.

'I am going to make use of our waiting time to decorate that hare. I am excited to show both animals to Iorwerth.'

With that, he was gone.

Rachel sighed as she put her spoon to her bowl. Silas slowed his own eating to keep her company. His impulse was to finish it quickly and to lick the bowl clean, like Wolf. He knew he could not at this table.

'My apologies for my brother,' Rachel said between slow, deliberate mouthfuls. 'When he has an idea, something that seizes his imagination, he becomes so focused on it that he neglects all else. Visitors included.'

'Please don't apologise. You and your brother have shown me nothing but kindness, and me, a complete stranger. You even shared your stories with me last night, without asking to know anything about me.'

Rachel paused and looked at him directly. 'Do you want to share your story? I would listen without judgement.'

For a moment, Silas nearly gave in to the urge to tell her all. She was so kind and gentle, but his story was not.

It was messy, painful and violent. He was ashamed to tell it, because unlike their stories, his was yet to have a redemptive ending. He dared to hope it would have, in time.

He gave her a small smile. 'Thank you,' he said, and shook his head slightly, surprised to feel his eyes pricking.

Rachel put her spoon in her empty bowl. She rose from the table and looked at him kindly, just for a moment more, before collecting the empty porridge bowls and whisking them away from the table.

In the two hours or so that it took for the rain to stop and the ground to begin to dry out, Silas tried to usefully occupy himself. Matthew was alone in his workshop for the whole time and Rachel busied herself in the kitchen. Silas donned his damp cloak and boots again and ventured outside. He found the pony standing in sodden straw and cleared it out as best he could. The back corner of the stable seemed to have stayed dry, so he spread dry straw there for her, and replenished her feed bag from a store of oats he found in a barrel. She allowed him into her space without complaint, whinnying softly as he did what he could to make her more comfortable.

Finally, the clouds began to disperse, and a watery sun began to peek from behind the grey.

True to Rachel's prediction the standing water in the compound drained away quickly, leaving behind compacted mud that soon became a rutted mess as Silas and Matthew led the pony out and put her into the traces of a small cart. She seemed to be happy that the rain had stopped too, as she raised her head, snorted and shook her mane.

Matthew climbed into the cart and held out his hand to help Silas up beside him. A cloak-shrouded Rachel trudged over to open the gate for them, both sodden doors resisting her as she tugged on them. They drove out into the open street, still running with rivulets of water, but firm enough for them to drive the cart forward.

For God so loved the world that He gave His

only begotten Son,

that whoever believes in Him should not perish

but have everlasting life.

For God did not send His Son into the world to

condemn the world,

but that the world through Him might be saved.

John 3:16-17

12

Iorwerth

The charcoal camp was strangely quiet as they approached. Unsurprisingly, with the still prevalent dampness, there was no smoke rising. Wood was stacked in an almost complete pile, but it had not been finished with earth. There was no sign of Iorwerth, and even more surprising, no bark of greeting from his dog.

Something felt wrong as Matthew pulled up the cart, and both men alighted. There were fire remains, but they were cold and rain-soaked. Iorwerth was not in his shelter, or anywhere they could see. The handcart was where Silas had last seen it. The clouds were parting above them, revealing more blue sky, and the sunlight was pleasantly warming. If Iorwerth had taken shelter from the storm, he would have been back at camp as soon as the rain stopped. His charcoal piles were awaiting his attention.

'I think we should go to his cottage.' Silas could not get rid of the feeling of unease.

'Which way is it?' Matthew was making his way back to the cart.

'I am not completely sure.'

Silas looked around and could see several narrower tracks than the one they had arrived on, leading away from the camp clearing.

'I think it could be this way.' He moved towards one that seemed familiar. 'But you won't be able to bring the pony cart. The track is narrow and the ground sodden.'

Matthew came to join him. 'Lead on, Morgan.'

Silas took a few steps, his boots squelching in the mud, but he didn't feel confident. They walked on until suddenly the track narrowed, and they found their way blocked by a fallen tree. One that had been there for some time, judging by the ivy growing over it.

'We will have to turn back. I think we have followed the wrong path.'

Silas chastised himself for not taking more notice of the way Iorwerth had led them back from the cottage not many days previously.

They found themselves back in the clearing, contemplating the other paths on offer to them. Silas was getting increasingly anxious.

'Iorwerth! Wolf!' He called as loud as he could, but the only sound he heard in response was birds startled into flight by his shouts. He had another thought, unsure of where it had come from, he put two fingers to his mouth and whistled high and loud and long.

Nothing. Then, suddenly, there was the sound of an animal crashing through undergrowth, accompanied by a frenzied barking. Wolf ran at them both full pelt and then seemed to check himself as he saw Silas, screeching to an ungainly halt in front of him and dropping his belly to the ground.

'Wolf!' Silas bent down to ruffle the dog's hair in relief, but then the dog was up and off again, back in the direction he had come from. He only paused briefly once to look back, and Silas got the message.

'We are coming, boy,' Silas yelled, and started to run, hearing Matthew's footsteps pounding behind him. They were heading through the trees, brushing twigs and branches aside. Wolf had slowed to make sure they were still following, but he was still moving at some pace. Eventually the trees opened into the familiar clearing where Iorwerth's humble cottage stood. There was no smoke indicating a fire of any sort, and the windows were shuttered. The door, however, stood ajar, and Wolf pelted inside, with Silas and Matthew hard on his heels.

The room was dark and smelled dank. As they moved further inside there was another less than pleasant aroma, the rank smell of human sickness. Iorwerth lay on one of the platforms, wrapped tight in a thick blanket. The floor around was soiled, and the man didn't move as they approached.

'Iorwerth? It is Morgan.' Silas bent over, relieved to feel the man's rancid breath on his cheek, but there was no response. Iorwerth's hand, where it gripped the blanket tight around him, was cold to the touch, but the man's forehead was burning hot and peppered with beads of sweat.

'We need some air and light. Unshutter a window and open the door wide on its hinges.' Silas was giving orders, but Matthew didn't hesitate to comply. It was obvious that the charcoal burner was in a bad way, and there was no comfort, nothing to aid him, in that dilapidated cottage.

Silas bent again to put his fingers to the man's neck. The pulsing of his heart was rapid and weak. Iorwerth groaned and coughed violently, but his eyes still did not open.

'Iorwerth?' Silas tried again. 'It's Morgan. Can you hear me? Matthew the goldsmith is here with me. We are going to help you.'

No response.

'He can't stay here,' he whispered to Matthew. 'I am going to impose on you and your sister's kindness and ask if you will take Iorwerth in. If we can get him out of here, that is.'

'You do not even have to ask. I can't get the pony cart to the cottage, though, and I don't think we can carry him.'

'Iorwerth has a handcart. If we can get that here, perhaps we can carry him back to the camp in that. It is a bit undignified, but at least the poor man will be insensible. Do you think you can find your way back to the camp? The track should be obvious from this direction. Or shall I go?' Silas didn't want to leave his friend's side.

'I will find it. Do you think Wolf will help me?'

'Wolf! Take Matthew to the camp.' Silas spoke to the dog in a commanding tone.

Wolf looked at him, and then looked at Matthew and mercifully seemed to understand. He pushed his hairy body past them both and sped out of the door. Matthew followed the dog. Silas sent up a quick prayer that Wolf would indeed follow his instructions and not lead Matthew deep into the forest and leave him there.

He bent down to Iorwerth again and used his sleeve to wipe the poor man's brow. He could not even offer him a sip of clean water. One eyelid flickered, and a hand shot out and grabbed Silas' sleeve.

'Mair's box.' It was rasped out breathily, but Silas heard and understood. He placed a hand over Iorwerth's. 'It will come with us, I promise.'

The charcoal burner coughed again and released his grip on Silas' sleeve. He did not speak again and thankfully it was not long before Silas heard Matthew approaching, pulling the handcart behind him. It was Wolf who appeared through the open door first, tail wagging and tongue lolling, looking pleased with himself.

Matthew entered behind him, blowing hard.

'That dog took great delight in moving so fast that I had to run to keep up with him!' He bent over and put his hands on his knees for a few moments and then stood and stretched his back. 'I am not as fit as I was,' he grimaced, and wiped the sweat from his forehead.

The handcart would not fit through the door.

'Do you have energy enough to help me carry him to the cart? He is not a big man, but he will be a dead weight.'

Matthew nodded. 'With God's help, we can do it,' he said.

With more puffing and blowing, Matthew and Silas lifted and carried the charcoal burner from his bed and out of the cottage. They tried their best to be careful, but he was half-lowered and half-dropped onto the handcart, and his legs had to be bent up, so they did not drag on the ground. It did not look comfortable, but it was the best they could do for him.

'I'll pull,' Silas offered, taking up the handcart handles. 'Can you steady him with your hand so that he does not topple off? The track is not exactly smooth.'

Matthew took his place without complaint and lent his strength to help push the load as Silas pulled. They were both almost at the end of themselves by the time they reached the charcoal camp and manhandled Iorwerth into the back of the pony cart.

'Wait!' Silas called as Matthew released the reins of the pony from where he had tied them and made to climb back into the driving seat. He stumbled over to Iorwerth's shelter and bent to retrieve the box containing Mair's precious carved figures. Matthew had followed him, and his gasp was audible. Silas turned to find him examining Iorwerth's carvings stacked around the shelves.

'So many!' It was an awe-filled whisper. 'What I could do with these. The man is so gifted.' Then Matthew seemed to come to himself and glancing back at the sick man now lying in the back of his pony cart, dropped his hands from the treasure-filled shelves.

'Let's get him home, and pray that he survives to create yet more,' he said, and moved purposefully towards his cart.

The pony cart wasn't a large one, and Silas rode cramped in the back, alongside the prone figure of the charcoal burner with a not-so-small dog laid across his legs and a fair-sized wooden box shoved behind his back.

Rachel welcomed them home and into the yard. After what seemed like the slightest moment of surprise at their unexpected cargo, she swung into action to help them unload its human burden. Iorwerth had not roused at all, apart from to cough and groan periodically. He was burning with fever, and as soon as he had been carried into Einion's easily accessible room, he was laid carefully on the bed and the soiled blanket removed. Rachel looked down at him, her face filled with pity.

'He needs cool water passed through his lips and warm water to bathe his head, chest and limbs. I think he needs to be stripped of those rank clothes. I can't do that.' She glanced across at Silas, who stood by the man's bedside.

'I will nurse him,' Silas said quietly. 'Matthew and I will strip and bathe him, if you can provide the warm water, and a clean tunic or shirt of some kind. If we can get water into him, he might also swallow a thin broth. Can you make some, with animal bones, if you have some?

And if you have access to feverfew or rose water, that might help with his fever?'

'Do you have knowledge of the healing arts?'

Silas nodded. He had stood by many sickbeds and aided Infirmarers enough times to know the basics, but he wasn't going to divulge that information to Rachel and her brother.

She waited an instant to see if he would answer, before twirling and disappearing into the kitchen.

Silas found himself naturally giving orders again, as between them, he and Matthew wrestled to divest Iorwerth of his soiled clothing. It was thrown in a heap outside of the door, and already the smell emanating from the man improved. Once they had bathed his face, neck, chest and arms, with rose-scented water, he smelled even better and looked very different as well. His cheeks were flushed with fever, but his skin around it was whiter than it probably had been for years. His hair and beard still carried soot and charcoal dust but washing those was a task for another time, if the man survived.

Iorwerth stirred a couple of times at their ministrations and uttered a few unintelligible words. Wolf sprang up from his place at the foot of the bed every time his master mumbled, but sank back into his sentry position, lying with his head on his front legs, when he sensed he wasn't being summoned.

A cup of water was held to the man's mouth, and he involuntarily parted his lips and swallowed, each sip followed with a paroxysm of coughing. Silas persisted over the hours that followed, as he encouraged the man to take water, and then a few mouthfuls of broth, with the finely chopped dried leaves of feverfew added to it. Rachel had run to the house of the midwife who had given her some from her collection of dried herbs at an exorbitant price. She had also sacrificed one of their egg-laying hens to make the bone broth, using the stringy flesh to make a stew that fed them all as the evening drew in.

Silas did not leave the charcoal burner's side. He continued to bathe his burning skin and offer him life-giving fluids. He tried to pray, comforted that Matthew and Rachel also prayed. He could hear their whispered words as they sat together at the kitchen table through the long night hours. He was thankful, as he thought God was more likely to hear their prayers than his.

Morning came and Silas woke sitting on the hard floor with his back against the wall. He had been sat on a stool by the man's bedside with Wolf at his feet. But as the night had worn on, he had been increasingly unable to sit upright. He feared he would fall off the stool, which unlike Iorwerth's, had its full three legs. So, he had quietly lowered himself to the floor sometime before dawn, and he must have dozed.

He looked over and was pleased to see Iorwerth's chest was moving, and his breathing was regular. His cheeks were still flushed, but he seemed to be sleeping peacefully. Silas stood quietly, knowing he needed to go outside. The dog moved with him and followed him out into the yard. The air was fresh and cool, and Silas breathed deeply. Apart from a few fluffy clouds, the sky was pale blue and the sun warm on his aching back. He took his time, waiting for Wolf to do his business and have a quick sniff around. As he stepped back inside the room, he was surprised to see Iorwerth lying with his eyes open.

'You are awake, thanks be to God!' He meant it.

Silas hurried over but the man did not turn his head. 'Iorwerth?' He placed a hand on the man's shoulder. Only then the charcoal burner turned to him, and Silas was startled to see that the man's eyes were a deep sapphire blue. He hadn't noticed before, perhaps because charcoal dust had just made his whole face, eyes included, appear dark.

At the movement, Iorwerth coughed again, lurching his chest upwards. Silas moved quickly to support him as he hacked and then helped lower him to his bed. He tried to speak.

'Where...?' he wheezed. 'Where am I?'

'You are being cared for in the home of Matthew the goldsmith and his sister, Rachel.'

Iorwerth coughed again. 'Wolf?' he whispered, and the dog was right there, his long tongue licking his master's face. Iorwerth raised a hand to feebly lay it on the dog's neck. 'I can't see clearly, but you sound like Morgan.'

It was obviously an effort, and Silas raised a cup to the man's lips.

'Yes, it is Morgan. We found you and brought you back here. But now you need to rest, and we will talk more later.'

Iorwerth took a deep drink from the cup and then laid back down. He had not removed his hand from Wolf's neck and the dog lowered his body so that his head rested on Iorwerth's chest. Silas left them to go and tell Matthew and Rachel that their prayers had been heard. It seemed that for now, at least, God had spared the charcoal burner.

By evening, Iorwerth was able to sit up in his bed, well-bolstered by cushions, to take some broth. He needed to be fed by spoon, and he was still coughing, but the fever seemed to have subsided, and his chest did not rattle as ominously as it had. After he had taken a few sips of the bone broth, he laid back and watched as Wolf noisily finished the bowl. A small smile crossed his face and Silas smiled with him.

Silas made himself a makeshift bed on the floor, in the space between Iorwerth's bed and the opposite wall. Straw, blankets and one of Rachel's fine sheepskins for a pillow would make for a much more comfortable night than the one he had just endured. He was hopeful that Iorwerth would sleep soundly, and that he too would be able to rest.

'Thank ye.' It came as a croaked whisper.

Silas was sitting on his bed, removing his boots. He shifted so that he leaned against the wall.

'I am just glad we came back to the camp when we did.'

'Why did ye come back?'

Silas didn't want to trouble the charcoal burner with that just yet. He had seen Matthew's reaction to the carvings at the camp, and he had seen his face when he had opened the lid of Mair's box. That box was now safely stored in Matthew's locked cabinet, but Silas guessed that he already had designs on the figures it contained. He did not think Iorwerth would part with those. Although he might let Matthew work his craft on the animal carvings.

'What happened, Iorwerth?'

The man grimaced, coughed and then took a few strained breaths.

'After ye left with the charcoal, I was going to go and catch up on some sleep, but I thought I would try to finish the pile first. I could see the weather was closing in.' He paused, and Silas handed him a cup to sip from, so that he could continue his tale. 'It was strange, I could not seem to get my limbs to work. My head began to pound, and I was coughing, but then I always cough. I stopped trying to work and wrapped myself in my blanket. I thought about lighting a fire, but I just didn't have strength enough. Then the rain started…' He coughed again and closed his eyes, before continuing hoarsely. 'I woke sometime later, and it was dark. I was soaked and shivering. I knew I was in trouble and somehow, I forced myself up and staggered to the cottage. I remember heaving the door open and emptying my guts onto the floor with the effort. I don't remember much else.'

'Wolf led us to you.'

The dog wagged his tail at the sound of his name, but he did not lift his head from his master's lap. Iorwerth reached down and stroked the dog.

'Good job he likes ye, Stranger.' He tried to laugh, but it turned into another cough.

'Liked me enough to lead me to you. But I think it's obvious that the dog loves you.'

Iorwerth grunted, but he also smiled as he moved to lie a bit flatter. He was soon snoring.

Silas lowered himself onto his own bed and pulled a thick blanket up over his legs, but he could not sleep. He lay listening to Iorwerth's noisy snores, grateful that he slept and that the worst seemed to be over for him. Wolf had laid his long body alongside his master's, on the bed and was snoring softly too.

You love Me.

He heard it. It wasn't audible but he recognised the voice because he had heard it before, deep in his heart. He almost sat up but forced himself to stay still. He found his fists were clenched as tightly as his eyes, and he willed them both to relax.

Again, he heard it, and it was unmistakable.

You love Me.

He knew whose voice it was. He had longed to hear from God. Pleaded with Him for a word of promise or of hope, for a reassurance of answered prayer or deliverance. He had heard nothing, felt nothing, for so many months. And now, when God did speak it was to say something that seemed so... incomprehensible.

It hadn't been a command, 'Love Me', that would have made more sense. Or even, 'I love You', which he might have struggled to believe, coming from God. No. The voice had whispered, *You love Me*.

It touched something deep within him to hear those words, and he lay with tears quietly rolling down his cheeks. God saw, and God knew, and God understood. At the heart of it all, beyond his doubts and fears, beyond the confusion in his mind and the dulling of his emotions towards God – beyond all of that, God was exposing the true position of his deepest self. He could not escape it. His heart still belonged to God.

A new commandment I give to you, that you love one another; as I have loved you, that you also love one another.

By this all will know that you are My disciples, if you have love for one another.

John 13:34-35

13
Rachel

Silas would wonder, afterwards, why he did not leave the goldsmith's home as Iorwerth's health improved. There was no suggestion from either Matthew or Rachel that he had outstayed his welcome. They were as kind and generous as always. And he felt reluctant to move on, feeling that he owed it to the charcoal burner to care for him as he recovered, giving back some of the kindness he had received.

When Einion the blacksmith returned a few days later, there was no question of moving either Iorwerth or Silas from his room. A tall, broad man with thick arms and a shock of red hair, Einion insisted he would be happy to spend his nights in the stable. He joked that the pony and his own horse would be more amiable company than his complaining mother had been, and that he would sleep more peacefully than he had for many nights.

Even after his fever had broken, it was obvious that Iorwerth was severely weakened by his illness. Or perhaps he had not realised how his lifestyle had left him weak and vulnerable until forced to rest. His cough persisted, and sometimes it left him completely spent.

His appetite was improving, but he still slept for long periods. When he was awake, Silas would sit with him, and they tried to converse. But talking soon exhausted Iorwerth and brought on more coughing.

One morning, after Silas had helped Iorwerth to break his fast and wash, Matthew appeared, with an object in his hands.

'For reasons I am not sure of, I assumed that you might be able to read, Morgan?' He raised his eyebrows in question, while handing Silas a leather-bound book. 'This is a thing of great value to me, a gift from my good friend Abbot Julian. It was in his own personal library, and I asked to borrow it so many times that finally he insisted I keep it!' Matthew laughed. 'It bears my name.'

Silas turned the heavy book over and lifted the cover. Inside he could see neat script in uniform lines, with highly decorated capitals, and the title 'Gospel of Matthew'. It was a fine book, a valuable gift, and as he lifted each page, he could see the beautiful decoration continued. This was an object of great workmanship that talented monks had laboured hours over.

'It is beautiful.' He turned his face to Matthew and recognised the same gleam of appreciation in the man's eyes that probably glowed from his own.

'It is.' Silas heard the catch in the man's voice. 'So precious that it spends much of its time locked away with items of silver and gold and precious stones. And it is the most valuable of all to me. It does not get read often enough. I thought perhaps you could read it to Iorwerth? It might soothe and comfort him?'

Soothe and comfort. Silas held the book in his hands, pausing to open it. He knew reading the words it contained might well challenge and convict him, but might they soothe and comfort his soul as well? It seemed a long time since he had held, read and meditated over, any portion of the Bible. He used to love his times of Lectio Divina, sitting to study the biblical text, waiting on God for its meaning and application. That was before Grace Dieu robbed him of the time, energy and will to do so.

Matthew turned to leave. Silas perched on the stool beside Iorwerth's bedside. The sickly man laid with his eyes closed, his chest moving up and down, his breathing thankfully quiet, until the next paroxysm caught him. He had not stirred during Matthew and Silas' quiet conversation, but as Silas rested back against the wall, and opened the book, Iorwerth lifted an eyelid.

'I would love to hear it,' he whispered hoarsely.

Silas cleared his throat and began to read. He had opened the book in the middle and found himself reading of how Jesus reacted with compassion to the crowds that thronged to be with Him, how He taught them and healed all that were brought to Him, how He cared that they were tired and hungry, and fed them miraculously.[6]

Silas paused as tears blurred his vision. As he read, his heart was reacting to the words on the page. This was

---

[6] See Matthew 14.

the Jesus he had sworn to follow all those years ago; the Man of Galilee, whose love compelled people to follow Him, the Saviour whose life displayed so much good, whose words changed lives, whose healing touch set so many free. This was the Son of God who had given His whole self, even His very life, for him. This Jesus had offered him salvation and had asked for his life in return. And he had given it, willingly. Given himself to serve Christ and his fellow men. It was good to remember why he had done that.

He read on, and there was Jesus, walking on the water, calling Peter to come to him, catching him as he sank, helping him back to the boat and stilling the storm.

'O you of little faith, why did you doubt?'[7]

The words shot like an arrow into Silas' heart. It wasn't condemnation he felt, just an overwhelming sadness, as if he had let both himself and Jesus down. Peter had only been human in his moment of doubt. He had been walking on a stormy sea, and the roaring wind and waves had been real and terrifying. It was no wonder the man had floundered. God knew how storm-tossed Silas' life had been. The wind and waves had been real – terrifying raids, constant fear, struggling to keep going with so little, feeling a failure, being kidnapped, losing Abbot John, losing Grace Dieu. Was it any surprise that he had doubted, that his faith had failed, that he

---

[7] Matthew 14:31

had found himself sinking? But no divine hand had pulled *him* out of the waves.

He closed the book sharply, shutting his eyes against a sudden wave of grief. He leaned his head back against the wall. Iorwerth coughed but did not speak, and Silas assumed he slept. When he eventually opened his eyes, it was to find the man staring at him intently from his bed. Wolf also raised his head from where it had lain on his master's feet, and two sets of eyes seemed to bore into him.

'Are your eyes tired, Stranger?' Iorwerth spoke and then coughed again. 'I was finding the words and your voice so calming. I could not understand the language but still the words soothed. I recognised a few words only. It is Jesus ye be reading about?'

Of course! Silas hadn't thought. He had read the Latin text out loud, not considering that the charcoal burner had not been educated to understand it.

'Yes.' He sat upright, resting his elbows on his knees with a sigh. 'My apologies, I did not think to translate for you. I read the stories of the feeding of the 5,000, and of Jesus walking on the water.'

'Ah. I know those stories well enough. Mair told them to our children.' Iorwerth was trying to pull himself up. Silas placed the book on his bed and offered his hand to help Iorwerth sit. The movement resulted in another fit of coughing, and Silas handed him some water to sip.

'I think I will try to get out of bed today.'

That was not what Silas was expecting the man to say.

'Are you sure you feel strong enough?'

Iorwerth grunted. 'I am about done with this bed, and with this room, Morgan. Despite your good company.' He twisted about and painfully slowly lowered first one, then a second, bare leg to the floor.

'Wait. Do not move. Let me get help.' The man was obviously determined, but Silas worried that he had underestimated his weakened state.

The charcoal burner sat perched on the edge of the pallet, his bare feet resting on the floor, his hands gripping the side of the bed to keep himself upright, his face pale with the effort of moving.

Silas went first to the kitchen to inform Rachel, and to ask for a clean cloak to cover the man to maintain his dignity. Then he went to Matthew's workshop, but finding it empty, sped out into the yard. Einion was there, dressed in his thick leather apron, his face and arms flushed red from firing up the forge. He dropped the bellows and followed Silas at his request.

Between them, and with some effort, they eventually had Iorwerth upright. His feet were shod in a pair of Matthew's old slippers, and his body covered by a finer cloak than he had probably ever worn before.

'Now what?' Einion asked, one eyebrow almost disappearing under his wild fringe. He was standing one side of the charcoal burner while Silas stood on the other, each holding on to the swaying man.

'I can walk!' Iorwerth insisted.

'But where to, Iorwerth?'

Rachel's face appeared around the doorframe.

'Come here into the kitchen. I have brought a high-backed chair through. He can sit by the fire and keep me company for a while. Wolf too.'

The dog was standing, gazing lovingly at Rachel, or perhaps at the bowl in her arms, his tongue drooling and tail swishing.

Einion laughed. 'Come on then, Iorwerth. It might be easier if I carry you.'

'No. I can walk.' It was said through gritted teeth, as he painstakingly lifted one leg and then the other, leaning heavily on his two companions.

Iorwerth stopped as he reached the kitchen doorway, breathing heavily. He coughed once and leaned into Einion's strong bulk for a moment.

'Are you sure you can do this?' Silas asked. 'We can help you back to your bed and try again later?'

The charcoal burner turned a flushed face towards him. 'If Jesus helped Peter walk on water, He can help me walk a few more steps into the kitchen!'

The seat beside Rachel's hearth became Iorwerth's favourite place. Each day he grew stronger, until by the fourth morning, he could walk almost unaided into the kitchen. He did not need Einion's strength, just Silas' arm.

He would sit for a few hours, and Rachel or Silas would keep him company. Then he would go back to his bed to rest for the afternoon, before coming back to the kitchen to sit and eat supper in the company of them all. Matthew and Rachel had given up using the parlour and now an odd collection of fine chairs and kitchen stools sat around the rough kitchen table. It was convivial and Silas enjoyed those evening meals, with their lively discussion and laughter, not to mention good food and wine.

'Einion and I have been to the camp today, Iorwerth. And to the cottage.' Matthew was using a piece of bread to sop up the last dregs of a very tasty lamb caul that they had finished between them.

'Good. I thank ye. Is all well? Did ye find what ye went looking for?' Iorwerth was able to both eat and speak more freely without coughing. He dipped his own piece of bread into the pot, but lifted it out dry, a brief look of disappointment crossing his face.

'All is how you left it. Except the cottage. Einion has already begun cleaning it and doing some vital repairs to the roof.'

'And the carvings?'

'All here. In the workshop. You can examine them for yourself later. I have Mair's box secure too.'

A sad smile crossed Iorwerth's lips. 'It is for the best.'

Rachel leaned over and placed her hand on his sleeve. 'You are sure?'

'I am. It is time.'

Silas looked from Matthew to Rachel, to Einion and to Iorwerth. They all seemed to know something he didn't.

Iorwerth glanced over at him and must have read his confusion.

'I think, Stranger, that your unexpected arrival in my camp might well have been the hand of Providence. If ye hadn't come, and if ye hadn't left and brought my carved animals to Matthew, if ye hadn't brought him back to the camp to speak with me, then I might have died alone in that cottage.'

Silas swallowed back the lump in his throat. The words Iorwerth spoke rang true. Was it God who had led him to the charcoal burner? Maybe.

Iorwerth was still speaking, his hand around a cup containing the strong sweet wine that Matthew had served them earlier.

'Matthew and Rachel have offered me a home here with them.'

This was news, and Silas wondered at it. Not at the hospitality and kind-heartedness of the goldsmith and his sister, that was not in doubt. But at the drastic change of life it would mean for Iorwerth.

'You look surprised?'

'I am, a little. What will become of your camp? And your charcoal business? And the cottage?'

'All taken care of. Gruffydd Ddu will take over my charcoal piles. Although whether he will burn them as well as I did is unlikely. And Einion here, he will have the cottage for his mother.'

Silas looked to the blacksmith, who sat in a high-backed chair, his large frame dwarfing it, and with his thick legs stretched out in front of him.

'My mother cannot cope with the farm anymore, and I cannot cope with having to be away from my forge for days on end, whenever she imagines herself sick unto death. She is old, but not as frail as she makes out. I think it is the loneliness that makes her call for me. So, I will move her into Iorwerth's cottage, and she can have some hens and a goat, and that will be enough. I can stay my nights there with her, and Iorwerth can keep my room here. It is time for a change for me also. There are both sad and happy memories for me in the room that Sarah and I shared. Now Iorwerth and Wolf can share it!'

They all laughed at that, and Wolf woofed his agreement.

'It is all settled, then?'

'It is.' Matthew spoke. 'Iorwerth will work with me. He will continue to carve, and I will beautify his creations with my stones. I have seen inside Mair's box, and I have commissioned Iorwerth to make more figures. Another crucifix, and another Madonna and child. I think there will be more commissions to come, especially when Abbot Julian sees them. I daresay abbeys and churches alike would appreciate such fine and yet simple representations of Christ and His holy mother.'

Iorwerth, Einion and his mother, Matthew and his new venture, even Wolf lying stretched out beside the fire, were all settled. What of him? Silas looked around the room again, at the relaxed happy faces, and was grateful for his part in bringing change into these good people's lives. But this wasn't his home. He could not settle here. He was still a stranger.

'Will you come to the abbey with me tomorrow, Morgan? I have told Abbot Julian about you and would love to introduce you to him. He is eager to meet the kind stranger who saved Iorwerth's life and helped him to discover a new purpose.'

Abbey? Abbot? The hairs on the back of Silas' neck tingled, and he wiped a sweaty hand across them. What answer could he give? The abbey was the last place he wanted to go. What if Julian or some other brother recognised him? It was likely enough. The thought terrified him. If he were discovered, he would have to go back to Dore. He would return in shame, and he was not ready for that. Not yet.

Matthew was waiting for an answer, but Silas could not open his mouth to speak. He motioned his head in what looked like a nod, and that must have been enough to satisfy Matthew, who turned his attention back to Einion and the discussion about how to make the cottage more habitable.

Silas drank deep of his own cup of wine, and as he placed it back on the table, he looked up to find Rachel watching him. Her eyes were kind, but her forehead was creased in concern. He dipped his eyes quickly away from her, and mumbling some excuse, stood from the table and took himself out of the kitchen, through to the room he shared with Iorwerth and the dog, and into the fresh cold night air. He lifted his face to the star-spotted darkness and let out a long deep breath.

'Why, God? Now where do I go?' he whispered into the night.

But no reply came.

He did not think he would sleep, but the wine and good food must have had some effect, and he eventually drifted off. He trusted his internal clock to wake him well before dawn. He may have abandoned the Prayer Offices, but his body still remembered. Vigils was the Office where silent monks shuffled, half-asleep, down the cloisters, willing the prayers to be done quickly, so they could return to their beds for a few short hours more.

Iorwerth and Wolf both snored soundly, undisturbed as he rolled onto his knees from his bed on the floor. He had not divested himself of his tunic, and his boots, gloves, hat and cloak he had left in a neat pile by the foot of his bed. He gathered them, noiselessly, feeling around in the dark for his scrip. It was not there. He sat back on his heels trying to remember where he had last seen it. It was too late to go looking. He would have to leave without it and worry later about what he would do without the cup and knife it contained.

He rose to his feet and crept towards the door. Wolf lifted his head and whined softly as he tried to silently lift the latch. Silas put his finger to his lips to make a shushing action, and then smiled at his own stupidity. Wolf was clever, but not that clever. He managed to lift it, the door creaking slightly as it opened into the yard. Then Wolf was by his feet, tail wagging, ready for a nightly excursion. Silas sighed as he stepped through the door. He would wait for the dog to do what he needed and then let him back inside before he tried to leave the compound himself. It was mercifully dry, and a bright half-moon hung in a cloudless sky.

'He is not the only one watching out for you.' The voice was quiet and instantly recognisable. She stepped into his line of vision, but he could not see her face clearly. She carried no light, and a dark, hooded cloak covered her head and shoulders. She was holding something out to him. 'This is yours.'

He reached out and took his scrip from her.

'This is for you to take with you. Did you think you could escape my hearth without at least some provision for your journey?'

He took the small sack from her hand and felt its bulging weight.

'I must go.' He didn't know what else to say.

'I know.'

'Forgive me.' He felt the guilt of sneaking away without proper farewells to those he had shared so much with. But he could not chance the questions or having to lie. It was better this way.

'There is nothing to forgive. Perhaps when you have found peace, when your journey has come to an end, then you will return to visit us again? Maybe then you will be able to tell me,' He heard her gently sigh. 'Tell *us* your story?'

He could not answer, but felt her move subtly closer to him, close enough that he could smell the rose water she had bathed her work-roughened hands in. He had grown fond of this gentle, godly woman. Not in the same way as he had felt drawn to Hannah, but he would always remember her kindness.

'I will miss your company, Morgan. If that is what your name truly is. You came into our home a stranger, but you leave a friend. God go with you.'

'Thank you.'

It didn't seem words enough, but he could say no more for the lump in his throat.

She moved noiselessly away from him. He heard her lifting the wooden plank, and the gate swinging on its hinges.

Silas walked out of the yard past Rachel, and into the street beyond, not looking back until he had heard the gate swing back into place behind him. He paused to say a silent grateful farewell and then turned and walked away.

And when Jesus went out, He saw a great

multitude;

and He was moved with compassion for them,

and healed their sick.

Matthew 14:14

14

THE STRANGER

Silas stood at the crossroads of the four roads that led out of Rhaeadr Gwy. To the south was the way he had come. To the east was Abbey Cwmhir, and he would not be taking that road. He looked west, and pondered taking it, but the road north seemed to draw him. The track was wide and easy to follow with just the light of the moon to guide him. He walked slowly, the familiar weight of his scrip hanging from his belt, the bag of Rachel's provisions tucked under his arm. Past homes and other buildings, all shut up and silent against the night air.

He felt weary, even before he started out; a bone-deep weariness that he suspected had little to do with several restless nights sleeping on the floor, disturbed by Iorwerth's cough; more a weariness from having to move on. He could have stayed at Matthew and Rachel's, continued to be a part of the little community that had formed around their kitchen table. He knew he would have been welcomed. But he would not have brought much to that table. Not Einion's skill or Iorwerth's craftsmanship. He could work, but his skills at carpentry and farming would have limited use here.

Even Wolf had proved himself useful by catching vermin in the stables. It did not feel right to stay on, enjoying fine food, a warm place to sleep and good company, without being honest with his hosts.

Could he have told Rachel all his story? And Matthew? Would they have understood and let him stay? They did not seem the sort to judge a man. Yet knowing where he had come from, and why he had left, they might have tried to persuade him to return to his calling. Especially knowing the close relationship they had with the abbey and its abbot. No. He was better to keep his secrets, and to keep moving. Keep running. But running from what? Or who?

He tried to walk with more purpose as he left the final few scattered buildings of the town behind him. The road was creeping upwards, and his calves began to burn. The track surface was potted, and he tripped more than once in the dim light. Ahead of him, he could make out the shape of high, dark treetops that seemed to lean in menacingly. The track narrowed. He sighed. He needed to leave Matthew's house under the cover of night, but he did not need to be travelling without seeing clearly where he was going. He could not get lost in unfamiliar woods again. He looked for a gap in the trees and found a clearing, the grass growing high beneath the boughs of a cluster of oaks, elms and horse chestnuts. The trees formed a rough circle and beneath them was as good a place as any to shelter.

Silas stepped off the path and into the grass, which was wet from dew, and soon soaked the toes of his boots. He found a spot beneath a tree that was more earth than grass, and lowered himself to the ground, tucking his sack in beside him and then wrapping his cloak tightly around. He rested against the tree and stretched his legs out in front of him, closing his eyes. A barn owl screeched somewhere close, and further away, he thought he heard the distant howl of a wolf. A real one. He smiled to himself at the remembrance of Iorwerth's dog. What he would give now for the warm weight of that hairy beast lying alongside him.

The sun was already high in the sky when he woke with a start. He had not meant to sleep, merely to wait for the dawn. But he had slept soundly. The night air and the damp soil beneath him had chilled him, but warming sunlight was streaming in through the tree branches.

He gazed in wonder at the sight he awoke to. All around him was not long grass as he had thought, but a carpet of bright blue bell-shaped flowers. Swathes of them, stretching out in all directions under the trees, their delicate heads swaying and bobbing in the light breeze. Silas choked back a surprising wave of emotion. Such natural beauty had always stirred his soul in the past, before the cares of life had taken their toll. Now, here, miles away from his past life, days and weeks on from his last battle lost, he felt it afresh, that deep sense of the extraordinary wonder of creation. The handiwork of a God, who expressed His own beauty through what He had created.

He sat and enjoyed the place for a while, shifting so that his legs were touched by the warmth of the sun. He reached for Rachel's food parcel, but he felt no compunction to eat. His belly had been well fed the night before, and now his soul was taking a moment to feed itself. Finally, he became too aware of the cold, hard ground beneath him, the way it had numbed his flesh, and he knew he needed to move. He stood up slowly, plucking a long, low branch from the tree he had sheltered under. It wasn't perfectly straight, but it was sturdy enough for him to lean on. He had a journey of unknown length ahead of him and he needed strength to walk it. He had no idea where he was going, but at least now that the sun had risen, he could see his way more clearly.

Stepping back onto the road, he could see the path it took through the trees ahead. It was a rough, flattened earth track, wide enough for a single wagon, perhaps, or to herd a small flock of sheep along. As he walked, he passed both. First a shepherd driving his reluctant sheep to town, with the help of a small, snapping dog. Silas stepped out of the way and called out a greeting, but the shepherd seemed in no mood to speak, except to swear at both sheep and dog. Silas felt a pang of sympathy for the sheep. They looked a bedraggled lot, and it was unlikely they were being driven to market for their fleeces; more likely to end up as mutton in the butcher's shop, or on someone's table. His stomach rumbled, but he didn't want to stop and eat yet. He had already wasted enough daylight hours.

The cart passed him a few moments later, pulled by a broad-chested horse. A bearded man with a huge floppy hat sat in the driver's seat and he called out a friendly greeting as he drove past. Several pieces of wooden furniture were tied to the back of the cart with ropes, and a young lad, no older than perhaps fourteen summers, sat among them, his feet dangling over the edge.

Silas lifted his hand in greeting, and the lad waved back, laughing as the wagon went over a pothole and he was almost thrown from his perch. Silas drew a sharp intake of breath. The furniture was clearly not the same quality, and the lad was not the same boy, but it brought Samuel and Hannah to Silas' mind again. He allowed himself to wonder about them. Were they doing well? Was Samuel still prospering under Roget St Germain's sponsorship? Had Hannah given in to John Boatman's advances? A pang of jealousy was followed swiftly by a humbling realisation. He could not be jealous of a life that he had purposely turned away from. Even if Hannah did choose to marry again, it was none of his business. He wished her well, desired nothing but happiness for them all. He lifted his face to heaven and turned his thoughts into the briefest of prayers.

The trees, with their cooling shadows, gave way to broad, open grassland. The track had descended and risen again, and the sun was now high in the sky. Silas felt the warmth of it on his back, and alongside the effort it took to navigate the undulating path, he was perspiring. He paused to remove his cloak, securing it around his waist. He tied the food sack to the top of his makeshift walking stick and placed that over his shoulder, so that it dangled behind him. It had grown increasingly heavy, and it would make sense to stop soon to relieve the bag of some of its edible weight. He needed to slake his thirst too, that was an even more pressing need.

As the path came to the top of another steep rise, he heard the unmistakable sound of running water. A mountain stream was just what he needed. He followed the sound, clambering awkwardly down a slope. Between some large rocks, he found it. He had come some distance from the path but was sure he would find his way back.

The last few steps were so steep, he was barely able to stop himself from falling headlong into the narrow, fast-flowing white water, but he managed to grab a young sapling. It bent under his weight but was rooted strongly enough to slow him so that he could plant his feet and come to an unsteady halt. Cautiously, he lowered himself onto a flat rock at the water's edge. He placed his cloak, stick and bag behind him and leaned over to cup his hand into the water, but it was flowing so fast that by the time he withdrew his hand and lifted it to his lips, only a few drops of water remained in his scooped palm.

He released his scrip from his belt and opened it to find the cup that had travelled with him all the way from Abbey Dore. Dipping that into the water was much more successful, and after two or three attempts Silas had drunk enough of the cool, clear water to satisfy his thirst. Now he really was hungry, and he sat back on the rock and reached for Rachel's food parcel. Opening the sack, he was no longer surprised that it had felt heavy. He fished out a large, round loaf of crusty bread. Beneath that, wrapped in linen he found a lump of hard, waxy cheese, a couple of sweet and spicy-smelling buns dotted with dried fruit, and then, to his delight, a savoury treat. Wrapped in boiled cabbage leaves, tied with strips of leek, he knew what the two small square parcels contained. Lamb meat cooked until soft, with herbs and chopped leeks added. Rachel had served them before, and here she had made some especially for him, probably keeping back some of the meat from the caul she had served the night before.

He laid the feast out before him on the surface of the rock, thankful again for Rachel's kindness. He would not eat it all. He would make it last. One of the lamb parcels, half of the cheese, a piece of the bread, maybe one of the buns. His mouth was salivating as he reached once more into his scrip, hoping that his knife was still there. He hadn't thought to check the contents when Rachel had handed it to him or stopped to wonder why she had it. As he reached his hand in, his fingers closed around something metal, but it wasn't his knife. He drew out his hand and there in his palm was the pewter cross he had given to Matthew. He didn't know why it had been returned to him, but the wave of gratitude almost overwhelmed him, as he closed his fingers around it and brought his hand to his mouth to kiss it.

Lowering his hand, he saw the cross had been cleaned, polished and hung on a new chain. Where the crossbeams met, a shiny red agate sat. It was his cross, his simple cross, but Matthew's kindness had beautified it. Silas felt so humbled by what the goldsmith and his sister had done for him. He did not merit such grace.

As he gazed at that cross in his hand, he knew his Christian friends had followed the way of their Master. The Son of God had lowered Himself, even to death on the cross, for all undeserving people. He had extended His fathomless grace to everyone, including Matthew and Rachel, and... Silas. He knew he was an unworthy recipient of the grace of God. Not just Christ's death on the cross, but over and over. God had provided, and blessed, and never once did Silas deserve it. Yet he had thrown that grace back in God's face, shaking his fist and denying His existence. Why? Because life had got tough? Because following Christ had become too difficult? It was the way of the cross – Jesus had promised no other life for His followers.

'May I join you?'

The voice startled Silas out of his reverie. He had not heard anyone approach, which was strange, knowing how precarious a descent he had made to reach the stream. He looked up to find a tall, slender man standing over him. He was leaning on a long staff, his feet placed wide apart, but Silas could not clearly see his face, as the sun was behind him, casting it into shadow.

His voice sounded friendly. Silas could not very well refuse him. He did not own the rock he sat on, or the water that ran fast and free below it. The stranger did not wait for an answer. He lowered his tall frame onto the ground beside Silas. He kept a respectful distance between them, but as his features became clearer, Silas could see that he was looking intently at the feast laid out on the rock between them. His stomach sank as he realised that he was going to have to share his precious food. The stranger was not carrying a bag of any kind, not even a scrip.

'Would you like to borrow my cup to take some water from the stream?' That was a painless enough offer.

The stranger smiled and reached out his hand to take the proffered cup. Silas watched as he bent a long arm into the water to fill it. The man took a deep drink and then dipped the cup again.

Silas observed him, noting that he was dressed in good-quality clothes, and sturdy leather shoes, both seemingly unsullied by the elements. His hair was pale yellow and cropped close to his head in the Norman style, his face clean-shaven and naturally tanned. His eyes, when he turned back to Silas to thank him, were the palest of blues, but the look they carried was kind.

'Thank you, I was in need of refreshment.'

The stranger's eyes were drawn back to the food and there they seemed to linger a moment, before he turned his open face back to Silas.

Silas sighed inwardly. 'Please, won't you join me? There is plenty of food here.'

'I would be glad to.' The stranger's voice was deep and melodic. Silas couldn't put an age to him, he seemed neither old nor young. When he began to eat, it was with enthusiasm.

The two of them shared the meal in silence, until all that was left was a quarter of the loaf and one of the sweet buns. The stranger sat back and ran his hand over his stomach, grinning.

'A fine feast, and good company. My thanks to you and to the hand that prepared it.'

Good company? Hardly a word had been exchanged between them, but it was not uncomfortable to sit and eat with the man. He seemed in no hurry to leave, looking out over the stream to the hazy outline of mountains in the distance. The sun shone out of a clear blue sky, and it was pleasant enough to rest awhile. Silas didn't feel in any hurry to move on either, but he should at least attempt conversation.

'Can I ask you your name?'

'I have been called many things.' The stranger let out a small laugh and turned to smile at Silas. 'But you can call me Cennad.'

It was not a name he was familiar with, but it seemed to suit the man.

'I am Silas.'

He wasn't sure why his true name had sprung to his lips, but it didn't seem to matter to a fellow traveller. They were strangers who would soon be parting ways.

'Where are you travelling to, Silas? Or perhaps you have no particular destination in mind?'

Cennad turned his attention back to the mountains and sat with one knee raised, his arm leaning comfortably on it. He was twiddling a piece of long grass in his hand. Silas did not know how to answer. He mumbled something noncommittal.

Silence lingered between them for a while.

'Are you a man on the run?' Cennad turned to him and gave him such a look of intensity that Silas drew back. He broke eye contact and tried to busy himself packing away the remnants of the food. When he looked up, the man was still staring at him. This time, something closer to compassion was shining from his eyes.

'You are, I think. Running from someone or something? It matters not to me. I see kindness in you, Silas. It is not every man that would willingly share his lunch with a complete stranger.'

Silas had not shared willingly, but there had been more than enough for both of them. He felt satisfyingly full. He would rest only a while longer and then move on again. There were still some hours of daylight left. He needed to get down from this elevated high ground and find somewhere more sheltered if he were to spend the night in the open. He had no money to pay for lodgings. The only thing of worth he had was his pewter cross, and he was not willing to part with that again.

The stranger got to his feet, towering above Silas.

'I wonder, may we keep company as you continue your journey, Silas? It is always better to travel in pairs than on your own in wild, open country like this.'

Silas scrambled to his feet in a much more ungainly fashion than Cennad had. He picked up his belongings and brushed down his crumpled tunic that looked like rags alongside the fine clothes of his new companion.

He began to make an excuse, but what came from his mouth instead was a simple 'yes.' The stranger reached out a surprisingly strong hand to help Silas clamber back up the steep, rocky slope.

'I was heading north.' He turned to question Cennad, as they stepped back onto the wide track he had been following.

'Then I will head north also,' the stranger replied with a smile, and fell in beside Silas.

Let brotherly love continue.

Do not forget to entertain strangers, for by so doing some have unwittingly entertained angels.

Hebrews 13:1-2

15

Cennad

They talked little, but that suited Silas. This was the sort of company he preferred, the warm presence of a friendly companion. Cennad seemed content enough to walk quietly at his side, moderating his long stride to match Silas' shorter one. The sun was warm and came with a refreshing gentle breeze. A pair of kites swooped, dipping and diving in the sky above them, and spring lambs chased each other, their uncoordinated frolicking causing both Cennad and Silas to smile.

As they continued to walk, Silas felt his earlier weariness drop away. He wasn't sure if it was the warmth of the sun, the spring-like feel of the landscape they were walking through, or strangely, something to do with the man by his side. Cennad seemed to exude energy, and just his proximity energised Silas. They walked several miles, but Silas did not feel the need to stop. More than once, he wondered where Cennad was headed, and whether it would be a good thing to continue on with him. After all, he had no real destination of his own.

The road began to widen, and as it crested yet another hill, below them Silas could see a collection of buildings making up a sizeable settlement. In its centre, alongside a slow-moving river, was the unmistakable outline of a rectangular church. Stone-built and whitewashed, it stood stark against the wooden thatched buildings that surrounded it.

'The church of St Idloes.' Cennad must have read his mind.

'You know it?'

'I do.'

Was this where Cennad was headed? They were drawing closer; the road they were on would take them right through the heart of the town, if you could call it a town. It was not as established as Rhaeadr Gwy, but there were some signs of industry; shops selling their wares, a pen full of bleating sheep waiting to be sold, and a tavern with a collection of men sitting on stools and upturned barrels outside.

'Market day.'

It wasn't like any market day Silas had ever experienced before. 'There doesn't seem to be much buying and selling going on.'

Cennad turned to him and grinned broadly. 'Oh, there is! All aided by a cup or two of ale!'

He nodded in the direction of the tavern. So that was where all the business was taking place.

'You know this town? Is this where you were headed?'

Cennad didn't answer straight away but stopped outside the tavern.

'I know the ale is good! Would you like to try it?'

Silas suddenly felt very thirsty, and a cup of ale would be most welcome. But he had no money to pay for it, and if Cennad carried any coin on his body it was well hidden.

'Wait here.'

He hadn't even answered, but the man was already striding towards the tavern. Silas did as he was told. He found a patch of grass and sank down onto it, feeling strangely weary again.

Cennad disappeared into the tavern and seemed to take his time to reappear. When he did so, it was with a smile on his face and a jug and cup in his hand. Silas didn't like to ask how he had paid for it, but that didn't concern him for long, once he had drunk some of the ale. It was good, and it did the trick. Cennad poured himself a cup, drank it quickly and then poured a second cup for Silas. The first cup he had drunk thirstily, this second one he savoured more. It was scented with herbs that he could not identify and slightly sweetened with honey to temper the bitterness.

'Good, yes?'

'Very. Thank you. I appreciate you spending your coin on it.'

Cennad gave him a strange look and Silas suddenly felt a little overawed. His companion was an unsettling kind of man, but not in a bad way. It wasn't that Silas didn't feel safe in his company, more that he was somehow different to anyone he had ever met before. He knew nothing about Cennad, and yet the way he looked at him made Silas feel like the man could see deep into his soul.

He finished the ale and let out a long breath. He handed the cup back to Cennad, who had dropped to sit beside him. Silas stretched weary legs out in front of him and rubbed his knotted calves. He could feel the ache now, and his feet were also beginning to throb.

'Do you want to find lodgings here, in Llanidloes, Silas? Or do you want to continue your journey? There are still a few hours of daylight left, but if you are weary, perhaps you could stay here and recover your strength before pressing on.'

'Are you staying here? Or perhaps this is your home? I haven't thought to ask where you hail from.'

'This isn't my home.' Cennad finished the cup of ale and then sprung to his feet. 'I must return these.' He indicated the jug and cup in his hands.

Silas watched him go. He hadn't answered the most important question. If Cennad were planning to stay here, then Silas would stay too. He was intrigued by the man and wanted to know him better. He had no coin to pay for lodgings, he reminded himself, and he couldn't expect Cennad to pay for him.

The man reappeared but did not sit.

'I'm not staying here, Silas. I must keep walking. If you will accompany me, we must leave now.'

'Oh.' Silas began to lever himself to his feet. He felt Cennad's strong arm beneath his elbow, and at his touch, a strange wave of strength surged through his body. Suddenly he felt he could walk further. He didn't know for how long, or where he would finally let his body rest. But for now, he wanted to stay in the company of his new friend, and that meant moving on.

Cennad did not speak again until they had reached the top of the hill behind the town. Silas breathed heavily as he climbed, but even that seemed to invigorate him further.

'I know of a place where you can find rest tonight. It will mean walking a fair distance more. Not as far as you have already travelled today, but the sun will be close to setting by the time you reach it.'

His words startled Silas. Had he told Cennad where he had travelled from? He couldn't recall it, but he must have done. He didn't relish the thought of journeying until the sun set. It had begun its slow descent, but that still meant several hours of walking.

'I have no coin to pay for lodgings.'

'I know. You will not need them.'

How was it that almost every sentence Cennad uttered left Silas with so many questions? Questions that somehow didn't need to be answered.

'Will you be resting there yourself? It would be good for you to show me to this place.' He didn't add how much he wanted to stay in the man's company.

'I will happily show you the way, Silas.' He turned a kind smile in his direction, and for a moment Silas forgot that yet again he hadn't answered his question. He opened his mouth to repeat it but couldn't bring himself to say the words. Cennad was striding on, and Silas fell in beside him.

The sun was getting ever closer to the horizon, and a deep orange and purple glow had settled over the distant mountains, Silas knew that hours had passed, but somehow, his body was no more tired than when they had started out. They had talked on the way, but about nothing consequential. Silas still did not know much about the man walking beside him, except his appreciation of the scenery and his knowledge of woodland plants and birds. Perhaps, when they stopped for the night, hopefully under a roof and beside a hearth, they might share deeper conversation. Not only did he want to know Cennad's story, he had a surprising urge to tell him his own. All of it. The whole truth.

They reached a fork in the road. The main road had narrowed after they had left Llanidloes, and now one path went uphill and the other downhill.

'Over the crest of that hill, you will be able to see the place. It stands on its own, an inn with its own smithy attached. There will be smoke from the fire and the forge, and probably lights in the window by the time you make sight of it. You will find a welcome there, whether or not you have coin to pay.'

Silas stood stock still, with a sudden realisation.

'You're not coming with me, are you?'

Cennad stopped at his words. He wore such a kind and compassionate expression that Silas almost wept.

'No, Silas. The next part of the journey you will travel alone. I must leave you and take my own path.' He indicated the lower track.

'Where will you stay?' Silas wanted to urge him, persuade him to change his mind. 'The sun is almost setting and there is no habitation in sight in that direction. What if you are set upon by outlaws or ruffians?'

Cennad smiled and reached to place his hand on Silas' shoulder.

'You do not need to worry about me, friend.' His hand lingered for a moment, and Silas felt its warm weight, along with a feeling of inexplicable peace. 'But you need to make haste, while you still have light enough to see your way. Go well, Silas, and God bless you.' With that he lifted his hand from Silas' shoulder and walked away.

Silas turned to take the other path. He had only taken a few steps when he was aware that the heavy weariness was returning, and he had to will himself to keep going. He felt Cennad's absence and turned to wave farewell. His hand had barely lifted from his side when he realised the futility of the action. Cennad had vanished. He saw the lower path clearly and he could see no figure walking on it. He shivered involuntarily, and stood watching for a few moments more, trying to catch a reassuring glimpse of his travelling companion. The hairs on his arms bristled and he closed his eyes. Opening them a moment later, there was still no sign of the man. Silas crossed himself, took a steadying breath and trudged on.

He was grateful when, just as Cennad had said, a long, low building came into view, smoke rising into the darkening sky. The steps he took to reach it seemed to require as much effort as all the walking he had done since meeting Cennad. When, finally, he reached his destination, he found the door wide open, the light from blazing candles issuing a warm invitation. He peered inside and called out a cautious greeting. The room was cosy with a good fire, and a large table filling the space. Something bubbling in a pot over the fire was giving out a wonderful aroma and the table was already laid.

'Oh! Forgive me, I didn't realise we had another guest. Welcome, traveller.'

Silas spun at the voice and found himself facing the tiniest of women. She was definitely no child, her face wrinkling around her eyes as she smiled kindly.

'Please, go in.'

She gestured towards the open doorway. He stepped aside and made way for her to pass him, following her into the welcoming room.

'Take a seat at our table. Help yourself to the ale in the jug. I will be serving supper soon, when my husband and our other guest are done sorting out the horses. Please,' she gestured to the table at Silas' hesitation, and he took a seat on the bench. Before he could reach for the jug, she had done so and poured him a cup of ale. 'You look weary. Have you travelled far? And on foot, too; you must be exhausted.' She didn't wait for him to answer. 'I can find warm water for you to soak your feet and there is a comfortable bed for you to take your rest on, just through there.' She pointed to a partition with an opening to the far side of the room. 'I am surprised to see a man travelling on his own in these parts. You are brave, indeed. We have been much plagued by rogue outlaws.'

'I was not alone.'

'Oh?' She looked to the door expectantly.

'As in, I have come to your door alone, but I did not walk on my own for most of the way. Cennad, I think you may know him, he pointed me in the direction of your inn, but then had to go his own way.'

He couldn't bring himself to explain the strange circumstances of their parting. He still couldn't quite work out what had happened.

'Cennad, you say? Hmm, I don't think I know anyone of that name.'

'I didn't know him until today. We met on the road. He was good company, if a mite strange. A tall man with fair hair, and a kind look about him. Perhaps he stayed here before?'

'It is possible. Where did you say he was going?'

'I am not sure. He didn't say. He just vanished.' The last was said half under his breath as he brought the cup of ale to his lips. But she must have heard him.

'Strange indeed. Except... no, that couldn't be it.' She stood gazing out of the door towards the night sky, which was now almost completely dark. 'Cennad means messenger,' she whispered, and then with a slight shake of her head, she turned back to Silas with a smile. 'Well, I am glad he recommended our inn to you. I hope you find our hospitality pleasing.'

Silas swallowed the full mouthful of ale he had taken and cleared his throat. 'I cannot pay. In coin, I mean. I am willing to work in payment.' He began to raise himself from his seat, but his legs objected violently.

'Now, don't be worrying about that,' the woman said firmly, turning back to tend her cooking pot.

Silas sank back thankfully onto his seat. He heard the sound of male voices and laughter approaching, and he was grateful that supper would soon be served. He was eager to eat and then to excuse himself to a bed, as soon as was polite. He realised he hadn't even found out his hostess' name before sitting at her table and drinking her ale.

'My apologies, I didn't ask your name?'

'I am Anwen, and you are?'

'Silas?'

It wasn't his voice that answered, and he swung around in surprise. In through the door had entered two large men. One was obviously the smith, with his leather apron and fire-reddened face. The other man was not quite as large, but was tall enough, and dressed head to foot in the unmistakable garb of a Cistercian.

Silas felt panic in the back of his throat. His palms began to sweat, and his head throbbed. The urge to run was almost overpowering. He gripped his fists tightly closed and held his breath as the monk approached and sat his large frame down beside him.

His face was familiar, and Silas tried to place him. He wasn't from Dore; he was sure of that. Yet he knew they had met.

'You don't remember me, do you?'

Silas swallowed and his voice came as a whisper, 'No.'

Was he about to be exposed? The monk smiled, and the smile reached to his warm, dark eyes, bright in the candlelight. He placed a hand on Silas' arm and squeezed it gently.

'No matter. I remember you and the memory is a good one. We will talk more after supper. Our hostess is ready to serve us, and my stomach is ready to be fed. Samson here is also famished, I am sure. He eats like a horse. No, he eats more than any horse I have met. And I have met a few.' He laughed, deeply and warmly, and Samson joined in with a loud guffaw.

A flash of a memory and Silas suddenly placed him. Brother Hywel. He had arrived with horses, fine horses, and a second younger monk, at Grace Dieu many months ago. They had stayed just long enough to see for themselves the state of things – and had left a generous gift behind; wine that would have been sold for provisions if it hadn't been stolen in a raid just a few nights later.

He didn't admit to recognising him. He could not bear to mention the name of Grace Dieu out loud, especially in such jovial company. A thick broth had been served into bowls, and bread was being cut into chunks and handed round. Brother Hywel bowed his head and said a short prayer, and the others at the table began to tuck into the food.

'Please, don't be polite,' Anwen sat opposite and gestured towards his spoon. 'You will need to eat quickly to keep up with these two.' She smiled, but concern etched her face as she leaned towards him.

He swallowed the nausea that threatened. He had lost his appetite, and yet he needed to eat. And he needed her to stop looking at him like that. He forced a smile onto his face and picked up his spoon, dipping it into the broth and bringing it to his lips. It had smelled good when he entered, and no doubt tasted good as well, but his stomach roiled, and he let the spoon drop.

'I am sorry. I find myself too weary to eat. My apologies.' He could not meet Anwen's eye and was aware that Hywel was staring at him. 'If you will excuse me.' He tried to stand and found he needed to grip the table to prise himself up.

'Here, let me help you.' The monk was up and behind him and had his arm around his waist before he realised what was happening. 'Come through to the sleeping area and rest yourself.'

Silas felt himself propelled along and was grateful for the other man's strength as he forced his legs to carry him the few steps it took to get past the partition to a room furnished with two pallet beds. Hywel helped him sit, and before Silas could protest, had pulled one boot and then the other from his throbbing feet, lifted his aching legs up onto the bed and covered him with a soft, clean blanket.

'Rest, my friend,' Hywel whispered. 'And do not fret. You are safe here, among good people.'

Silas grabbed Hywel's hand and drew him close. 'You did not call me Brother.'

'What? When we were sat at the table?' Hywel covered Silas' hand with his own. 'I am not here to judge.

I am surprised to meet you here, and to see you... different to when last we met, Silas. But rest now and we will have time to talk later.'

Silas released Hywel and let his body relax onto the bed. He heard Hywel leave the room, the sound of whispered conversation, and of spoons scraping bowls. He wondered what Hywel was telling them. Then he chided himself. Hywel had been all kindness. He had promised not to judge. He had not exposed him when he could have, and he trusted him not to speak against him now.

Silas turned to face the wall, turning his back on the warmth and friendship he could imagine being enjoyed the other side of the partition. He closed his eyes and willed sleep to come.

You are My friends if you do whatever I command you.

No longer do I call you servants, for a servant does not know what his master is doing; but I have called you friends, for all things that I heard from My Father I have made known to you.

You did not choose Me, but I chose you...

John 15:14-16

16
STAY-A-LITTLE

He was back there, the heat of the flames burning his face, and the smoke stinging his eyes. The terror was the same. Someone was calling for water but all he had in his hands was a flagon of fine wine. He tried to throw some on the flames, but they just responded with greater ferocity, driving him back. He could see other figures trying to beat back the flames, and then through the smoke he saw a pure white stallion gallop at speed towards him. The horse stopped and reared, tossing its head and whinnying. On its back sat a tall man, with blazing eyes and a flashing sword in his hand, his hair aglow in the light of the flames around him. Then another horse appeared – a bay, snorting and blowing, and on its back was Hywel, drawing on the reins, dropping to the ground and running towards the flames.

'Hywel!' Silas cried out in panic, 'Hywel, no!'

'Hush, Silas, hush.'

A hand on his shoulder startled him awake, the gentle voice whispering close to his ear. He lay long enough for the pounding in his temples to slow and his breathing to settle. Then he opened his eyes.

Hywel was there, crouching beside his bed, a lit candle stump in his free hand. Enough light for Silas to see the concern in the monk's eyes.

'Hush now. All is well.'

'Sorry. I was dreaming. Did I wake you?'

'Do not trouble yourself. I was yet to retire. Samson and Anwen are abed, but I wanted to check on the horses one more time. One of them is a bit skittish.'

'Not as skittish as the horses in my dream,' Silas laughed drily, lifting himself up so that he half-sat, his head resting against the wall.

Hywel stood and placed the candle on a stool that sat between the two pallets. On it was also a trencher with a hunk of bread and a cup. Hywel reached down and offered the trencher to Silas. The cup contained thick, creamy milk.

'I thought I would see if you could eat something, so that you would sleep through the night. I did not mean to wake you, if you were already asleep, but I think you might be glad to have been woken from whatever terrified you in that dream.'

'Yes.' Silas grimaced at the remembrance. It had been too real. 'I am glad for the food too.' His stomach rumbled in agreement.

'Please, eat, drink.' Hywel lowered himself onto the other bed and pulled his long legs up, but he didn't lay his head down, watching until Silas had eaten the bread and emptied the cup.

'Your dream. Do you know what it was about?'

Silas returned the trencher to the stool and wiped his hand across his mouth.

'It was confusing. I was back at Grace Dieu. It was ablaze, and we couldn't fight the fire. That part was true enough. We couldn't save the abbey last time.'

'Grace Dieu? The abbey has been destroyed?'

'Didn't you know?' That was surprising to Silas.

'I have been away from home for some weeks, travelling; sourcing horses and ponies for our princely benefactor.'

'Ah. Then you would have heard nothing of my desertion either. How I led my brothers away from the fight and retreated myself. How I ran, feeling the failure that I was, and despairing of it all. I thought news of my treachery would be widespread by now.'

Hywel shifted and laid himself down. 'I had not heard, but I would love you to tell me. Tell me what you wish, Silas. We have all night if we need it.'

Silas looked over at the man lying on the other bed, his hands clasped relaxed about his middle, his legs crossed at the ankles. He wondered if he could trust Hywel. He had wanted to bear his soul to Cennad, drawn in by his kindness and gentleness, but he had not been given the chance. Now another man, seemingly as kind and gentle as his travelling companion, was offering to be his confessor. Suddenly, the weight of it seemed too much for him to carry alone.

'Can we put out the light?' He would talk but he did not want to be able to see the reactions that might play across Hywel's face.

Hywel leaned over, a knowing smile on his face, and blew on the candle, throwing the room into complete darkness. As his eyes adjusted to the dark, Silas could see that Hywel had resumed his relaxed position. It gave him courage as he began to tell his tale.

It was so quiet that Silas wondered more than once if Hywel had fallen asleep. Yet every time he paused for any length of time in the telling of his story, he heard a whispered encouragement to continue. He told it all. From what he had been through in Grace Dieu's dying days, to the abandonment of his vows. His journey away from Abbey Dore and its falsities to his fight with the River Wye. He told of Hannah and Samuel, of the things he did to help them – but not of his growing feelings for the widow. How he had run away again, and his extraordinary encounter with the charcoal burner. He told of meeting Matthew and Rachel, and their kindness to both him and Iorwerth.

At the mention of Matthew's name, Hywel let out a strange little laugh. 'Matthew?' He whispered. 'Who would have thought? I met him once, on a pilgrimage, many years ago.' Silas heard him chuckle softly.

Soon he was nearing the end of his story, as he described meeting Cennad, and the strangeness of the journey that had brought him to Anwen and Samson's Inn.

'What is this place called? I never even thought to ask.'

'Stay-a-Little.'

'A strange name for such a welcoming place?'
'Indeed.'
'So, here is where my story ends.'
'For now.'

The silence stretched between them. Silas felt a sense of relief in having unburdened himself, but he was anxious too. He was expecting a reaction, waiting for it to come. Hywel was a Cistercian, after all. A man of faith, from what he remembered of him. Yet Hywel said nothing. Perhaps he had drifted off? Finally, Silas could bear it no longer.

'What will you do with what I have told you?'

Hywel shifted so that he was lying on his side facing Silas and pulled up a blanket to cover his legs.

'Pray, Silas,' he said softly. 'I will pray, and see what God wants me to do with what you have told me, if anything. I will speak to no one else but God, of that you can be sure.'

Silas whispered a relieved, 'Thank you.'

The silence was soon marked by the sound of soft snores, and Silas readjusted himself in his bed and closed his own eyes. He did not fall asleep quite so quickly. Instead, he found himself praying.

Silently, he opened his heart to God and thanked Him for the people He had put in his path, the provision He had made for him, the kindness of strangers, the unseen protection. Finally, he thanked God for the gentle, non-judgemental Cistercian who lay sleeping beside him.

Silas woke to soft daylight streaming through the gap in the partition. The window in the room where they had slept was still shuttered closed, but either the door or windows had been opened in the main room. It was early and it felt chilly. Silas pulled the blanket up over his shoulder and closed his eyes but could not find sleep again.

A cockerel crowed outside, and there was obviously a nesting pair of birds somewhere under the overhang of the thatch. He could hear them scratching and tweeting. He could not hear his companion, and sure enough when he turned over, he found the bed opposite him empty and tidy. He sat up, pulling the blanket with him, not yet willing to put his feet to the cold floor. His legs felt heavy, and he didn't know how well they would support him when he did try to rise, or whether he would be able to walk on them. He hadn't actually thought about what he would do after spending the night here. He could not allow himself to stay and accept Anwen's hospitality for more than the one night without payment. Yet the thought of moving on, especially walking anywhere, was not appealing.

He heard a door creak and then thud shut and the large figure of Brother Hywel appeared in the partition doorway.

'Good morning, Silas.' He spoke with hushed tones. 'My apologies if I disturbed you. I am used to rising early and was awake well before dawn.'

'I usually wake in time for Lauds,' Silas admitted guiltily.

'It was better that you slept,' Hywel smiled as he lowered himself to sit on the edge of his bed.

'You have been praying?'

'God and I have been talking, yes. Talking and walking. I needed to stretch my legs before I get back on my horse today.'

'You are leaving?'

'After I have broken my fast, yes.'

Silas was strangely disappointed but not surprised. This was an inn, after all, and although it seemed Hywel was at home here, he would be expected back at his abbey community.

Hywel was staring at him. Waiting for him to comment, maybe? He could not read him. He felt uncomfortable under the man's perusal. He fidgeted until he was sitting on the edge of his own pallet, his head lowered so that he did not have to meet Hywel's gaze.

'Do you not want to know what God said to me about you?'

Silas' head shot up. Hywel's eyes twinkled.

'What did He say?' It was croaked out.

'He told me that you had been lost, but now you were found.'

Like the sheep in the story that Samuel had reminded him of. The lost one that the shepherd had not given up searching for.

'He also told me to bring you home.'

Silas lowered his head again. He had come to a point of decision. Did he say yes? Yes to Hywel and yes to God?

Or did he keep going? He was tired, he knew that much. Tired of running. And God, through Hywel, seemed to be offering him an end to his journey.

'Home?' He lifted his head and met Hywel's eyes.

'Cymer. My home. God told me to take you home with me to Abbey Cymer. Will you come, Silas?'

Silas looked into the kind eyes of the man in front of him and knew that he no longer had a choice. His heart needed to find peace again, and a home – a permanent one. Yes, it was time to trust that this man had heard from God. It was time to trust God again.

'I didn't think to ask you if you rode. Are you comfortable on horseback?'

They were standing in the inn's enclosed yard with its extensive stabling and well-built forge.

These were fair questions for Hywel to ask him. He knew nothing of Silas' background. There was not much opportunity for monks, once cloistered, to ride fine horses such as the ones Hywel had led out of the stables. But Silas had taken his vows as a grown man, and he had ridden horses and driven wagons, raised to inherit his father's merchant trade. Before he had chosen another way.

'I can ride well enough, but it has been some time since I sat on the back of horses such as these, and I have never ridden without a saddle.'

Hywel had led out three horses. A sturdy-looking piebald stood quietly, alongside a slightly smaller grey, the only one of the three that had been saddled. Hywel was hanging on to the reins of a pretty bay, but she was not happy. Silas watched as Hywel moved to her side and placed his hand on her flank, leaning in to whisper to her. She tossed her head and stamped her front hooves, but Hywel did not move away. He continued stroking her and speaking calmly until she quietened, dipping her head finally to lean into him.

'Remarkable, isn't he?' Samson had moved up beside Silas. 'He has a way with horses, a God-given gift. He is also pretty good with humans.' He clapped a large hand on Silas' shoulder. 'He will make a good travelling companion, for however long you choose to journey with him.'

So Hywel hadn't told them he was going to Cymer with him? The monk had kept his word and not shared any of his secrets with their hosts. Hywel had explained over the table that morning that he had invited Silas to ride a way with him to let his legs recover from his walk. Samson had laughed at that, and pointed out that his legs might recover but other parts of him might ache instead after a few hours in the saddle.

Anwen had fed them well. More crusty baked bread, soft, pungent goats' cheese flavoured with wild garlic, and freshly boiled hens' eggs had graced the table, as they had broken fast together. Silas wondered if perhaps he had eaten more than he should have as he contemplated heaving himself up onto the back of one of Hywel's horses.

'You can ride this one. She seems docile and is obviously used to being saddled. She is a new acquisition, and I am yet to name her.' Hywel led the grey forward and handed the reins to Silas. He still held the reins of the bay in his other hand. 'I can ride Quint there, without a saddle,' he indicated the piebald. 'He and I go back a long way and he will behave well for me. This lass, though,' he indicated the bay, 'she will not let anyone ride her, and I think will be a challenge to gentle. But she follows behind Quint quietly enough when we are on the move. I'll lead her.'

Silas looked up at the grey and then down at his legs. He wasn't sure he had the muscle strength to hoist himself up into the saddle. Samson must have understood, as he chuckled and bent down beside him. Silas grabbed hold of the saddle and put one booted foot into the big man's open hands. The smith was strong, and he was suddenly up and fumbling to lift his other leg over the horse's back. He settled himself into the saddle, placed his feet in the stirrups and straightened his back. Already he could feel the strain in his shoulders, lower back and thighs, and his seat would no doubt be complaining soon. Still, he was glad not to be walking. The grey stood quietly, despite all of Silas' fidgeting, and he leaned forward to pat her neck, whispering his thanks.

Eira[8]. The name whispered in his mind, and he knew it suited her. Gentle as freshly fallen snow. 'Eira.' He said the name out loud.

---

[8] Welsh for 'snow'

Hywel smiled over at him from the back of Quint. 'Yes, that will do nicely, and I think we will keep the weather theme and call the bay Storm!'

'Here, for your journey.' Anwen appeared with packages wrapped in cloth. She handed them to Hywel who had draped a pair of saddlebags over Quint's neck in front of his knees. 'Those are for you. This,' she fished out a smaller package, wrapped in hessian, from her apron pocket, 'this one is for Pedr. His favourite, honeyed oat cakes. Can you secrete them to him? So that he doesn't have to share them – especially with Prior William?'

Hywel grinned as he took the package and added it to his bags. 'I will find a way,' he winked.

'Thank you, my friend,' Anwen patted Hywel's hand. 'Take it with our love.'

Samson had come to stand beside her, towering over her, but placing a large hand ever so gently on her waist. She leaned into her husband, and her eyes sparkled with tears.

'You will see your boy again soon, dear friends,' Hywel said gently. 'And now we must make our farewells, with grateful thanks for your hospitality as always.'

He nodded to Silas and then nudged Quint forward with his knees, expertly leading both his own horse and the bay through the yard gates. Silas twitched his own knees ever so slightly and clicked his tongue, but Eira needed little encouragement to follow the other horses out of the yard. Silas looked back and raised his hand.

'Thank you,' he called, and then turned back in the saddle to face what lie ahead.

They rode a while in silence until the track widened enough for Hywel to slow and allow Silas to pull up beside him.

'How is it?' He grinned across at Silas.

'I am beginning to remember. Both the joy of sitting astride a well-behaved horse, and the effort that is needed to stay upright!'

Hywel laughed, then his face grew serious. 'I want to push the horses today. It is a long ride, and we might be in the saddle for some hours without a break. It is rough terrain, lacking in safe shelter, and a steep climb in places. You will feel the strain almost as much as the horses do.'

Silas followed his gaze ahead to the mountains that seemed to loom darker the closer they got to them.

'I have longed to see these mountains all my life. I never thought I would be riding over them.' Silas felt a thrill of excitement at the thought, and not a little trepidation. 'Are we safe on this route?'

'We should be. We are entering Prince Llewellyn's home territory soon, and I carry his seal, which will lend us some protection.' Hywel patted the scrip at his belt. 'But there are those who might be watching out for unsuspecting riders and what they can take from them. Those who see themselves as subject to no one. We won't want to be lingering long anywhere.'

Silas looked around them nervously, at all the places outlaws could easily be hiding in the mountain foothills. Maybe even now they were being watched? But Hywel did not seem unduly worried. It was enough reassurance.

'I will follow your lead, Hywel. The horses seem to trust you, and so will I.'

He wondered if they would stop to enjoy the food parcels Anwen had gifted them. He hoped so. Surely Hywel would allow them a meal break at some point?

'This Pedr that Anwen mentioned, is he a brother monk at Cymer?' He remembered that she had mentioned the prior by name in her instructions to Hywel.

'Yes, he is. And he is Anwen and Samson's only son. A kind, gentle soul, like them, gifted in design and making, like his father.'

That made sense as to Hywel's obvious close connection with the pair.

'So that is how you know Samson and Anwen?'

'I have known them for far longer than the years of Pedr's life, but that is a story for another time. They had lived through tragedy and pain, and still their faith beams bright. It is their joy that their longed-for son is now committed to God's service. But it pains them that they cannot see him more often. That is why I always try to divert to Stay-a-Little on any journey I take back to Cymer, to see them and be the means of exchanging greetings, news and, invariably, gifts. Now, we must push on.'

Hywel pulled forward, picking up the pace slightly as the path began to climb.

Silas followed, encouraging Eira to keep pace, which she did without complaint. He found he could relax into the saddle and let her lead, loosening his hold on her reins to reach up and pull the hood of his cloak over his head. The sun was now obscured by thick grey clouds and the air temperature had fallen markedly. He could feel the dampness in the air, and as they drew nearer to the mountains, a light rain began to fall. Hywel did not slow the pace; he was obviously serious about pushing on.

Silas bent his head to keep the rain from his face as much as he could and concentrated on the road ahead. He was nervous as to where it led – not just the mountain crossing, but what would greet him on the other side of those high peaks. Was Abbey Cymer going to be a place of refuge, or a place of retribution? Would he find peace there, or more turmoil? Was he ready to recommit to abbey life? Was he ready to be Brother Silas again?

My sheep hear My voice, and I know them, and

they follow Me.

John 10:27

17

MOUNTAINS

Hywel had not been wrong about his intention to move at pace. Despite the terrain and the now persistent rain he drove them on, until at last they were deep into the mountains. Each peak seemed bigger than the last, with Cader Idris, the largest of them all, now close. From what Silas could see, the track ahead of them wound steeply up the mountainside. He was tired, aching and soaked through. Eira must have been feeling it too, as she stumbled slightly.

'Hywel,' he called ahead, and then called again a little louder.

Hywel turned his head and thankfully pulled Quint to a halt. Storm had been plodding along behind Quint, with her pretty head lowered. As they came to a stop, she almost ran into the back of the other horse. She jumped back and tossed her head, but Hywel soon had her under control. Silas pulled Eira up beside Quint.

'Eira is struggling, Hywel. She might not be sure-footed enough with my weight on her back to tackle that mountain track.' He indicated with his head the path ahead.

'All the horses need a break, and I daresay you and I could do with stretching our legs. I had already planned to stop.'

Silas grimaced as he shifted in his saddle. He ached all over, especially his back and thighs. He wanted desperately to dismount to relieve the pressure on his backside, but wasn't sure how his legs would react to being 'stretched' either. He hadn't even considered how he would get himself back on the poor horse, who had bent her head to take what sustenance and moisture she could from a clump of wild grass.

'I was hoping to take us to a spot by a stream I know of, but we are already wet enough, without having to sit on sodden grass.'

Even as he was speaking, the rain was getting heavier. And it was icy cold, pricking like sharp needles where it hit unprotected flesh.

Hywel dismounted, landing in a puddle with a splash. He stepped as close to Eira's flank as he could while still holding the reins of Quint and Storm. He had to raise his voice over the sound of the rain hitting the ground. It was torrential now, flowing down the track beneath them like a stream.

'I know a place where we can shelter, but you will have to dismount and help me lead the horses.'

Silas eased his leg over the horse's back, sliding to the ground less than gracefully, and letting out an involuntary cry of pain as his back jolted with the effort.

Hywel didn't linger. He set off with the horses, drawing away from the well-marked track they had been travelling, onto what looked more like a sheep trail. It seemed to be heading towards a sheer rock face, but Silas followed on trustingly, pulling Eira behind him. As they got nearer, Silas could see that the lower part of what had looked like a solid wall of rock was made up of several large boulders. Each of them was taller that the height of most men. The narrow track fed in-between the huge rocks and an almost smooth mountainside. It was only just wide enough to lead the horses through in single file, but as soon as they stepped behind the boulders, the shelter from the worst of the rain was immediate.

It wasn't easy for either man or horse to navigate, but Silas followed on until Hywel raised his hand and they all came to a stop.

'Wait here,' Hywel said, his face unnaturally serious. He handed all the reins to Silas, who took them reluctantly. 'Please, I won't be long.' Then he was gone, disappearing around a bend in the path.

The horses were unsettled, and Silas felt it too. They stood huddled together, shivering and cold.

A few minutes passed and Hywel reappeared. 'All clear!' he smiled as he took control of Storm and Quint. 'This way,' he called as he led the horses around the stones.

All clear of what? Silas tried not to imagine too much as he trudged behind Hywel and his horses, Eira trailing behind.

'Look,' Hywel stopped again and pointed ahead. Silas could see what looked like a dark opening in the rock face. Hywel clicked his tongue and led Quint and Storm into a wide cave. He pulled the horses to one side, and they took their places, Quint against the side wall of the cave and Storm half-leaning against him. Silas followed with Eira and led the horse to stand with the others, leaving just enough room for Hywel and Silas to shelter. The cave was not deep, and it narrowed considerably towards the back. It was cold and damp, but better than being out in the rain that continued to lash down outside.

Hywel removed Eira's saddle and took the blanket from her back to lay on the floor at Silas' feet.

'Sit on this,' he said. 'We will wait out the worst of the rain in here.'

'I appreciate the offer to sit, but I think I might be more comfortable standing,' Silas replied, rubbing the offending area of his body, and twisting his face into a grimace.

Hywel chuckled. 'I had forgotten what it feels like to sit for long hours on a hard saddle when you aren't used to it. I'm sorry for your... discomfort. Would you prefer to lie down?'

That actually sounded like a very good idea to Silas, as he gingerly lowered his sore body down onto the blanket. The cave floor was packed earth, and none too soft, and Eira's blanket and his own clothes were both damp. That did not matter as Silas turned over to lie flat on his back. He brought his knees up to relieve the ache in his spine and closed his eyes. He could hear Hywel scrabbling about at the back of the cave and opened his eyes a few minutes later to find him piling up some bits of sticks and dry leaves.

'We aren't the only people to know of this place. Whoever sheltered here last kindly left some kindling. It seems someone may have even lived in here for a while.'

'Not outlaws?'

'Possibly. Most likely. I was half-expecting to find them here when we arrived.' Hywel looked at Silas.

Hywel had led them to a known outlaw hideout? Was that why he had gone ahead? What if he had found them here? Hywel was grinning. He had to smile back, despite his discomfort.

Hywel took a flint and a small broad-bladed knife from the scrip at his belt and picked out a piece of dried moss from the pile he had collected. He struck the flint on his knife blade, and after several attempts produced a spark that lit the moss. Carefully he blew on it until it was smoking, and then he pushed it gently under the sticks. Thankfully it took, and soon they had a small glowing source of warmth. Hywel went to the saddlebags and retrieved Anwen's food parcels.

Silas reluctantly turned onto his side and leant on one elbow so that he could eat with his free hand. A few mouthfuls of bread and cheese was enough before the urge to change position and rest became more pressing than any need to eat. Hywel handed him an unstoppered flagon and he took a swallow from it. It was mead; thick, sweet and warming. He took another drink to help the bread and cheese down, enjoying the inner glow the mead produced, but then he really had to lie down again.

'Sorry, Hywel. I need to stretch out.'

Hywel came to sit beside him. He grinned around a mouthful of bread, before lifting the flagon to his lips and drinking deeply.

'I was hoping we could talk to pass the time. I don't think this rain is going to ease off soon.' Hywel packed away the remains of the food and added more sticks to the fire.

Silas closed his eyes and pondered all the questions he still had for God. He wondered if a deep conversation was what Hywel had in mind. If he asked Hywel any of those questions, would the monk be able to answer for God? He had proved himself a wise listener already. There were still things that Silas had to settle, preferably before they reached Hywel's abbey home. The thought of how close they were to that destination propelled him to speak.

He didn't open his eyes; it was easier not to see Hywel's reaction.

'Why did God abandon me?'

Hywel didn't answer straight away. Silas heard him shifting, heard the fire sparking and felt its warmth begin to seep through his damp clothes.

'I don't believe He did.'

That wasn't the answer Silas wanted. What did Hywel know of what it felt like to call out to God and hear nothing? To see none of his prayers answered. To have sought and not found the God he had once trusted.

Hywel hadn't finished.

'Sometimes, from my experience...'

So perhaps he did know what it felt like.

'... when we go through traumatic and difficult things... in those times, God chooses to stop speaking to us in the ways we are familiar with. Instead of appearing close, and whispering His word into our hearts, or opening the words of scripture to speak into our need, it is as if He goes silent. Our prayers seem to go unheard and unanswered.'

Silas did not respond, but he was listening intently.

'Instead, God finds other ways to show us that He is there. Less obvious ways, perhaps, but ways that will speak to us if we let them.'

'Like what?'

'All manner of things. He might speak of His care for us through the kindness of others. He might show His love through provision for our needs. He might demonstrate His power through unexplained miraculous happenings. He might whisper of His greatness through a glorious sunset or display His creativity through the beauty of an object made by the hands of a gifted craftsman. He may remind us of things our hearts once knew by stirring our spirits to feel what our emotions struggle to. And then, just sometimes, He puts people in our paths who are so like Him that we know we have been in His company.'

Silas opened his eyes as the truth behind Hywel's words touched his soul. He looked at the big man, still sat hunched over the fire. He was concentrating on tending the flames.

Remembering his journey since leaving Dore, he knew that he had experienced all that Hywel had described. Kind strangers had taken him in; Hannah and Samuel, Iorwerth, Matthew and Rachel. Good food filled his belly when he had no coin to pay for it. The bread and wine mysteriously left on the church doorstep. He recalled his reaction to Iorwerth's carvings, and especially to the beautiful crucifix; how it had caused him to weep. He thought of the bluebells – was that only yesterday? How the sight had moved him. He recollected Cennad, his calm, life-giving presence and the protection his company had unknowingly afforded him. Here, too, in Hywel, he saw a reflection of the Christ he had come to know. The Christ revealed in the reading of Matthew's Gospel.

Why had he failed to see God in all of it? What had made him run in the first place? He prided himself on being a man of faith, and yet he had been prepared to throw it all away, to turn his back on God, and on his life in Him.

'Why?' He choked as he tried to voice it.

Hywel looked over his shoulder at him.

'Were you angry with God, Silas? Did you raise your fist to Him? Did you take offence at Him?'

'I had reason to.' He still hadn't forgotten Grace Dieu's failure, the crushing of all his dreams.

'That may be. We can all do those things when we don't understand why God allows us to experience pain. If we allow the offence, the disappointment, to dominate our thoughts and feelings, then we can stop hearing God. He has things to say to us that perhaps we are unwilling or unable to hear, because our hearts are broken. God will never force Himself on us, Silas, but likewise, He will never stop pursuing our hearts. We might run from Him, thinking that will ease our pain, but eventually He will find us. Or perhaps it is more accurate to say, He gives us the grace to find Him again.

'I know He didn't abandon you, Silas. I believe His promises, and He says He never leaves the ones He loves[9]. Whatever you may have felt, He never left your side.'

Silas levered himself up, the pain in his body forgotten. Tears rolled unbidden down his cheeks, and he didn't stop them. As Hywel was speaking, it was as if someone, or something, had been drawing the torn edges of his heart close and stitching them back together. He pictured the prodigal son and hoped that the Father's embrace was just as open to him.[10]

'Will He forgive me?' he whispered.

'Always.'

The rain stopped eventually. Hywel stood outside the cave and looked to the sky.

'Are you able to continue?' He addressed Silas, who had curled into a ball on his side. He had been weeping quietly, processing all that Hywel had said. He asked

---

[9] Hebrews 13:5
[10] See Luke 15:11-32

God for forgiveness, and peace came. He still had questions, but at least now he could sense God's closeness, and he had missed that for too long. He didn't want to move, from his position or from that dank cave. He feared the feeling would leave him if he did, and he couldn't bear that thought.

Hywel, though, was obviously keen to go, and the horses were restless, especially Storm, at the confinement of the cave. Silas rolled into a sitting position and was surprised that his muscles felt easier. He stood up slowly and stretched his back.

'Ready?'

Silas nodded his reply and helped Hywel resaddle Eira. They put out the last embers of the fire with their boots and walked out of the shelter of the rocks and back onto the mountain path.

Hywel aided Silas back into the saddle, and they headed uphill again. The horses seemed glad to be back in the open air and moved with renewed energy. Silas felt good too. God hadn't left him. As he looked at the beauty of the craggy landscape, at the mountain grandeur all around them, and the broad sky above, he felt His closeness still.

They didn't need to reach the peak of Cader Idris, but the mountain pass took them close. The path wove around the mountain until finally they could see beyond: the outline of more mountain peaks against the darkening sky and a wooded valley below. Hywel pulled onto a broad area of grass, and nimbly dropped to the ground to let Quint dip his head to feed. Storm was let loose to find fodder too.

Hywel wandered over to Eira's head and offered Silas his hand to dismount.

'We'll let the horses rest and feed before we descend. They have done well. We still have some daylight hours.'

'Can we see Cymer from here?'

'No, it is masked by the trees, but you might be able to see the line of the river that runs from the sea and past the abbey. There...'

Silas followed the line of his pointed finger.

'Hywel?' How did he say this? The monk looked at him expectantly. 'I am not sure I am ready to go back.' He knew that he was on the way to making full peace with God, but he wasn't sure that meant returning to a way of life that had brought him such pain.

Hywel didn't answer. He went to Quint's saddlebags and took out some bread and the flagon.

'You didn't eat much in the cave. Finish these, and then we will move on.'

As Silas took them from him, Hywel placed a hand on his arm.

'We will not make it to Cymer before nightfall now. We will take shelter somewhere warm and comfortable. Somewhere you can be Silas and not Brother Silas. You can stay there as long as you need to.' He smiled. 'Hopefully not for too long.'

Silas felt the peace return and finished the hunk of bread he had been given, flushing it down with the last of the mead. He shivered. Despite the burning of the drink that he could feel all the way down to his stomach, the air at this height was near freezing.

'Come on.' Hywel was back by his side. 'We should get going. It's lovely up here when the sun is shining, but not so nice when that cold wind gets in under your habit!'

The path down the other side of the mountain was steep at first but straightened and evened out. The horses sped from a walk to a trot as they reached the lower slopes. A large stone building with an attached range of wooden stabling came into view. Sitting by itself at the edge of the woods, a plume of smoke rising from a hole in its thatched roof, Silas hoped it was where they were headed. Sure enough, Hywel reined in Quint and Storm as they approached.

A man appeared. He was not tall, and a large paunch indicated he lived well. His flushed cheeks and a balding pate indicated he was neither young nor particularly healthy. He was puffing with the effort of coming out to greet them.

'Brother Hywel!' It wasn't said with much warmth, but he took the monk's proffered hand and clasped it briefly. 'What can I do for you?'

'A bed for me and my friend, and stables for our horses, Osian. If that could be arranged.'

Silas watched as a silent conversation was played out in front of him. Neither man spoke, but their eyes did. It was as if they were assessing one another.

'Unusual. When the abbey is but five miles down the road.' It was Osian who spoke first. He stood with his hands on his belt, feet splayed.

Hywel didn't waiver. His posture remained relaxed as he turned to wink at Silas. He turned back to Osian.

'Well, do you have room for us, innkeeper? I can pay. Generously.'

The man sighed heavily and dropped his stance. He turned and raised his arm vaguely in the direction of the stables.

'Stable the horses, and I'll make space for you inside.'

'Friendly fellow,' Silas whispered, as they led the horses into the stables.

'Oh, Osian, he's alright. Doesn't like monks much, thinks we put off the other guests. But he will take our money sure enough and feed us. The beds will be clean. He is used to hosting the prince's men, and so keeps good standards.'

Hywel removed the horses' headcollars, and all three of them were soon helping themselves to hay that had been strung up in bundles inside the stables. He removed Eira's saddle and blanket, hanging both from a large hook.

'The horses need a good brush down, but I'll pay Osian's stable lad to do that. We need to go inside and get warm and dry.'

Hywel led the way, and as they entered the inn's stone building, the warmth hit them. At that moment, Silas didn't really care how good the food was, or how clean the beds. It was just good to be out of the cold and the rain, and good to be off the back of that horse.

But when he came to himself, he said, 'How many of my father's hired servants have bread enough and to spare, and I perish with hunger! I will arise and go to my father, and will say to him, "Father, I have sinned against heaven and before you, and I am no longer worthy to be called your son. Make me like one of your hired servants."'

And he arose and came to his father. But when he was still a great way off, his father saw him and had compassion, and ran and fell on his neck and kissed him. And the son said to him, 'Father, I have sinned against heaven and in your sight, and am no longer worthy to be called your son.'

But the father said to his servants, 'Bring out the best robe and put it on him, and put a ring on his hand and sandals on his feet. And bring the fatted calf here and kill it, and let us eat and be merry; for this my son was dead and is alive again; he was lost and is found.'

Luke 15:17-24

18

The Inn

One large room greeted them, warmed by a blazing fire contained in a central hearth. Rush lights dotted the walls, set into purpose-built sconces. To one end were eight pallet beds, lined up in rows, most already made up. At the opposite end was a large table with bench seating. A single high-backed chair stood at the far end of the table and a supper place had been laid, for one. There was a flagon and cup, and a trencher, on which stood a steaming ham hock.

Osian waddled across the room, carrying a huge iron pot. He grunted as he lifted it to fix it to the chain that hung over the fire.

He glared at Hywel as he passed by again, this time with a huge fork in his hand. He went to the table and speared the hock with the fork, carrying it back to dump it into the pot. It fell into the water with a splash.

'I think we may have stolen his supper,' Hywel whispered, and Silas couldn't help but grin.

Osian wasn't smiling. He was grumbling under his breath as he added a handful of dried lentils, a sprig of herbs and what looked like the outside leaves of a leek to the pot and stirred it with a large spoon.

'You will both have to wait for your supper. As will I now.'

He looked full at Silas for the first time, running his eyes up and down his bedraggled state.

'You'd be better to get those wet things off you and hung up, rather than stand there dripping on my floor. There is a rope strung along that back wall for the purpose of drying things. No point trying to hang them outside tonight.' The rain had begun to fall in earnest again, pelting the thatch above them. 'They will be dry by morning, if a bit smoked by the fire. Have you got something clean and dry to wear?'

Silas shook his head.

'Humpf. Well, I daresay a blanket wrapped around you will keep you warm and decent enough until you have eaten and retired. You won't be so precious of your modesty as this here *monk*.' He had turned his attention to Hywel and was giving him the same appraising look.

Silas wondered what the innkeeper's reaction would be if he knew the truth, as he removed his wet clothes and hung them as instructed. He helped himself to a blanket from one of the pallets. It was rough on his skin, but warm and large, covering his shoulders and damp undergarments adequately. He kept his boots on, not sure of the cleanliness of the rushes beneath his feet, or whether there might be vermin scurrying about. The inn looked clean enough from what he could see, but he would not be taking chances with exposed toes. His feet could stay shod until he finally laid down for the night.

To his surprise Hywel had also undressed, removing his soaked habit to reveal a linen undershirt and trews. He hung his habit up next to Silas' bedraggled tunic and also availed himself of a blanket. He was a most surprising monk.

He grinned at Silas as they both made their way over to the table and took their seats on one of the benches, sitting side by side, huddled in their blankets.

'I don't know about you, Silas, but I do hope we are Osian's only guests tonight! I'd hate to have to greet anyone attired thus!'

'At least you were wearing something under that habit!'

Hywel snorted. 'Thankfully, with the amount of horse riding I do, I am given special dispensation to wear something to cover my more delicate body parts! I suspect Osian was half-hoping that I was bare-bottomed as is the Cistercian way, and that I would have been forced to sit and sleep, uncomfortable, in my sodden habit.'

The smell of the cooking ham and lentils was enticing now, and Silas hoped they wouldn't have to wait long to eat. Osian had left through a side door but returned after a few moments with fuel for the fire. Whatever his feelings towards his unexpected guests, he was a good host, placing cups on the table in front of them, and pouring into them generously from a jug of ale. He returned to the cooking pot and stirred it again.

The hock, when it finally appeared in front of them, was delicious, the meat falling from the bone. The lentils and leeks that Osian spooned onto the trencher to accompany the meat were soft and tasty, salty from the ham, and fragrant from the herbs. It was delicious and much needed.

Osian sat to eat with them, and his mood seemed to improve the more he ate and drank. He was drinking wine from his own flagon, which he didn't offer to share. His cheeks turned even rosier in the glowing light from the rushes.

'Just one night you will be staying, then?' he asked over a mouthful of meat, chewing it noisily.

Silas was interested to hear Hywel's answer.

'We are very grateful for your kind hospitality, my friend, so we might be tempted to stay longer!' Hywel grinned.

'Better food than you get in that monastery, I should wager.'

'The meal was excellent, Osian, and we are grateful that you were willing to share your supper with us.' Hywel took another long drink of his ale and pushed the now empty trencher away. 'Do I need to go and check on the horses?'

Osian looked at him long and hard, before sighing loudly.

'No. You had best stay in here in your state of undress. I will go and make sure the boy has done his job and made things comfortable for them, and that they are secured for the night. You two can take your pick of the beds. I will clear this lot away,' he indicated the remains of their supper, 'and the fire can be left to die down naturally. I am not expecting any more guests at this hour, so will away to my own bed when I have seen to the horses. You will fend for yourselves well enough?'

'Yes, of course, thank you,' Hywel replied, as the man turned to busy himself at the table.

Hywel stood and Silas followed suit as they made their way over to the beds and picked the ones they had already taken blankets from. Silas patted the straw; the mattress was well-filled, and the linen was unstained. He sat on the bed, letting his supper digest before he laid down; he had fed well again. He unconsciously put his hand to his stomach. Despite all the walking of the last few weeks, the fine fare he had eaten had put flesh back on his bones, and a round stomach had begun to form. He sighed. He had always had a propensity to roundness. He supposed it was a good thing to not be skin and bone any more, but he must keep it in check. The restricted Cistercian diet would help with that, no doubt.

He was surprised that he was even thinking of life back in an abbey. He had to face it. God had told Hywel to bring him home, and the monk had to return to Abbey Cymer soon. Silas would have to move on too; he could not stay at Osian's inn indefinitely, however good the food. Could he leave with Hywel? Could he face going back to his old life?

'Are you well, my friend?'

Hywel glanced at Silas' hand, still held over his midriff.

'Yes, just ruminating about how well fed I have been lately,' he patted his stomach, 'and how that might change if I come with you to Abbey Cymer.'

Hywel lowered his tall frame onto the neighbouring bed.

'Oh, the food isn't too bad there. No meat, of course, but we do have fresh fish caught from the river on high days and holidays. And our cook is good with vegetables and herbs.' He paused and looked at Silas, his eyes glowing with kindness. 'Cymer isn't Grace Dieu, Silas,' he said quietly. 'We are well-established and we flourish, although not large and prosperous like Abbey Dore, Cwmhir or Tintern. We are small and will remain so and are a family who care well for one another and for those who live close to us. God has given us a generous benefactor in Prince Llewellyn, whose name also offers us protection. We breed horses for him, and our modest fields produce grain and support sheep. Our gardens are also fruitful. We may not feast, but we have enough, and I am not just talking of the food, Brother.'

It was the first time he had used the title, and Silas turned to meet his eyes. He understood Hywel's words and the meaning behind them. Returning to abbey life at Cymer was not the same as going back to the life he had left. It wasn't just a failing abbey that Silas had abandoned, he had run from his own sense of failure as well. God might have forgiven him, but he still had questions, still needed to make sense of what had happened, and then maybe find the grace to forgive himself and start afresh.

'Why did God let Grace Dieu fail?'

An unexpected wave of emotion hit him as the words left his mouth, and he pulled the blanket tighter around his shoulders. It was the question he had been wrestling with, putting it to the back of his mind, from long before it all ended, long before he had fled. He had gone through all the options. Had he been slaving away at something that God hadn't ordained? Had the calling to build a new community been just in his own mind? What of his brothers, and those who had sent them out on their mission? Of Abbot John, who gave his very life for it? Had they all got it wrong? Had God never favoured their endeavour? Never granted His favour and protection?

He covered his face with his hands as he leaned forward, waiting for Hywel to confirm his darkest fears.

Hywel did not speak for some time. When he did, he touched Silas' shoulder with such gentleness that tears threatened again.

'Do you remember the story of Job, Silas?'

Silas lifted his head and met Hywel's eyes. He did remember, the charcoal burner of all people had reminded him.

'I do. Not one of my favourite stories.' He attempted a smile, but Hywel wasn't smiling in response. The monk closed his eyes momentarily.

'It is tough to read how God allowed a man He loved dearly to go through such terrible loss and heartbreak.

None of it was Job's fault. It says clearly that he was a blameless man[11]. Do you understand that, Silas?'

He held his gaze and Silas looked away. He wasn't ready to answer. If he didn't understand why Job had to suffer, he was no closer to understanding why he had to. He had been faithful, not perfect, but had felt secure in God's love, before it went wrong.

Hywel shifted and let his hand drop from Silas' shoulder. Silas took the opportunity to prise off his boots and lift his legs onto the bed, lying down and covering himself completely with the blanket. Hywel stayed sitting, his arms folded across his knees.

'Job didn't understand why, Silas. His friends thought they understood, but all they did was compound his physical pain with mental suffering. No one needs friends like that, however well-meaning they might be,' he paused. 'I am not one of those friends, Silas. I am not here to tell you that you failed, that your sin somehow caused the failure of a work you invested so much of yourself into. I am not going to tell you that it was your fault, because I don't believe it was. It is too simplistic for me to believe that suffering is always a direct result of sin or disobedience. It wasn't the case with Job, despite how his friends counselled him.' He paused again, but Silas didn't have a response. 'When his friends finally stopped speaking, and Job finished trying to defend himself, God spoke. Do you remember, Silas? Do

---

[11] See Job 1:1

you remember what God said? Not word for word, but the message that he wanted Job to hear?'

Silas tried to go back into his memory to retrieve it, but all he could recall were the words that Iorwerth had quoted. Job's words, not God's: 'The LORD gave, and the LORD has taken away; Blessed be the name of the LORD.'[12] It was a call to praise God in all things, even things beyond understanding. Iorwerth had said them with a conviction Silas was struggling to emulate.

Hywel was still waiting, and Silas finally remembered something that had always intrigued him. God had spoken to Job about the Behemoth, and Leviathan, the great beast that no one could tame? Creatures of such size and strength that no one could really imagine what they referred to. He had tried to picture the beasts when he had first read about them, and he had failed. Nothing in his world had looked anything like the descriptions God had given, yet God Himself knew what beasts He was talking of.

Of course! That was the point. God knew. And if only God knew, and no one else, that needed to be enough. He looked up at Hywel, realisation shining from his eyes.

'I don't need to know why, do I?'

Hywel shook his head gently. 'We think we must have all the answers, and we look to God for them. We want to understand everything. But God is so much bigger than us, Silas. He was so much bigger than Job. We

---

[12] Job 1:21

cannot begin to comprehend just how big He is, and how small we are in comparison, yet He stoops down to be with us. He wants to be involved in our lives. He wants to care for us and provide for us. Provide for all of creation – even the Behemoths!' He smiled.

'This is what Job said, once he had heard God declare His greatness and majesty,

> I know that you can do anything.
> No one can keep you from doing what you plan to do.
> You asked me, 'Who do you think you are to disagree with my plans?
> You do not know what you are talking about.'
> I spoke about things I didn't completely understand.
> I talked about things that were too wonderful for me to know.[13]

And then Job repented, before God.'

Silas opened his eyes and watched the shadows from the fast-dimming rush lights playing on the thatch above his head.

'You have given me much to ponder, Hywel.'

He lay and listened as Hywel made himself comfortable on the bed beside him.

'How did the story end, Silas?'

'Remind me.'

---

[13] Job 42:2-3, NIRV.

'God restored Job's health and his wealth, blessing his later life with much more than he had had before. He gave him a new family and extended his years, so he lived to see four generations of children and grandchildren. He gave him back what he had lost, and so much more.'

'That's good.'

Exhaustion pulled at him. He wanted to stay awake and think, and talk more, but he was struggling. He was glad that he had asked Hywel the question that had troubled him for so long and for the first time he was beginning to understand that perhaps he didn't need the answer. Perhaps he could just let it go and accept God's peace in exchange. He closed his eyes and began to drift off, but not before he heard a whisper from the next bed.

'I believe he will do the same for you, Silas.'

Silas awoke with the sensation of a gentle weight on his arm. He opened his eyes slowly to find Hywel sitting on the bed he had slept on, fully clothed in his familiar habit and black cloak, and leaning forward to touch his arm. It was not pitch black in the room; the rush lights and fire had long since burned out, but it was no longer fully night. Silas knew he had slept deeply, without dreams to trouble him, and he felt rested. He could not see the expression on Hywel's face, but he heard his whispered question clearly enough.

'Come celebrate Lauds with me?'

Silas slowly lifted himself up. He may have slept well but still his body felt stiff, and his back and limbs complained as he sat upright and swung his legs around.

'Here.' Hywel handed him his tunic and cloak. They looked even more worse for wear, but they were surprisingly dry, and only smelled slightly of fire smoke.

'We must be quiet. Osian will be up soon to tend to the fire and prepare food for us to break our fast. But I want to be outside before he appears through that door.'

He nodded towards the door that their host had left through the night before; obviously it led to some sort of private accommodation.

Hywel rose quietly and Silas stifled a groan as he stood to pull his tunic over his head. Hywel was already unlatching the door by the time Silas had donned boots and cloak and caught up with him. They exited as soundlessly as they could, pulling the door closed behind them.

Thankfully, the rain had stopped sometime in the night, and above them the sky was clear, the pinprick lights of thousands of stars fading as the dawn approached.

'This way.' Hywel strode out and Silas hobbled after him, willing his legs to cooperate. It was chilly, but the air felt fresh and invigorating. On the far side of the inn, the road they had been travelling on met two others at a junction.

'That way is Cymer.' Hywel pointed eastwards, to where the faint rays of early morning sunlight were beginning to appear above the trees. He turned instead westward, towards the sea. They walked for a few hundred paces until Hywel suddenly came to stop at an outcrop of rocks.

'Let's climb up here; it won't be as good a view as we had from the mountain yesterday, but we will see the sunrise better for being higher.'

He didn't wait for Silas to answer before he was nimbly climbing onto a rock and reaching up for the next one. Silas watched him. He moved well for a big man and had the advantage of long arms and legs. Hywel wasn't young either; Silas had estimated him to be close to his own age. Still, he moved swiftly and easily and was halfway up the climb before he looked back to see that Silas hadn't moved. Silas looked down at his own tired legs and short arms, looked up at the large rocks before him, and let out a huge breath. He approached the rocks, and his friend was ready for him. Hywel reached down a strong hand and Silas grabbed onto it gratefully. Between them they got his body up the rocks until Silas was level with Hywel, and then they climbed together until they reached a spot where the rocks formed a natural seat. They were now more than the height of four tall men above the ground, but Silas chose not to look down. He focused instead on the scene before him.

The sky had erupted into a glory of pale-yellow gold tinged with pink, as the top curve of a glowing sun appeared from behind mountains and dark-tipped trees. He sat transfixed at the beauty of it and found his arms naturally rising out from his sides, his palms uplifted, as if to welcome the sun as it rose. It was a spontaneous expression of praise, not to the dawn, but to the God who was far above him in power and in understanding. The God who had created the universe and who instructed the sun to rise. The God who cared enough about him to pursue him, and find him, and to direct his path to converge with Hywel's.

With Job, his heart cried out in faith, 'Blessed be the name of the LORD!' And this time he meant it.

My sheep hear My voice, and I know them, and they follow Me. And I give them eternal life, and they shall never perish; neither shall anyone snatch them out of My hand. My Father, who has given them to Me, is greater than all; and no one is able to snatch them out of My Father's hand. I and My Father are one.

John 10:27-31

19

Sunrise

'I don't sing.'

Silas glanced sideways at Hywel's words. The monk sat, gazing at the sight before them with deep appreciation. His face seemed to glow in the reflected early morning sunlight.

'I wish I could on mornings like this, but I will not try. It would disturb the peace.'

Silas chuckled. He liked Hywel more and more. 'I don't think we need to sing, there are other ways.'

Hywel smiled at him, before turning back to the sunrise. Quietly he began to recite the words of a familiar psalm:

'O Lord, our Lord,
How excellent is Your name in all the earth,
Who have set Your glory above the heavens!

Out of the mouth of babes and nursing infants
You have ordained strength,
Because of Your enemies,
That You may silence the enemy and the avenger.

When I consider Your heavens, the work of Your fingers,
The moon and the stars, which You have ordained,
What is man that You are mindful of him,
And the son of man that You visit him?
For You have made him a little lower than the angels,
And You have crowned him with glory and honor.

You have made him to have dominion over the works of Your hands;
You have put all things under his feet,
All sheep and oxen –
Even the beasts of the field,
The birds of the air,
And the fish of the sea
That pass through the paths of the seas.

O Lord, our Lord,
How excellent is Your name in all the earth!'[14]

At first Silas just let the words wash over him. They were there in his memory too, and so fitting. He joined his fellow monk in a moment of worship more poignant than perhaps any he had experienced before. He felt at peace, he felt a quiet joy, he felt... at home.

---

[14] Psalm 8

This simple act of worship in communion with another soul reminded him of what he had been missing. It was so simple, after all, where he had made it complicated. It wasn't about achieving or doing great things for God. It was about him and God, and their relationship; the Almighty Creator God who had bowed down to visit him with His love and grace. The Father in heaven who had given His Son so that Silas could know Him, love Him and walk with Him. He needed to rediscover that intimacy with God. The relationship that he had purposely walked away from but was his very reason for living. He bowed his head and prayed silently, feeling the touch of Hywel's hand on his shoulder. And in that moment, it was like God Himself was sitting beside him, His own strong arm about his shoulders.

The sun had completely risen and the sky above them had turned from yellow to pale blue, before Hywel spoke again.

'I think I must return to the abbey today, Silas. It won't be long before news gets to Cymer that I am here.' He paused. 'Are you ready to come with me?'

Silas sighed softly and nodded. 'I will come,' he whispered. There was still some apprehension but less so. He needed to take that final step. 'I don't want to return like this, though.' He looked down at his clothes, lifting the skirt of the rough tunic that was almost threadbare now. 'I need my head shaved.' He looked at Hywel with a wry grin. If he was going back to abbey life, he was going to go back looking like a Cistercian.

'I understand.' Hywel thought for a moment. 'I will leave after we have broken our fast. I will ride Quint and lead Storm to Cymer but leave Eira here with you. I will return with the things that you need, as soon as I can.' His eyes were kind.

'Thank you,' Silas said softly. 'What will you tell your fellow brothers?'

'I will not lie, Silas, but neither do I think they need to know the whole truth. I can tell them honestly that I met a fellow brother on my journey home, but that he was exhausted by his journey and needed to rest at the inn before we continued. They can make of that what they will. You will find most of the community will not even question us. We all carry secrets, and we are all redeemed only by the grace of God. Only Prior William might pry. He is not a bad man; he just enjoys his position of superiority. I advise you not to be too open with him.'

Silas smiled. 'Thank you for the warning. I am happy to stay here until you return. By here, I mean the inn, not this cold, hard rock.' He shifted uncomfortably.

Hywel stood and reached out to help Silas up. His stiff muscles complained as he stood.

'I actually think we might be better descending the rocks on our backsides.' Hywel looked back at the route they had climbed. 'I did not realise how high or how steep it was.'

'You go first, then if I slip you can catch me.' Silas was also looking down, and his head was swimming. The ground below began to pull at him, and he stood back from the edge instinctively, stumbling slightly. Hywel caught him by the arm.

'We will be fine, Brother. Trust me, trust God, and don't look down!'

Hywel lowered his large frame and slowly inched his way down the first large rock. He waited as Silas bent his legs and rested his backside on the edge. Silas focused on Hywel's face rather than the drop and began his descent. Bit by bit, they clambered down until they were both standing on solid, flat ground. Silas laughed, a mixture of relief and exhilaration, his legs still wobbly. Hywel clapped him on the back.

'Not quite as elegant as the mountain goats, but we made it. Now, after all that excitement, I need to eat!'

Smoke was rising from the hole in the inn's roof, indicating that Osian was up and a fire already burning. The innkeeper looked up from stirring his cooking pot as they entered.

'Thought for a moment you two had left without paying. Then I realised the horses were still here, and I reckoned that was payment enough.'

It was hard to know whether or not he was joking.

'Here.' He began to ladle thick porridge into a bowl, and handed it to Silas, who took it and sat down by the table. There was bread and a small dish of honey already laid out. A jug, filled to the brim with milk, accompanied it.

Silas poured some of the creamy milk onto his porridge and spooned a trickle of honey over the top, before bringing a spoonful of the steaming food to his mouth. It wasn't at all bad. In fact, the porridge was almost on a par with what Rachel had made. He remembered her cooking and her kindness with fondness. His heart twinged as he thought back to Hannah too, and her son. But he had to look forward now, not back.

Hywel made short work of his own breakfast, before making his way out to the stables. He made swift work of saddling up Quint and attaching Storm's headcollar.

Silas followed him out and Osian also appeared.

'You are leaving, monk?'

'I am, Osian, but Silas here will be staying a few hours more. I will leave the grey here with him. The horses look as if they have been well cared for, as have we.'

Osian grunted. He looked over at Silas. 'You are heading out later, then? I don't blame you for wanting to part company with a monk. Although this one isn't so bad.'

Was that the semblance of a half-smile that crossed his face?

Hywel must have seen it. 'Thank you for the compliment – I think!' He laughed.

Hywel leapt easily onto Quint's back and sat poised ready with Storm's reins in his hand. He dipped his head, and Silas raised his hand in response. Then he was gone, out of the stable yard and down the road at a fair pace. He didn't look back.

The innkeeper turned to go back inside the inn. Silas followed him.

'Can I do anything to make myself useful?'

Osian stopped and eyed Silas suspiciously. 'It is not normal for me to expect my guests to work for their keep. Brother Hywel paid me well enough.'

Silas hadn't seen the exchange of any coin.

'I would rather work than sit idle, and these stiff bones need activity.' He glanced around the yard, spying some uncut timber and an axe beside a depleted pile of firewood. 'I can cut wood for your fire?'

Osian seemed to appraise him for a moment, as if assessing his competency for the task.

'Go ahead.' He gestured towards the axe. 'But don't injure yourself,' he muttered as he walked away.

Silas found the work was just what he needed. At first, his back and shoulders complained, but the axe was well balanced and once he got into the swing, he began to enjoy the exertion. The sun was warm on his back, and sweat poured off him, but the wood pile grew, and he felt a great deal of satisfaction in seeing it.

Osian reappeared after some time, and handed him a cup of ale, which he downed thankfully. The innkeeper stood with his hands on his hips, nodding his approval.

'You will be needing a wash down and a change of clothes.'

He was right. His old tunic was now sticking to his back uncomfortably. Silas didn't care. He would not be wearing it for much longer. He peeled the fabric away from his chest to let air in. When he was done with the wood pile, he availed himself of some clean rainwater that had been collected in a half-barrel, to rinse off his face and arms. The rest of him would have to wait.

Osian called him inside, and he was glad to get out of the sun. It was a warm spring day, the sky a deep blue, with only a hint of small wispy clouds high above them.

'You have done enough. Come, sit and take a rest.' Osian indicated the bench at the table. He took his own seat and poured them both another cup of ale.

'You have travelled far? You are not native to these parts.'

'A fair distance, yes.'

'Do you have far to go?'

Silas smiled to himself. Was the man fishing for information or just being friendly? He suspected the innkeeper kept abreast of all that was happening around the vicinity and wasn't slow to pass on information. It was a question that he was happy enough to answer. He was done with travelling; he knew his journey was almost over, in more ways than one.

'Not far, no.'

'Humph.' The innkeeper didn't seem satisfied.

'Did you travel with Brother Hywel the whole way? I was surprised to see that only one of the horses had a saddle. It seems he has taken the saddle and left you and the grey without it. Is the horse yours or his?'

'Brother Hywel is returning for the horse.'

'Oh.'

'Is he returning for you as well?'

Silas pondered before replying. What did it matter if Osian knew his plans?

'I am going with him to Cymer Abbey.'

Osian examined him with beady, inquisitive eyes, but Silas wasn't going to give him anything more.

'Thank you for the ale, innkeeper.' He stood from the table, his back and legs feeling surprisingly much looser than they had before. 'I will go and see Eira and see if she needs anything.'

He moved quickly, and Osian thankfully made no move to follow him.

Eira was happy to be out of the stables. He led her from the stable yard to a spot where a swathe of sheep-mown grass opened up beneath the rocks they had climbed earlier. He let the horse go and she lowered her head gratefully, nuzzling around to find the longer tufts of grass that grew at the base of the rocks.

The landscape was so soothing. The mountains loomed in a way that made Silas feel safe and protected. The trees, some with fresh green leaves, others with dark evergreen needles, seemed to offer their own embrace. Silas leaned back against the sun-warmed rocks and closed his eyes. He would remember this place, and the way God had met him here. He no longer felt lost, he realised. He still had some way to go to rebuild his life with God, but here, in this strange and yet comforting place, he felt he was almost home.

He opened his eyes and saw Eira lift her head and prick her ears. There was the sound of a horse approaching. He pushed himself away from the rock, and taking hold of her headcollar, led the grey back in the direction of the inn. Sure enough, it was the familiar shape of Hywel, on the back of Quint. The horse was laden with bulging saddlebags. Hywel dismounted easily and came to meet them.

'Are you ready to leave? Or do you need more time?'

Silas thought about it, but not for long. 'I'm ready. But I want to leave here as I am. We don't need to give Osian anything more to wonder and talk to others about.'

Hywel smiled in understanding. 'You go and get the rest of your things, and I will transfer the saddle onto Eira's back. And unload some of the weight of Quint's saddlebags.'

He lifted a bulging sack from one of the bags and as he placed it on the ground, it opened to reveal a collection of leeks, spring cabbages and a variety of dried beans.

'I raided the garden and the kitchen stores... with permission. Brother Aldred, the almoner, agreed that a small gift might sweeten Osian's opinion of the Cistercians. A little, anyway.' Hywel grinned.

Silas headed into the inn to gather his meagre belongings – his scrip, which he reattached to his belt, his cloak, gloves and hat. The scrip was the only thing that he really wanted to keep now. Hywel followed him in and deposited the bag of vegetables on Osian's table.

Osian tried hard to hide his appreciation but then allowed himself a brief smile, and for a moment his face was transformed. He proceeded to examine the contents thoroughly.

'We will be taking our leave, then. With grateful thanks for your hospitality.'

Osian left his perusal of the gifted vegetables and offered his hand to both Hywel and then Silas.

'Thank you for your generosity in the vegetables, Brother, and to you, Stranger, for growing my wood pile for me.' The innkeeper nodded and turned away as his cheeks flushed pink. 'God go with you,' he mumbled.

Hywel and Silas left the room, exchanging a smile. They were leaving well.

They rode together in companiable silence. The road took them downwards until they met the valley bottom, and Silas could see the river flowing wide and full from the recent rainfall. Hywel pulled to a stop where a cluster of tall trees met the riverbank and dismounted. He took hold of Quint's reins and began to lead him into the trees. Silas slid from Eira's back and they followed.

At first, the way was narrow and uneven, crisscrossed by ancient tree roots, but they encouraged the horses through until the track widened out into a small clearing at the waters' edge.

'You knew of this place?' Silas asked. It was well hidden.

'One of my favourites. Secluded enough to be alone with your thoughts, but not too far from the road that you can easily get lost.'

It was a lovely spot, especially with the sunlight sparkling on the water. Hywel unburdened both horses and left them to graze contentedly on yellow dandelions and lush grass. He carried the saddlebags over to a spot close to the river, where a group of medium-sized stones sat clustered around a darkened patch of grass.

'Others have lit fires here, but I don't know that we should if we want to remain hidden.' He looked at Silas, handing him the bundle of clothes in his hand. 'This is a private moment, no?'

'Yes, thank you.' Silas took the bundle and unrolled it, to find a clean white habit and familiar black cloak inside. 'Where did you get these? Did anyone ask why you needed them?' Silas suddenly felt uneasy. He held the habit up to his body, and it seemed to be a reasonable enough fit. It definitely wasn't one of Hywel's. His would have been long enough on Silas to trail behind him. Could he wear stolen clothes, and do so when in his heart he was renewing his vow to God?'

'Brother Aldred. Silas, he is a good man, and an old soldier who knows more of life than most of our community. I told him enough, but not all, and he did not question further. He is a good man to talk to, if you ever need to share your story further. This is one of his habits, an old one, but clean. The cloak he found in the stores. There will be sandals and a scapular waiting for you too once we get back to Cymer.'

Silas swallowed hard. Kindness had already been shown to him by another member of Cymer's community, before he had even crossed the threshold of the abbey. Cymer was becoming more appealing the closer they got.

'I will change into these shortly.' He laid them out on a rock beside him. 'But first we need to do something with this...' He ran his hand over his rough hair. 'And this...' He pulled at his beard.

'Yes. We thought of that too.' Hywel scrabbled around in the saddlebag and pulled out a tiny glass vial, and an item wrapped in rags. The vial he placed on the ground as he unwrapped the rags to expose a razor with a shiny blade. He seemed to be turning it in his hand to feel the weight of it.

'Have you ever shaved a tonsure before?'

Hywel looked up from examining the blade and winked. 'No. But I am willing to have a go.'

Silas didn't have much choice. Yet again he would have to trust Hywel. The monk stepped ominously close, razor poised.

'I'll do my beard myself first, I think.' Silas stepped back hurriedly out of Hywel's reach and held his hand out for the razor. 'I'll go to the river and use the water from there. Hot water would have been better.'

'I thought about that too. I cannot warm water for you, but I did bring you some oil to soften your beard, if that helps.' Hywel picked up the vial and unstopped it, sniffing the opening. He screwed his face up.

'It's anointing oil, isn't it?'

'Yes, it is quite fragrant, but at least it will improve the smell of you.'

'I daresay. But still I would like to know where exactly you *borrowed* that from? I doubt it came from the almoner's store.'

Hywel grinned but did not answer.

Silas contemplated the razor in his hand but made no move closer to the water's edge. Hywel must have seen his hesitation.

'Shall we eat first?' he said, digging another package out of his saddlebag.

Silas smiled gratefully and put the razor down beside the habit. Both could wait a while longer.

Come to Me, all you who labor and are heavy laden, and I will give you rest. Take My yoke upon you and learn from Me, for I am gentle and lowly in heart, and you will find rest for your souls. For My yoke is easy and My burden is light.

Matthew 11:28-30

20

HOME

They sat on the rocks and shared the bread and dried fruit Hywel had begged from the almoner's store. Something else was playing on Silas' mind, and he needed to find a way to ask Hywel about it. He trusted the man's wisdom, or rather his obvious connection to God and the wisdom of the Almighty.

'When I told you my story at Stay-a-Little, you surprised me. You did not judge or condemn me.'

'As I said before, we all carry secrets. There are things in my own past that I am not proud of, that I would hesitate to share for fear of being judged. God's grace towards me has taught me that I cannot take the place of judgement. That belongs to Him alone.'

Silas looked at the man before him and could not imagine him ever having done anything to be ashamed of. Although he had demonstrated such understanding and empathy towards Silas, it made sense that he had been on his own difficult path, and that he had come through it.

'You said that you would pray, that you and God had talked, and when you came back you seemed to have had a clear answer from God.'

'Yes, I did hear God clearly.'

'How did God speak to you? I mean, did you hear His voice?'

'I suppose I did. Not with my ears, as such, but with my heart and mind. He talks to me like that from time to time. Other times, when I ask for His wisdom, I get an impression of what is the right thing to do, or He uses His Word in the scriptures to speak to me. On that occasion I heard Him telling me clearly to take you home, and I knew in my spirit what that meant.'

Hywel helped himself to another mouthful of bread, and Silas paused before he spoke again, waiting for Hywel to finish eating.

'I used to hear God speak – before I failed.' He lowered his head.

'Before Grace Dieu failed, *not you.*'

He glanced up and found Hywel staring at him. Had Silas just heard God's voice through Hywel's? The words '*not you'* seemed to go straight to his heart. Could it be that God did not consider him a failure? It *felt* true.

'I don't think I hear God speak as often or as clearly as you do, Hywel, but I do think I heard him one time during my journey, unexpectedly, at a time I had convinced myself that He was nowhere close.'

'What did you hear Him say?' Hywel was now sitting relaxed on his stone seat, his long arms resting on bent knees.

Silas thought back to that moment lying beside Iorwerth's sick bed, observing Wolf's devotion to his master.

'I heard the words, "You love Me."'

He remembered the emotion, the deep longing it had evoked in him the first time he had heard the words. Tears threatened again because as he sat there in that sunny copse, with a new friend, and an already healing heart, he knew those words were exactly what he had needed to hear. Words that had begun his journey back to God's heart, that had begun his journey home.

'Beautiful words to hear.'

'Yes,' Silas took a deep, steadying breath. 'I knew God was reminding me that He was inescapable, despite all that had happened, despite my fear, doubt and disappointment. I had tried running from Him, but in truth I was also running from my true self.'

He glanced up and saw only compassion in his brother monk's eyes. It gave him courage to continue.

'I gave my heart to God, out of love for Him, many years ago. His love for me had drawn me to Him, the love that sent Jesus to the cross. Once I had experienced that love and understood the depth of it, it was easy to give my heart completely to Him. Following Jesus was not easy, even in those early days, but I loved Him so intensely and devotedly that nothing else mattered.

'I don't know when the intensity of that love for God faded. Perhaps it was just dulled over the years. Perhaps it was because I believed the greatest expression of my devotion to God was to build something great for Him. Was my desire to see Grace Dieu prosper, my determination to work hard at all costs to keep it from failing, truly out of love for God? I wonder now, looking back, if pride did not come into it. At least partly. I did genuinely want to do something great for God, to honour Him. But I also wanted to prove myself.'

Hywel sat upright, stretching his back. 'Whatever your motives, you poured yourself out for your community, Silas. God saw that.'

'Maybe so, but it wasn't enough to save it. In losing Grace Dieu, I lost my trust in God, I...' He shook his head. 'I didn't think I loved Him anymore. I didn't even like the God I thought had failed us. At least, I told myself that.'

'But God thought differently?'

Silas nodded.

Hywel had returned to his relaxed pose, watching the river flow past, and the white-bibbed birds dipping at the water's edge.

'We were both called to a life of service, Silas, to God and to our fellow man. Others might look at us and consider us devoted to God, but our hearts are fickle. We are human, after all. When things are going well, it is easy to declare our love for God, and to act out of it. When things are tough, it is harder. Especially when our hearts are wounded.

'You told me your story, Silas. You told me of your journey and the people you met. In every one of those encounters you gave of yourself. Lives were changed, transformed even, because of you, because of your compassion, and your desire to help. What propelled you to finish the furniture for Hannah? To find employment for Samuel? What motivated you to improve Iorwerth's life by finding a market for his carvings? What made you stay and help nurse him back to health? Yes, you found warmth and shelter, food and fellowship in return for your kind acts. But I don't think that is why you stayed and helped those people.'

Silas closed his eyes and remembered.

'I think God whispered to you in that moment, Silas, out of a Father's pride for His son. He said, "Look, Silas, you love Me, in loving these." You went beyond yourself, put your own heartbreak aside, compelled by His love within you. He flowed out of you as you loved those people. You walked in His compassion, grace and wisdom. You could not help it, because it is who you are. You are His son, Silas. You may not have felt it, or even believed it for a time, but it was, it is, the truth. He loves you, and yes, you love Him.'

Silas didn't stop the tears as they dripped onto his clasped hands. He felt the truth of Hywel's words go deep into his understanding. He was so grateful to God for this man and his godly wisdom. So grateful for this brother – in every sense of the word. Finally, he sighed deeply and sat upright, reaching for the razor.

'Shall we do this?' He smiled warily over at Hywel, who grinned in response.

'Yes,' he said, standing to his feet as Silas made his way over to the river edge.

The skin on his chin and on his scalp was red and chafed by the time they were finished with the razor. He had done what he could himself, but then had trusted Hywel to do the rest. Cold river water hadn't made the job much easier, but at least it was cooling to his flesh as he splashed it over his head. He knelt on the river's edge with his new tonsure, still in his old tunic. As he stared into the clear running water, he had a sudden urge. He stood to his feet, undid the belt from his waist, and lifted his tunic up and over his head. He pulled his boots off and stepped into the river.

He felt trepidation as he walked against the weight of water, feeling the pull of the current, but his fear was overcome with determination, and something else... a compulsion. He gasped as the cold water rose higher up his legs, the deeper he went. Finally, he stopped and steadied himself, digging his bare feet into the soft riverbed. Hywel stood on the riverbank watching him, his hands clasped together within wide habit sleeves. He was moving his lips, but Silas could not make out his words. Hywel released his hands from his sleeves and placed them together in a praying position, and Silas nodded in comprehension. He needed to do this for himself, but Hywel and his prayers were with him.

He turned his face to the blue sky above him, and the strength of light from the sun forced him to close his eyes. He bathed in its warmth for a moment, and then he sunk to his knees and dipped his whole body under the water. He felt the shock of it briefly, but then an indescribable peace flooded his soul. He staggered to get back to his feet, but he was no longer afraid of the river. Its water had washed his body clean, and he knew that God's grace had also cleansed his soul. As he stepped out of the water Hywel was there, ready to wrap his old cloak around him. He was shivering but he felt more alive than he had felt for months, years, even. The cold had stimulated his senses, but it was the symbolism of the act that caused his face to erupt into a broad smile. God had given him a new start, a second chance, and now he was ready to step back into his sequestered life a new man.

The habit felt good with its familiar roughness and loose sleeves. Silas secured his belt with his scrip attached around his waist. He had another sudden thought, as he delved into the scrip for his pewter cross. He brought the crucifix to his lips and then hung the chain about his neck. It felt right, the weight of the cross lying above his heart. He was still smiling as Hywel lifted the black cloak to his shoulders and helped him secure it. He slipped still damp feet back into his boots, wishing briefly for the feel of sandals on his feet, but their journey wasn't quite over yet. He still had to get on Eira's back and ride a few more hard miles with his feet in stirrups.

'How do I look?' He held his wide-sleeved arms out before Hywel.

'Like a Cistercian, Brother,' he smiled. He had the vial of oil in his hands. 'Would you let me use some of this on your scalp? It still looks a bit raw and with this sun blazing down, your poor skin will suffer yet more as you ride.'

Silas lowered his body to sit on the nearest stone, and Hywel stood over him. He felt the cool drops of oil land and felt Hywel's touch as he rubbed his scalp gently. He smelled the fragrance of the spices. It had been offered as an act of kindness, but in that moment, it felt more like an anointing. An act of reconsecration. Silas closed his eyes and Hywel began to pray words of blessing over him. It was a holy moment, as holy as any he had experienced inside of a church building. His heart was bursting with gratitude towards God, and with a bubbling joy that he was finding it hard to contain.

'There's just one more thing I need to do, Hywel, before we leave here,' he half-whispered.

'What is that, Brother?'

'I want to bury these.' He picked up his bedraggled tunic and cloak. 'I want to leave the last few weeks behind me. I don't want to carry these with me into my new life, even hidden in a saddlebag. I left my doubts and fears, my anger and my rebellion against God, in the waters of the river. I want to bury these too. Will you help me?'

Hywel smiled with understanding. 'I have no shovel to move earth, but I have an idea. Stand up Brother.'

Silas stood up from the large stone he had been sitting on. Hywel began kicking at the earth around the base of the stone, and Silas joined him, until they had formed a deep groove all around the edge.

'Help me push.' Hywel bent and put his shoulder to the rock, and Silas laid his palms flat on it. They pushed and then went to the other side of the rock and pushed from that side. Bit by bit the stone began to shift until it was loose enough that a final push lifted it from the ground. Hywel tipped it and held onto it as Silas made a slight dip beneath it with his booted foot, and then shoved his old clothes into it. Hywel released the stone, and the clothes were buried under the very rock where Silas had been blessed with anointing oil.

Hywel dusted his hands down his habit and smiled.

'Now, are you ready, Brother?'

Silas smiled back at him. 'I am, Brother. Let's go home.'

'There.'

Hywel pulled up and pointed. Through the trees, Silas could see the outline of a stone church with a modest tower. It sat nestled among the trees, surrounded by a series of compact buildings. The sun glinted off glass-filled windows, and whitewashed walls. The sound of a bell ringing to call the brothers to prayer rang out.

There was a moment of apprehension, but Hywel spurred Quint on, and Silas had no time left to ponder. Abbey Cymer lay ahead. The end of his journey, and the beginning of a new adventure with God.

Jesus answered, 'What I'm about to tell you is true. No one can enter God's kingdom unless they are born with water and the Holy Spirit. People give birth to people. But the Spirit gives birth to spirit.

You should not be surprised when I say, "You must all be born again." The wind blows where it wants to. You hear the sound it makes. But you can't tell where it comes from or where it is going. It is the same with everyone who is born with the Spirit.'

John 3:5-8, NIRV

Epilogue

Spring had long passed, summer was almost ended, and the trees were beginning to change colour, from green to a myriad of shades of gold, bronze and fiery reds. Brother Silas stood in a deep culvert, his feet immersed in water, steadying a contraption that Brother Pedr was working on. Samson and Anwen's tall, gentle son was a young man gifted in design and inventiveness. He had constructed a method of drawing water from the River Mawddach, along a series of channels that served the kitchens and bath house at Abbey Cymer. He was trying out a gate that could be used to control the water flow, and Silas had offered to help him, intrigued by the idea.

They were both so engrossed in the task, neither of them heard Prior William's approach, until the man cleared his throat loudly. Silas started and Pedr grabbed him by the arm to stop him toppling into the water flowing around his feet.

'Brother Silas.'

It was said with a distinctly supercilious tone, matching the look he sent down his long nose in their direction.

'Father Abbot has asked me to bring you to him – immediately,' he added, looking Silas up and down, taking in his habit tucked into his belt and his grubby scapular.

Pedr helped Silas clamber out of the culvert. The prior stepped back hastily, as if scared he too might be tarnished by the evidence of hard work. Silas stood up, released his habit from his belt and shoved his still-wet feet into his sandals.

'Unfortunately, it can't wait for you to make yourself more presentable.' The prior screwed his nose up, and swivelled round to stride back towards the stone abbey buildings.

Silas smoothed out his habit and scapular as best he could and exchanged a smile with Pedr. He felt a sudden apprehension. He had never been summoned to the abbot's rooms before, and the apparent urgency didn't feel good.

He had been welcomed to Abbey Cymer by Abbot Thomas. A small man, his eyes clouded with age, he had urged Silas to speak up or lean close if he wanted to be heard. He was Father Abbot, but due to his age and apparent incapacities, he left much of the everyday oversight of the abbey to the fastidious Prior William.

Silas had been welcomed by the other brothers in the community, and had felt at home quicker than he could have imagined. Brother Hywel's description of Cymer had been correct. It was different from Grace Dieu, but also not so different. Silas appreciated that it was small and the life simple. It had none of the ostentation of Abbey Dore, and yet in its own way was a fitting reflection of God's glory. It had a simple stone church, with high arches and tall glass windows. It also boasted well-built stone accommodation, a quiet cloister and well-kept gardens, all in a beautiful setting. Abbey Cymer sat close to a clean, wide, fish-filled river, in the secluded embrace of tree-covered mountain slopes.

Modest areas of pasture catered for the needs of their sheep, and a wide arable field was full of ready-to-harvest grain. Hywel had stables and paddocks enough for his horses. Eira had settled in well with the rest of the breeding herd. Storm was still a work in progress, but Silas enjoyed watching his friend work with the horse, impressed at Hywel's natural ability.

He loved it here, and as he climbed the steps up to the abbot's rooms close on William's heels, he felt an unfamiliar feeling rising in his throat. Panic. Perhaps brought on by his memories of the last time he had been summoned before an abbot, back at Abbey Dore. It felt like a lifetime ago, but the memory came flooding back as he stood outside another great wooden door. He even felt a momentary urge to run. He closed his eyes against the feeling and took a steadying breath. This wasn't Abbey Dore, and this wasn't Abbot Adam.

'Come.' The feeble voice was only just audible as the prior pushed the door open. He hadn't knocked or waited for the summons. The abbot's limited hearing had made the prior bold, maybe even presumptuous.

'Ah, Brother Silas.' The abbot did not appear angry, that was good. The look on his face was more of pity, which did little to allay Silas' fear.

'You may leave us, Brother Prior, and close the door behind you.'

'But you need me to read for you, Father Abbot.'

The prior's voice had raised a tone or two. His appeal seemed either unheeded or unheard, as the abbot raised a hand and gestured towards the door, dismissing him.

Abbot Thomas waited until the prior had left and pulled the door shut behind him. He was standing behind a table strewn with documents. A window above the table gave light enough for Silas to see the parchment held in the abbot's hands bore a broken seal.

'We have received letters today, Brother. One in particular.' He waved the parchment in Silas' vague direction. 'This, I think, concerns you. As you know, my eyesight is failing, so Prior William reads aloud any missive that comes for me. He began reading this but something about its content made me interrupt him before he read more than he needed to. I decided to summon you.'

The abbot handed Silas the letter.

'I wonder if you would read it for me, Brother, slowly, so that I can hear, if you please.'

Silas scanned the document before opening his mouth, and already his hand was shaking. He had recognised the words Grace Dieu and his own name. He began to read. There were the usual salutations, and the name of the author, Abbot Adam of Abbey Dore. And then the letter went on:

We mourn to inform you that the abbey at Grace Dieu has been abandoned and left in ruination, through the wanton disregard to our

> Rule and the perfidy of several members of our community. Most especially at fault are those charged with her founding and establishment, among them, one Brother Silas. He abandoned his position, leading other well-meaning brethren astray, rebelling against our holy authority, and has since made himself an outcast to our Order. We beg you all to pray that God would see fit to judge him according to his works, and to bring him to repentance. He is at present of unknown whereabouts, having broken his vows and stolen from the abbey to make good his escape from punishment.

Silas could read no further. The blood was pumping in his head, and the room span. He staggered.

The abbot moved surprisingly quickly to place a chair behind his knees. He grabbed Silas' arm as he fell into the chair and whispered into his ear, 'Give me the letter.'

Silas released his hold on the parchment and dropped his head to the level of his knees, waiting for the dizziness to pass. A trembling hand appeared beneath his face, holding a cup half-filled with strong-smelling wine. He took it gratefully, bringing it to his lips and taking a deep drink.

'Brother.' The abbot spoke gently, and Silas raised his eyes to meet his.

'Parchment is precious, and I could order this scraped clean and reused. But not this time. No one else must read the words it contains. Not here.'

Silas watched as the abbot dropped the letter into a glowing brazier and observed as the flames took hold. The sickly aroma of burning skin reached his nose as the letter crinkled and browned, the vile words melting into the fire.

'That missive spoke of a Brother Silas. I have to tell you, Son,' he spoke clearly and kindly, 'I do not know that man. Whoever that letter describes, it is not the man who sits before me. It is not the man I have observed serving his brothers, working hard for all, showing kindness and unwavering devotion to the Rule of Life here. It is not the man I have seen weep during sung worship, or smile as he encounters God through meditation on scripture. It is not the man I have seen fool around with Hywel, and his horses, or get his hands dirty in the soil of our gardens. You are not that Brother Silas.' He nodded towards the still smoking parchment. 'You are our brother, Silas, your home is here with us. And it always will be.'

The thief does not come except to steal, and to kill, and to destroy.

I have come that they may have life, and that they may have it more abundantly.

John 10:10

Historical Note

I love to weave real people and events into my fiction. I believe it adds an element of historical authenticity and helps set the story well and truly in the period I have chosen. As a lover of history, this also means that I can lose myself for hours in historical research – whether that is trawling the internet, reading fascinating books, or visiting atmospheric abbey ruins. Almost as much fun as writing!

Grace Dieu was a real place. It was the last Cistercian abbey founded in Wales, in around 1226, at the end of almost a century of rapid Cistercian expansion across Europe. Monks were indeed sent from the mother house of Dore Abbey in Herefordshire, to found an abbey over the border in Wales. Dore Abbey had been established in 1147 and was large and prosperous by this time.

Grace Dieu did not do well. It was subject to Welsh opposition right from its inception. In 1232, the abbot and a monk were taken captive, and in 1233, the whole abbey was razed to the ground by a Welsh raiding party. It was rebuilt a few years later at a different location, but never really prospered or grew. Nothing remains of Grace Dieu now except a muddy field alongside the tiny River Trothy.

Dore Abbey in contrast continued to prosper right up to the dissolution in 1536. If you visit today, you can still worship in part of the original abbey, now used as the parish church. I believe it is the only remaining Cistercian abbey building in the UK still used as a place of worship. The ruins are majestic, and it is easy to imagine the grandeur of the place in its heyday.

William de Braose, Lord of Hay, did get himself entangled with Prince Llewellyn's wife, Joan. He was captured and executed under Welsh law by the Prince, probably back at Llewellyn's northern stronghold, Abergwyngregyn. Llewellyn attacked Hay Castle in retaliation, and historical records show that King Henry III gifted monies to Lady Eve de Braose for the castle to be rebuilt. Readers of *The Healing* and *The Bride* might be interested to know that William was Philip de Braose's first cousin.

Abbey Cwmhir and Abbey Cymer of course existed and are both favourite places of mine to visit. Brother Silas and Brother Hywel, and most of the other central characters in the tale, come purely from my imagination.

As always, my apologies if I have corrupted or misrepresented people, places or customs in my storytelling.

Author's Note

The Stranger is my fourth full-length story full of monks and abbeys, Welsh mountains and landscapes. Readers of my other books will recognise some familiar names. It was fun including characters that have appeared elsewhere, and in some cases giving them more of a story.

Brother Silas first appears in *The Healing*, only briefly, but he and the abbey he was fighting to save stayed with me. When I visited the majestic ruins of Dore Abbey and the sad empty site where Grace Dieu once stood, I was struck by the contrast between the two abbeys – one large and prosperous, the other beleaguered from the start. The story idea for *The Stranger* started there.

Anwen, Samson and Pedr, and their story, is told in more detail in *The Healing*, where of course we also first meet Brother Hywel. Hywel's own troubled past is explored in *The Pilgrim,* where we also first meet Matthew – a very different Matthew than we meet in *The Stranger*. I loved being able to complete his redemptive story.

In writing this tale, yet again I have taken my inspiration not only from people and places of the past, but also from the story of God's dealings in my own life.

I can write about Brother Silas' pain, doubt and fear, because I have known those things. I have walked through seasons where I have felt abandoned by God, where failure and disappointment have caused perceived chasms of separation between me and Him.

But, like Silas, I have also found that it is not possible to outrun God's love. How He chooses to speak, how He chooses to restore, might not look like I might have expected it, but His kindness is without end. His mercy and grace are freely offered. He wants His children back and will fight for us.

I might never fully understand why suffering comes, why dreams are broken, why my best efforts sometimes seem to end in ruin, but I do know that God loves me. He wants the best for me, He is always good, and He can turn the worst of situations around in unexpected ways. He is a redeeming God, and with Him nothing is wasted. This is why I wrote this book, and why perhaps it will bless you in the reading.

He is, and always will be, worthy of all my praise.

More information on me and my books can be found at www.joymargetts.com

Acknowledgements

First of all, a very special thank you to my publishers, Broad Place Publishing. You have gone above and beyond! Thank you for your belief in this book, your self-sacrificial determination to produce something truly beautiful, and your meticulous attention to detail in all things. Thank you for putting up with me, and for all that we have learnt together. I honour you for what you are setting out to do with Broad Place, I see what it is costing you, and I am 100% with you and the vision. I am blessed to call you my friends as well as my publishers and pray God's continued favour on you and the work of your hands.

Thank you to Sheila Jacobs for editing, and David Salmon for another stunning cover. Thank you to those who read early versions of the story and gave me invaluable feedback, and to those who kindly endorsed the book for me. Your encouragement has really blessed me!

Thank you to Kingdom Story Writers, which is fast becoming a network of prayerful, supportive, like-minded people. You are all awesome and have encouraged me to go on writing Kingdom Stories, as we all pursue the dream of seeing more God honouring, faith filled, Holy Spirit inspired, Jesus centred books produced in this country. Thank you especially to my 'team': Joanna Watson, Joy Vee, Rachel Yarworth, Alex Banwell and Natasha Woodcraft for being a constant source of wisdom and inspiration.

My family deserve a mention. You have been so constant in your support, both emotionally and financially, to see my dream of writing books come to fruition. Special thanks to my chief book sellers – Mum and Aunty Pauline! Thank you, Tim, for your patience and love – you are a fantastic writer widower, and I couldn't do this without you.

Thank you to everyone who has read and loved my books and has told me so; for those of you who have signed up to follow my journey, and who have supported me in prayer and through buying my books! Thank you for every encouraging review, message and email. You have no idea how much these mean to me. I hope you have enjoyed this, my latest offering.

Lastly, of course, my deepest gratitude goes to God. He is my inspiration. My story is His story, and both are reflected in Silas' story. The gift to write has come from Him, and I do not take that lightly. He is the lover of my soul, the One who whispers His nearness even when I wander, and my heart's true home. Thank you, Jesus. This is for You.

J.M.

About Broad Place Publishing

Broad Place Publishing is a new Christian imprint whose aim is to bring Jesus-centred books to the market. We want to see good-quality books, inspired by the Holy Spirit, brought to life and made available across the world.

We work in partnership with the Holy Spirit at every step, encouraging our writers to listen to Him in their creativity, asking our editors to trust Him as they strive for excellence, and seeking Him for finances and marketing strategy.

We also strive to be an accessible publisher, using dyslexic friendly fonts and making the book available in multiple formats. Please contact us if you see any ways we can improve in this.

If you wish to support us in this missional work, either in prayer or financially, please see the website, or email us directly on:

support@broadplacepublishing.co.uk.

You can find out more about our work at:
broadplacepublishing.co.uk

ALSO FROM THE PUBLISHER

Books to encourage families in their walk with Jesus
by Joy Vee

The Kai Series (5-8s):
Kai: Born to be Super
Kai: Making it Count
Kai: Playing his Part

The Sienna Series (8-12s):
Love from Sienna
Left Out, Sienna?

The Petrov Series:
The Letters She Never Sent (8-12s)
They Whisper About Us (12+)

Bible-based Fiction
by Natasha Woodcraft

The Wanderer Series – *Cain & Abel Reimagined*

1. The Wanderer Scorned
2. The Wanderer Reborn

The Wardrobe by Alan Hoare

Encountering the Kingdom of Heaven through The Bible

BV - #0156 - 131124 - C0 - 198/129/18 - PB - 9781915034786 - Matt Lamination